For Richard T.
who spoke up!
Herb G.

Fathers

a novel in the

form of a memoir

by

HERBERT GOLD

Herb Gold 4 Nov '02

Creative Arts Book Company / Berkeley
1980

ISBN 0-916870-26-X

Library of Congress Catalog Card Number: 66–12012

Manufactured in the United States of America

Published by Creative Arts Book Company
833 Bancroft Way, Berkeley, CA 94710.

This is a book I have been writing all my life. Parts of it have been published in earlier versions since 1951. As I found the way to the end, or as the book found the way to its own end, the beginnings and middles have changed their shape. Therefore passages which have appeared in print before are here very much altered. I am grateful to the following publications: *Commentary*, the *Hudson Review*, *Midstream*, *Playboy*, and the *Saturday Evening Post*.

"Is the coin just gold, or is it the symbol of an action?
Is it merely truth, or does it mean something else?"

"We possess nothing but the metaphors of things."

Fathers

Preface

In the spring of 1966 my father and mother came to visit me in San Francisco. He was eighty years old and thought he ought to see Hawaii too, why not? while he was out there on the West Coast. Otherwise there is one thing and another. Things come up. He had this deal in Cleveland which could keep him pretty busy for the next few years.

They had planned to stay in a hotel, but the idea for an adventure occurred to them as they floated through the thin air between outer space and America. They would camp out with me in my apartment on Russian Hill. They could have the bed and I would use a sleeping bag on the floor in my study. My mother worried about my comfort, but I told her I can sleep or stay awake anywhere. She suspected as much. In our family, bed or floor, noise and confusion, sleep has never been a serious issue. Rather, insomnia is considered a diversion. This time, however, my father could not take his usual comfort in himself.

He had pulled a muscle in one leg and found it hard to tramp up and down the hills, casing the real estate, poking about in the supermarkets, noting whether the customers just buy or look first and then buy. When I awakened the first morning, I found him standing on my little terrace, pensive, frowning, blinking his old Tartar eyes, gazing out over Chinatown, North Beach, and the Bay. He was fully dressed already. He pursed his mouth, studied the situation, and said, "In Cleveland they don't like to build on hills."

"The engineers know how, Dad."

"Of course they know how. They get down to the rock if they got the rock. I said they don't *like*."

He was turning over in his mind the deal which was pending in Cleveland. "It's white propitty, a hunnert and eleven suites, plus the janitor," he said, "but it could get to be colored propitty overnight. Which it is how it is nowadays."

"Is that bad?"

"I didn't say bad. Who said progress is bad? I said that's how it is. It means trouble, but who said it's bad if I get clunked on the head some night? I don't mind for progress—just so I see him coming."

"Okay, Dad."

"Naw, I'm kidding. But I see him coming, I use my own hammer on him."

We went inside. It was early morning. Streams of fog were rolling off Twin Peaks, and the deep bass notes of foghorns were blowing at the Golden Gate. A Japanese freighter moved slowly under the morning sun toward the bridge. "What's that?" my father said. "Why the spyglass?" He took the binoculars out of my hands. "Tak-a-hashi," he read slowly. "What's that?"

"Japanese floating real estate, Dad."

"Hah. Transistors—funny little radios."

My father rubbed his hands. A little kidding in the morning was like the old days at the West Side Market in Cleveland. It got the blood moving. Talking about real estate made him hungry. Thinking about it made him thirsty too. My mother presented him with his breakfast—orange juice, corn flakes, bananas, sugar, and coffee. And toast. And more coffee.

"You got a funny coffee pot, why don't you get a Silex?" she asked me. "But you got the same kind of corn flakes out here we got in Cleveland."

"Well, I knew you were coming."

"Of course you knew we was coming," my father said. "We told you."

"Sam, but he didn't know we were going to stay here."

"Maybe he guessed. Good guesses run in the family. So he ran out and got corn flakes."

"Sam, put the spoon in. Your corn flakes are getting soggy."

"That's how I like them, I like them soggy," he said, "soft. I like the flavor sometimes."

"The tang," said my mother dreamily, quoting a word she must have heard on the radio while cooking. "Your father's worried about his deal," she said. "I couldn't hardly drag him out of Cleveland."

"I wanted to go," he said, "the West Coast, Hawaii, a

5

little swim. Frieda, you're always talking. But I got to take care of the business. Nobody else is in charge."

"Sam, drink your citrus."

I sat at the table and watched my mother moving about, serving even when there was nothing to serve. "Sam, the drops in your eyes, you know what the doctor said—he bawled you out last time. Sam, here's the honey, he's got Safeway honey in his white Sears Roebuck cabinet. Sam, he's got the same kind of corn flakes we got."

How many times had I been the guest in my parents' house and heard these soothing discussions of food, medicine, appliances, and money? It always made me feel like a child again to go home to visit my parents. And now they were my visitors, getting used to my bachelor quarters, seeing I could make do. I decided to ask, one more time, a question it seemed I had been asking my father, one way or another, all my life: "Dad, why are you taking chances on this deal? Why don't you take it easier? You're secure now."

A brilliant childish smile creased his cheeks. Flecks of light on his teeth, flecks of white on his jaw, needing a shave. "Secure! You know the answer to that one. Never secure."

"At your age, Dad—"

"But I tell you what, son. I'm not worried. I got it all figured out, the rate I'm going. In ten years, my deals go good, I'll be all set."

"You'll be ninety years old, Dad."

"Who said?"

"Your passport. Your citizenship papers."

"I never look at it," he said frankly. "I got better things to do with my time."

What would it cost, I thought, to yield once more to his intention? "Tell me about the deal, Dad."

"Listen, it looks good. Bricks. I like a lot of bricks like that. There's a hunnert and eleven units, plus one for the manager—Sawyer, you know Sawyer—all complete kitchens, semimodern, eighty-six per cent rented last year, a little less this year—which it's why the price went down. So I fix up a little, install some furnished, take out the semi-modern and put in some modern—look, it was management by a management firm, you think they know how to manage? Naw. So it's run down. It stands to reason. I know that. Look, I get my man to do the halls, I put Sawyer in there, I get my men on the job—"

My mother had her ear tuned to the deep sea growl reverberating through the morning. She ran to the balcony. "Sam, don't those ships ever hit in the fog?"

"Frieda, I'm talking business."

"This is a vacation. You're supposed to rest. You didn't drink your citrus. I want to know those ships how often they hit when it's foggy outside."

"Hardly ever, Mother," I said. "Also they have radar."

She clucked her lips. "All modern conveniences," she said.

"Never is pretty secure, ain't it?" my father asked. "For ships? For anything? In my home town, Kamenets-Podolsk, we never said an accident never happened. Eventually it did."

In San Francisco or in Cleveland we were six thousand

miles from Kamenets-Podolsk, or eight thousand miles, or twelve thousand, what difference does it make, an infinity of smoking ruins left behind along with the dream of Sabbath bread and a comprehended community, a distance memory or imagination crosses at deep peril to the sense of time now and place present. Moving on was my father's way, and it worked for him. He was still moving on. Success and security, those talismans, those palimpsests, those magic American words he liked to use, were still being worked through his darker intentions. Surely accidents might happen, but his cranky leg would heal in a few weeks. He would sit in the steam room at the Russian Bath and think. That was good for the pulled muscles, for the kinks, for the circulation, for the skin, for the knuckles and joints, and especially for the head. And especially for the part of the head that takes its ease and gives a blessing for pleasure. He liked the weight of steam boiling in his lungs and the weight of bricks on his mind. More security in bricks and steam than there used to be in iceberg lettuce and Castro Valley artichokes when he had the store, but he still liked them, too. For lunch. For dinner. To eat. He had very little to say about the past. Dwelling on what was over and done was not his style, even if he had to admit sometimes that it was not done and over. The store still came to mind. He wondered why he dreamed about it so much—those days of labor and doubt, racketeer demands and sudden spoilage, the hot spells of fruit and the icy silences of bank holidays. He had more to say about the future, but it was not necessary to talk much about that either. The future took care of itself, just ahead there, so long as you watched out for today. Yes, it was true, security only lay ahead, in the future, along with its unspoken shadow, which is oblivion. But today is what counts, and today a man is never secure. He can be healthy in the morning and crippled in the afternoon. He can be a gangster in the afternoon and love his children in the evening. There is always the lightning, the wars, the strokes, the matters a man in the world must deal with although there is no final dealing with them. Only in the game of risk is the dream of balance defined.

Once more I was willing to incite a son's ancient quarrel with his father. "Do you think you're a success, Dad?" It was like putting on the family's wedding raiment again. It was the worn quarrel, handled by many fingers, caressed and nearly transparent, letting through the light of grand occasions between father and son. "Do you think it was okay how you did, Dad? Did you get what you wanted—?"

"You sound like it's all over."

"Did you get what you wanted out of life?" I felt I had the right to ask him in this chill way. I was no longer a boy, either. We had been through a lifetime together, and only in this odd century can I still be considered young. The perpetual comeback, the perpetual fresh start, our famous male youthfulness may be the great innovation of contemporary American psychology. "I'm not saying you're so old, Dad. I'm saying: Do you think you're a success, you got what you wanted?"

"Still alive." He grinned. Staying alive a little while is enough; then we fail, we die. Is that what he meant? "Pretty loose, healthy," he said. "Still alive."

"When you look back, you think it was okay, Dad?"

"Who said I look back?"

"Was your life worthwhile?"

"Naw," he said. "I don't look back. What would I see? My shadow." He hit his sore thigh with the flat of his hand and it made a loud fat sound. "Which I got the rest of it here. You take care of the shadows. Your department."

"It's part of you too, everything that happened." His mouth was already opening in the sound of disgust. He had taken that guff from me before. *Aaach,* said the silent movement of his lips. "You're the creature of your own shadows, past, your parents, everything."

"Aach!" he groaned. "I got the next twenty years to worry about. A long mortgage, son. That's enough. A leash on life." He was getting angry. "You're trying to make me an old man, not just eighty—isn't that enough for you?—*old!* Well, I got my services."

"What?"

He grinned, eased by his outburst. "Faculties you call them. I call them services. A little word I use. They do for me okay. I'm satisfied."

"Are you satisfied, Dad?"

He stared at me and then at the Japanese ship heading eastward under the sun on the San Francisco Bay as if we were both determined to make trouble. Then he shrugged and looked inward and decided that *he* wanted no trouble. He tapped the deep reservoir of good humor which I had so often in the past taken for indiffer-ence—and been right in the past, and wrong, and right, and wrong. "I told you already," he said, "a thousand times or so, never counted, I'm not a mathematician—never satisfied. *Never satisfied!*" he shouted. He shook his head. Where was that reservoir? "Never satisfied, never secure. But still alive, son, still making trouble. Now I'm having trouble with the government. I can't die yet till we settle it. The government will have to elect a new Sam Gold, haha."

"You never wanted a quieter way? You could have had a quieter life, Dad."

The question seemed to stop him suddenly. He looked out over the glistening blue-and-white, watery and green, jeweled city of San Francisco which I had chosen for my own. We had talked about trade with China, but there was no trade with China; I had explained about the miners settling here, but the mines were mostly shut now, and the fortunes tamed. He liked brawling cities, and had no taste for this sweet air off the ocean, unbreathed by lungs, factories, smokestacks.

"I had a friend went to jail once. He had a quiet life. Maybe that's nice, must be good in jail. Thinking. Think a lot. Not for that boy, he got electrocuted, but someone else, maybe. It was never my way. Another chance I get, I'll tell you what, all right, I'll try it, son—a little quiet nice life."

And we shared the joke. He was only kidding. My life was not a prison; maybe it would only be a prison to him, even if I tried to define it as freedom. And his life?

His success? His failure? I could not define Man, though I invented about men. I could say, yes, a man uses his head, a man makes his decisions, a man masters his fate (strives to, perhaps fails at it), a man suffers his pains and despairs, a man takes his chances and explores his possibilities . . . My father was laughing and asking my mother to make some more toast, he was hungry again, and saying he was still alive, he needed nourishment, talking to his son made him hungry: "Hey, wake up in there. What kind of Toastmaster he got in that tiny no-good kitchen of his? Come on, let's have second breakfast."

He planned to consummate the deal in Cleveland, and the next one, and the next. At eighty he intended to pay court to poverty and riches both. He went out into Cleveland in his new Buick in search of efforts and chances. He had learned that pain and triumph cannot last, but he could ride with them as long as he could still ride. He watched his friends slow down, retire, or die, and he went to funerals almost every week, and he said: "Sometimes I get dizzy for a second and I hold on to my desk. Like a dizziness it gets black. But they never know. The person I'm talking to, they think I'm thinking. Maybe I am."

In April of his eightieth year he went on looking for the chance to exercise all his spirit and a little more. Otherwise a man is never secure, and knows nothing of success and failure, and takes the chance of knowing nothing, or perhaps too much, of his own life.

1

My father has never spoken his father's name. " 'He' hit me for whistling like a peasant, 'he' brought home a carp for the holiday, 'he' took me to the rabbi, but I didn't want to go." *He* did this or that. What my father has left me of my grandfather is a silent old man with a long white beard, a horse, a cart, a cow, a mud-and-log house—an old-country grandfather fixed in my mind like the memory of a painting. That's not enough, of course. This stylization of images does not satisfy the craving for history. I must try to tempt out the truth.

My father seems to have been his father's favorite child, perhaps merely because he was the eldest. I know this for several reasons, but here is the way I remember it: Sometimes my grandfather took my father to town with him. One of my uncles tells of clinging upside down, in a jealous rage, to the underside of the cart. Today, I have a double vision of the past, as if someone has forgotten to turn the film—this fat old Uncle Morris with a head that shakes, a nervous old head-shaker, peering through the slats of the cart as clumps of mud belt his behind—and a child, Moishe, wanting also to go to town. There was an even younger brother, still suckling, too young to want to go to town. In our family his name is now never pronounced. It is put aside for a different reason from the loss of my grandfather's name. But I have learned this name: Ben.

In their little village near Kamenets-Podolsk in Russia, just as the old century was ending, life was hard and dark for everyone, but harder and darker for Jews. The sons were taken away to the army forever, all except those crippled in some way which hurt the Czar's appetite. Holidays poured vodka into the peasants' mouths, and rumor poured poison into their ears, and the police stood by, smiling, when they poured fire over the Jewish houses. Cossacks gone mad, with white eyes, broke their weapons on children and inflicted their sons on girls, old women, nursing mothers. The Messiah was unaccountably delayed in the unfathomable future. The miracle of peace accompanied Him there. Within the fires which destroyed, there was a darkness which oppressed.

However, the human race does not permit utter darkness; the soul grows sharp sticks to point holes in the dark, stars in the night. Chassidism, the religion of light and drink, ferocious and funny stories, dancing and celebration, beat like a stick through the Jewish towns. It was also a religion of medals, magic, and charms. Jews raved and sang; Jews rolled in the woods in public ecstasies. They conquered the miseries of the police and a murderous peasantry by rocking and rolling.

Not all. My father, aged twelve, one year short of

being a man, was already a socialist, a freethinker, a revolutionist, and he wanted to ride away to America and pick up the gold in the streets of New York. He would carry a sack with him. The Czar's barbarous army or the golden freedom of America—is that a choice? His father knew that to stay in Russia meant conscription and death, but America was godless, a living death. He preferred the death he knew. My father's one-eyed grandfather threatened his son with a beating and a curse if he let the boy flee his fate. My father's father believed in the ancient maledictions and promises. This silent man sought to pass the remainder of his days with his children nearby, his wife, his cart, his horse, his cow, his hut, his fish on holidays. My twelve-year-old father clung to the idea that he would go to America to be a man, another man, another sort of man, inventing his own curses and his own fate. They must have fought over this. My father was beaten with a stick.

At last my grandfather grew weary of beating his eldest son. The boy was unknowable by stick; he was slow to learn, and my grandfather, who would willingly have spent his lifetime studying the Talmud with him, begrudged the hours he spent hitting him. Instead, father and son came to an understanding. They would travel to the nearby town to consult the wonder-working rabbi, a specialist in enigmas, about making a way across bogs and borders, past the Czar's police and the famous Dutchmen of western Europe, toward glittering America. They agreed to abide by the rabbi's judgment in the matter. My father secretly resolved that he would obey the wonder-working rabbi's decision only if it was the correct one. Thus, he reasoned, he had nothing to lose. Why quarrel with people who see the proper marvels? A wonder-working rabbi provided fair combat for a mentally working boy with constricted scruples and his mind made up.

My father was loaded by his father into the horse-drawn cart, along with eggs, a chicken, cakes, and other gifts for the rabbi, and silently they jolted across the irrational ruts of the mud road. At the local synagogue, two old men peered out, shrugged, and turned back to their discussion with God. My father thought: Does God answer? Then what kind of a discussion is it? His father said: "Hold on, child." In answer, my father stealthily lifted his hands from the rail across the cart. His father pretended not to see.

Animals and drunken peasants slowed their passage, but the divine guardian of roads and souls kept the stays in their wheels, the metal shoes on their horse, the patience in their hearts. My father wanted to whistle, but knew better. Instead, my father, aged twelve, silently rehearsed to himself the knowledge that he was an atheist, a socialist, and intended to go to America and take the name of Gold, in honor of the freedom given to men by the gold in the streets of New York; he thought all this through with great care, sorting it out and looking at the last star of morning, fixing it like the star in his mind in case the rabbi tried to work magic upon him in order to make him forget or deny or surrender. He had poked his own star in the night. With his own stick. It glittered. Inside, he was whistling. Silent whistles were emitted by his pursed lips and between his clenched teeth.

The wonder-working rabbi listened to both my father and my grandfather. He asked: how often beaten? He asked: did the boy study Torah from dawn to dusk? He asked: those cookies, did the little mother make them herself? He pulled his beard, turned his large veiny eyes on the two petitioners, and nibbled from the speckled cookies my grandmother had baked as a tribute to his wisdom. He must have been a very wise man. Many crumbs on his beard. And when he pulled his beard— many crumbs on his lap. He knew that his reputation for all-seeing foresight would suffer a decline in the district if he pronounced the wrong decision. An enigma-solver must select his enigmas with care. My father was burning, at the high temperature at which a twelve-year-old man burns, to go live under the limitless skies of America. In any case, he would go, with or without permission. The rabbi understood this. In one case, the father would be bitter and unreconciled, and the boy would steal away in the night, guiltily, with no lantern lit, with only his mother's sobs to wish him well. But if the Nameless One blessed the rabbi with a favorable word, father and son might still be reconciled. That could be the other case.

The rabbi said to the boy: Go to America, but wait two months until your bar mitzvah. Go as a man.

Even then my father was not a man of pure principles. He wanted to go to America right now, at age twelve, but he decided to wait until age thirteen, in order to please others and get all that he desired, which included the respect of his family.

The rabbi also said: And wear this medal around your neck, it will protect you from harm.

My father said: And my brothers? They too must go to America.

The rabbi said: Wear this. They are babies yet. Let be what God wills.

My father said: Give me some medals for the babies. For Ben too.

The rabbi said: They must come to see me at the proper time.

My father said: What is good for me will be good for them.

He needed no charms to help him go to America, but if fools said he needed one, he also wanted his brothers to have medals.

The rabbi took a cookie and did not deign to argue. Arguing at this point would be less a matter of principle— should a baby go to America who can barely dress himself?—than a matter of bickering. Bickering is unholy, an insult to the Word; anyone who is married knows this. God loves words—especially the silences between them. And so did the rabbi.

In due time, an appointment could be made to discuss future medals, travels, decisions. Solomon dealt coolly with twelve-year-old bickerers. He raised his hand. He reached his hand. He took a cookie. Sternly the rabbi chewed on the tribute sent with the supplicants.

My father, choking down his shame and disbelief, accepted the medal which the rabbi hung about his neck from a fairly clean string. All the other atheistic and socialistic ten- to twelve-year-old boys of the village would mock him, would accuse him of failing to whistle at rabbis, but my future father knew what he really wanted, and what he really wanted could not be altered by consenting to wear a medal under his blouse until he finally turned the bend in the long road that led from the Ukrainian village to the Western world.

My father's father paid proper respects to the rabbi, in words and in silences between words, and then the two went home, jiggling in the lightened cart, without the load of eggs, the chicken, the cakes, but with a decision that brought peace to the family. After they got back, by absent-minded habit, my grandfather peeked beneath the cart to see if any of his other sons was clinging to it. It would have made more sense to look sooner, but time and sequence were not his special talents.

My grandfather entered and said to his wife, "The boy will stay."

He would not spoil the Sabbath by adding, "But the man will go."

He went back outside to wash and prepare for evening prayers. He hugged his other son, Moishe, the one who always wanted to cling to the cart when my father went someplace. He dandled his third son, Ben, the babe in arms. Then he kissed his five-year-old daughter. His wife was worried by this show of affection. "What's the trouble? Are you deceiving me?"

"The boy will stay," he muttered. My father recalls

that his face was wet. He was weeping. He pretended it was wet from the basin of water, but there were fresh tears after he washed.

Two months passed. My father practiced the virtue of patience, and tried to tell himself it was a virtue. At his age it was hard to pretend to doubt what he knew, or to doubt what he wished; that is, it was hard to wait. He candled eggs for his father; he sold them to the peasant women, counting by twos and wishing his hand large enough to hold three eggs; he wandered down the muddy streets to the synagogue. Inside there were men at prayers or reading the Talmud, old men, or young men practicing to be old. He felt estranged from them by his magic intention. They loved God as one loves a woman. But already he believed there might be something else to love; he must have begun, at that age, by loving himself. The self is a secure devotion for a while, for a very young man, but only for a while. Time destroys this security. A safe place for one moment, but surely not for the next. He must have been very lonely with his idea.

His mother took this loneliness and love of self for a disease, and perhaps it was. She thought he had been poisoned. Flight in his stomach, the sinking of fear, dread, shock; ungratified desire was a gray weight always with him. His breath was hot, his eyes feverish, he soaked his clothes with sweat. It was the desire to flee or to take; to fight if necessary; to go.

Is this what happens when a boy stops loving God— again? When he stops loving his parents—again? When he discovers the hard way of being a man, and then will have the work of finding God, parents, and love anew? It was a sick passion, like jealousy, betrayed by life. And a terrible rage like lust—to possess the beloved far world of which he knew nothing.

He was abandoning everything that good men have always valued and trusted. For nothing. For a wisp of freedom without any clear sense of what it meant.

While my mind is absorbed in the meaning of the words I write, the melody of those words tells my heart a tale of its own.

Two months later, when my father, the thirteen-year-old man, left for America, smuggled away in the night to avoid the Czar's police, the first act of freedom which he remembers is tearing the medal from his throat and flinging it into the muddy tracks of the road. He didn't believe in charms. He knew who made his luck—himself. Not the child Ben, nor anyone, needed a medal to make luck in life. A man seizes it, he takes it, he forces it together or open, depending on which way it goes. If one way doesn't work, then a man tries the other. Or another. Or another. In the dank night of Russia, his last night in the bosom of family, the thirteen-year-old man pronounced a curse upon good luck. He would let the road lead him first one way, then another. The stars above would be his light and his adornment. If he needed more stars, he would poke them through the darkness; and if he couldn't, he would see without. Or go blind. Or find another way of seeing. Or make do with ears, hands, feet, and stubbornness.

He would not give the medal to any of his brothers.

If their father wanted one, let him take another load of cookies to the rabbi.

Carts across borders at night; money in the palms of deceitful peasants; brief passage through shrill cities of western Europe; the sour hold of a ship which burrowed into the heaving seas of the North Atlantic, towers of water higher than mountains. A storm blew white water sideways as if it wanted to slice off heads: a Cossack storm, using salt water like silver knives. What were the huddled ones doing in the hold of this ship? They came with feathers to make pillows, cloth to make hats, charms to melt into junk. Some rode happy and seasick through the storm, planning heaven in the promised land. A few had schemes and thought they knew what Columbus had found. Some merely sang, living through another day. And some feared they were noplace, nowhere, and dreamed of sinking in the sullen ocean.

My father had flung away his charm long before he saw the magic towers of New York, which were higher than storm water. He was strong. He found work. He hung about on street corners, in alleys, at the entrances of shops.

He studied the smoky gas lamps which lit up the streets almost like daylight, and listened to what people told him, and hurried to get in line for a better job. He needed nothing else for the moment.

If you can imagine the spirit of a thirteen-year-old boy cut away from his family like this, wandering in a strange land where a strange language was spoken, bearing a name not his by birth but now forevermore attached to him, you can also imagine what a dark and threatening world it must have seemed to him and how eagerly he could cleave to any promise of power. This was my father's condition in America. Love brings slow power, but violence, work, and money make it come quick. Or so a boy might think.

In New York, not speaking English, my father carried water to the workmen on the girders of the new sky-scrapers a-building; then he sewed pants and rented one third of a bed in a basement, eight hours a day of it, until the garment workers' strike. Hunger in the old country. In New York, on the winding way toward Cleveland, starvation. A famous strike cut down his eating. He consumed less food. He ate nothing at all sometimes. Sometimes he had a little more, for variety. He shared that bed in a basement on the Lower East Side. They slept in shifts. He had the bed for eight hours, then rolled out, then it was taken by another man, still damp and mussed, smelling of weariness. Owing two nights' rent, he had to give up his third of the bed. The time of famine had come.

Through the endless days he wandered the streets of Manhattan, picking up rumors of jobs, mumbling the strange language, English, hearing echoes of prosperity and comfort north of Fourteenth Street, far to the north. He had skipped a period in history—youth. He was a hungry man. He struggled to bring his brother Ben to golden America—in which he was starving. One week he could afford to eat only three rolls. They had delicious hard brown crusts, returned stale from the paradise north of Fourteenth Street. Inside there was the tender white flesh of bread. The silky fabric of bread. The sharp crumbs and poignant resilience of bread.

The dizziness of hunger mystified him. He was not uncomfortable or weak. It did not seem that way. No weakness, but flashing dreams. Strange New York must have been a more powerful stimulant than sugar or meat. Starvation in New York had no reality. His stomach was full of notions. Smoke in his head. The idea of prosperity floated in the air. It blew down the winds off the harbor; there were gusts of nourishment in the eddying swirls of East Broadway.

And yet, with all these blessings, sometimes he grew abruptly very tired in his wanderings. He slept at odd moments in parks, on benches, on any shadowed grass, at the Battery. He dreamed of what he had to do, bring Ben to America, make his move. He put his head on his cap, looked at the sky, kept his eyes open for a few seconds, and thought: I can do what I have to do. Whatever I have to do, I do.

Then he let himself sleep on a little patch of grass near the oily water licking at the pilings of the Battery. There was nothing anyone could steal in his pockets. He would wake up if they touched his shoes or his cap.

He came awake in many parks and basements. A cigar-maker took pity on him and thought he might have clever fingers. He was apprenticed in a little shop smelling of uric acid from the tobacco. Perhaps it was some other kind of acid. Finger, finger, press, and tongue. Pleasures for the rich and a boss oppressed by his own troubles, who turned silent after his initial kindness. But sometimes in the stillness of winters or the stony heat of summers, the boss would read aloud to his seven or eight deft rollers of cigars.

The work was murderously monotonous. One day he awoke and he had been a cigar-maker for six years. He fled this job.

When he left Russia, he left family, home, language, the threatening Cossacks and the Czar's cruel army. It was complicated to leave home, to abandon history. To leave New York would be easier. There was nothing but the wild tenements, the jungle of streets and alleys. The strike had brought him starvation, as if to mock his assumption of the name "Gold." There was no gold in the streets of New York. It was a myth, a joke, a lie like other myths. The myths try to keep a man from making his own way. As best he can, a man must thread his way through the vain promises and hopes.

In after-years my father used to tell his friends in the steam room of the Russian Bath in Cleveland, Ohio— see, he had nice clean feet, no calluses—that he was descended from rabbis and came over on the *Mayflower*. But this was a joke; his father was a Chassid, a believer in miracles, and not a rabbi; and the only Mayflower he came on was the Mayflower Moving & Storage, which carried him once from Indianapolis to Cleveland. My grandfather believed in miracles, and no miracles happened to him; my father believed only in decision and will, and made his own miracles. He accepted reasonable chances. He hoped for reasonable victories. My father's sister and younger brothers occupied most of his will and his powers of decision in the years until a grand duke's assassination at Sarajevo finally forced him to put away thoughts of his home village. That was the sensible thing to do.

One by one, thanks to the money he had earned in New York, his brothers and his sister were brought to America. The strikes were settled. A mountain of cigars arose toward heaven, but the smoke disappeared. A few dollars—one brother. A few more dollars—another brother. A few more dollars—a sister. Now they were all here, and soon the parents might be persuaded to leave their hut, their cart, their horse, their cow, their rabbi in Kamenets-Podolsk, their enigma-solving rabbi in the next town, for Hester Street in New York, where thugs in caps and policemen in blue and the stunned, dazzled, newly arrived immigrants strolled. Women sat on stoops with the sun on their thighs. Men worried about wives and children in the *shtetl*, back there, whom they would not see again for years, or ever, and the women with sun-warmed thighs looked over the fretful greenhorns. What a shame there was only the East Side sun to warm them on a fine afternoon. What a shame that so many healthy men looked so worried and unhealthy. Somehow there was a great deal of noise, though no one seemed to be shouting. A clamor of hope and desire filled the streets.

Each member of the family took my father's lead and accepted the name "Gold" upon arrival. It was simple and pronounceable, and it meant something. Mainly it meant they were American. They guaranteed their intention with a name that cut to the heart of America.

The only daughter was here, the oldest son was here, the youngest son was here, the miscellaneous son was here —Esther, Sam, Ben, Morris. There was no reason for the parents to put off the future with religious excuses. In 1912 my father had a gold tooth installed in his head by a dentist on Delancey Street who specialized in internal decoration; it replaced a perfectly adequate pale tooth. He then spent the rest of his money on a trip back to the old country. He wore fresh clothes, green shoes, and flashed a quick but modest smile to show the gold tooth. He whistled down the road. He whistled whenever he felt like it. Remembering that he had a man's task, to persuade his parents to come to America and take a new name, he felt like stopping his whistling. He told them about some of his adventures in the streets of New York, but he left out much. The conversations on the stoops and under electric bulbs in the hallways at night had no reality when he returned to being a child asking something of his parents. He tried to tell them about another way of dealing with fate. He asked them to let him deliver them from their fate. He showed the tooth in a smile; he begged them; because he had forgotten how to weep, he took his father's hand. His father disengaged his hand and wondered where the boy had learned such ways and cut his hair. Silence.

Then my father's father pointed out that the Ukraine was closer to Jerusalem than New York, and that when the Messiah comes, it will be just too far to roll from New York.

My father conceded this well-taken point, but remarked that it was a long roll from the Ukraine to Jerusalem too. And if you had to take a long roll, head over heels, or even sideways, more comfortably, why not take it from the Lower East Side, in the good company of the younger members of the family?

His father thought this one over. With lips pursed, but not whistling. He mentioned that he might discuss it with the rabbi.

"The rabbi," my father said, "will tell you only what you want to hear anyway, and eats all the cookies."

"Hanh?" said his father. *"Only?"*

"Mostly," said my father.

My father said never mind, the children were well, and they all wanted to see the family united in America. His mother spoke very little, but noticed that my father was skinny despite his gold tooth. If he had a gold tooth, he should also be fat. If not, is America a crazy place? Also he shaved his chin, cut his hair, and, in general, appeared to be in great danger.

"How is Ben, my baby?" she asked.

"Lonely. He misses you. He needs his mother. He wants to know when you're coming. Doing fine."

"Well, who put such ideas in his head? A baby like that."

"I did," my father admitted. "So now?"

Still and still, it was true that all the children had gone to New York. At last the old people promised to give up both holy tradition and easy rolling to Jerusalem in order not to lose their children. Maybe the Messiah would send skates too. My father thought that, but did not say it.

He returned to New York to earn the money to send for his parents. They promised. The spiteful fume of an Atlantic storm in midwinter attacked his stomach and ears. But he rolled with it like a sailor, dancing among the strewed, groaning bodies shipping themselves over for the first time. He sang to himself: Riding to America! All riding to America! No matter how sullen the ocean which lay between, they could all ride to America!

It took a while to find the money he needed because he was already working to keep his sister and brothers alive, and sometimes one or the other could not find a job, and there were depressions or strikes or layoffs or illness or one or another manner of disaster. Sometimes Ben was lazy and wouldn't sell his papers. Sometimes they went without eating. They ate stale bread or nothing at all. Like everyone else, they ate what was available during the occasional bad times in golden America. Ben, the youngest, sometimes said—foolishness—that he wished he were home. My father told him: America is now your home. The times will get better. There are new shops with old sewing machines opening in the basements of lower Broadway. There's a new place where you can rent pushcarts cheap and owe for the rent. But Ben had not been ready to leave his parents. Improving the times was not in his line.

On one terrible day, a day which grew worse in memory as the healing years passed, Ben again said to my father, "I want to go back."

"What's the matter, you crazy? There is no back."

"It was a mistake. I shouldn't have come. You made me come. I got no business here."

"Mama mama mama, you want to go to your mama."

Ben stood up. "That's right," he said defiantly.

My father wanted to hit him. Then he blinked; that was as foolish as going to the rabbi. He also had stood up, but he sank down in the chair of the dusty room they shared near the truck terminal. He said, "Ben, you try for a little while. You're just a kid. Why don't you try?"

"Okay," said Ben. "Maybe I'll go into the Army."

"You're too young. You're a foreigner."

"They'll take me. They make you a citizen."

"They won't take you." And then my father yelled at him: "Peasant!"

"Okay," said Ben, and picked up his cap and his book and went out to night school. He studied English every night, as did my father. This evening my father didn't go to class. He stayed home, drinking tea and brooding. The Army! Foolishness! (Later I asked him what language he thought these thoughts in, English, Yiddish, or Russian, and he looked at me in astonishment. "I *thought*," he said.) He decided, in whatever language, that he would hurry his parents; Ben needed them in America. And he would keep an eye on Ben. For some it was a great relief, a freedom, to leave home and parents and old wasting ways to make a life in which a man chooses everything, even his name. But for some, for Ben, it was a burden. My father, not understanding this, recognized it. He drank tea, ate half a loaf of bread with sugar, and waited under the bare bulb for Ben to get home from school. "You want to talk some more?" he asked.

Ben said, "You already told me," and went to bed.

My father sat up, figuring. The parents must be brought soon. There was the money and there was his father's stubbornness. But it must be soon.

If my father's will had been in control of history, the will of the family would have been done. Instead, the war of 1914 began. Before the parents could make the journey, they were killed in some obscure fashion. There was an unrecorded pogrom, followed by a fire. The maps had never recorded this village, and now what had never been recorded dropped out of fact. Ashes and ruins. A new time dug its heels into the bones of the old time. Gone were the ancestors, gone were the hut and cow and cemetery nearby, gone even was the wonder-working, cookie-loving rabbi in the next town. One ancient Jew survived, hiding in a chimney—my father's grandfather. But the mother would never see her baby Ben, who was not doing fine without her. The old name of the family was lost in the smoky fires of pogrom, war, and revolution. For good and all, the survivors were committed to America.

3

As long as they were in New York, and since there was no more hope of climbing a high building to see back to Kamenets-Podolsk, they had better look further into the subject of America. My father decided that Ben and he would finish the winter term in night school first, and in the meantime he would think around a little. The acquired habit of thinking toward the West troubled his body. It was like those Sunday morning dreams of women. It drove a man to thinking and walking and thinking again in his dark hole of a room, under the bare bulb, with the child's American primer spread open on his knees.

I am the Gingerbread Boy, I am, I am.
I can run, I can, I can.

Reading American could be as silly as the wonder-working rabbi's book of magic. He put on his cap and went out to buy a poppyseed roll for Sunday lunch. It was a gray, damp day, heavy with the Atlantic, and even the poppyseed roll had lost its flavor. A waste of a penny. But as luck would have it, at exactly this moment standing in a doorway, chewing the last of the poppyseed roll as the drizzle began—shaken from both earth and sky, it seemed, just shaking in the air—he met a man from Canton, Ohio. They discovered that they were cousins, or maybe not cousins, but they both came from Kamenets-Podolsk, or maybe not from Kamenets-Podolsk exactly, but nearby, in different villages, on opposite sides of Kamenets. In the Ukraine. Near Kiev. They had never heard of each other. Search as they did, mothers and fathers, and fathers of mothers and mothers of fathers, all the way back past miracles and pogroms, they could find no family in common. Not a single person. But nevertheless they were close relatives in a doorway as it rained with a fine mean drizzle on a Sunday morning in New York.

The cousin began to tell of the sleek, rich, golden city of Canton, Ohio. He pushed back the visor of his cap and lectured until the pale sun came out upon the joys of being a peddler in darling Canton. The new friends paced back and forth on the steaming sidewalks of Hester and Delancey streets while the cousin bragged about his brother, Shloimi Spitz, the king of Canton, whom even the Cossacks feared.

"There are Cossacks in your town of Canton?" my father inquired politely. He did want to insult his friend's city, but still, this could be a disadvantage.

"I refer to the police. That is the word I use."

"Ah," said my father. He would remember this. Though he had left his story about the gingerbread boy in his room, he was still learning American. Everywhere he went, he learned some more.

"Shloimi Spitz takes care of me."

"You need a nurse?" my father asked. "And there are Cossacks? In Canton? Where's Canton?"

He had already noticed about humankind that questions tend to draw a man out. All day and all night long the cousin who was not a cousin from Canton, Ohio, discoursed upon the joys of the peddler's life in that shining city on the steppes of Ohio. Long hours, low pay, no security. But it was the right time to talk with my father about moving westward. Also (went the cousin's rhapsody) fresh air and horse manure on the shoes. You have a baby brother? You can take your baby brother. You will live together like lovebirds in Canton, Ohio, and go to night school there, and borrow a cart from a jobber and pay him back a little every day, and get rich like me, as I will soon be, and eat prune pastries and fresh meat and forget your mother and father who will never now come to America, you had better just forget all about them . . .

My father listened very carefully, only occasionally interrupting with a question when the flow of promises grew thin.

In a few days he found himself, sure enough, with a borrowed cart, selling fruit in the streets of Canton. True to what the cousin had said, it was true, all true, he had manure on his feet. He could not be certain that it came from fat healthy horses in every case. He sometimes suspected dogs, pigs, and worse. Human beings. But his brother Ben was with him, and they could no longer see the ocean that led back to the old country, and the fertile hills and plains outside the village of Canton looked a little like the Ukraine. He was happy. He could whistle in peace. He wore a cap, corduroy pants, and heavy cork-soled boots. He spoke Yiddish, Russian, and a bit of English, which was the language shared by many of the inhabitants of Canton, Ohio. He attended night school to learn to read.

> I like to walk. I like to hop. I like to run.
> I am the Gingerbread Boy, I am, I am.

He explained to Ben in Yiddish, Russian, and English why it was important to read all about the gingerbread boy, no matter what Ben thought. In America many things are strange, but nothing must be foreign to young men learning to be Americans. He also tried to teach Ben how to sell oranges, apples, pears, and grapefruit from a cart. Tomatoes too, but there were dangers in tomatoes, and many people thought tomatoes poisonous. Eggs too—grave risks in the traffic with eggs.

He whistled and pulled his cart on a certain street at the edge of town which came to be known among the peddlers as his street. He sold fruit and sometimes a tomato or an egg. He saw very little of the talkative cousin who had inspired him to go to Canton, but why should he? The man wasn't even a relative.

There had been thugs in New York, willing to hit a boy on the head and take his dollar, but my father knew no gangsters yet. He had to go west for that.

One day a gangster named Shloimi Spitz sauntered twice around his cart on a gray November corner of Canton. Then, together with his kid brother, Moishe, the silent one, he tipped over the cart. While my father chased oranges, which run fast, and bananas, which wait, the Spitz brothers explained in detail the workings of the insurance agency which they represented. Shloimi did the talking. They would protect him from their impulses to tip fruit carts, and also from other insurance agencies. Some of those other insurance agencies were really mean; they tipped over people too. The Spitz brothers, lifelong gangsters, seemed much older than my father. They were men of the world. Their authority prevailed.

Oddly enough, despite the percentage appropriated by the gangsters, business suddenly began to prosper. My father bought a new pair of green shoes, learned arithmetic, and read fluently in English, only moving his lips a little. He swaggered up the boardinghouse porches to take girls out walking. He associated his prosperity with the intervention of his protectors, the gangsters. Also, although he barely heard of it, a war was beginning in the old country, and this had its distant repercussions in the liberal sale of fruit on the street corners of Canton, Ohio.

From one girl in a boardinghouse, a tailor's assistant, my father learned that green shoes are not really elegant; in return, she let him try to teach her something, too. Though he was just learning it himself.

He bought a motorcycle. That was truly elegant. The girl let him wear his green shoes. They drove out of the town of Canton on the dusty hilltop road. My father pointed out that the green of his shoes matched the green of the grass. The girl pointed out that the green of his shoes matched the green of the shimmering treetops. My father urged her to discuss it with him on the green grass just a little farther off the road. They shivered and hugged each other on the damp green grass. My father pointed out that the war might last forever or that a gangster might come to kill him. What could the girl answer to this? She answered what she had probably long ago and deep within decided to answer.

This was not the gold my father had expected to find in the streets of America. It was much better, rich as ripe fruit, as a squirting pear.

My father dealt bravely, like a responsible business-man, with his plague of gangsters. He stood up tall and proud and paid them off. It was only money. A man threads his way through the hills and valleys with feeling, with hope, and with an alert sense of the possible.

Then one day tragedy struck. But it did not strike my father; it struck one of his gangsters, whose sense of the possible had exceeded the actual. He had wanted to make an empire of the fruit carts of Canton, Ohio. Alexander was a boy when he conquered Greece. Moishe Spitz was a mere youth when he moved to consolidate several insur-ance companies into one. The discussion became ardent. Moishe grew insulting. The other insurance agent grew equally insulting. Amid all this impoliteness Moishe Spitz got hit on the head in an argument about insurance routes and neighborhoods. The other insurance salesman kicked him where he lay and went off to his own boardinghouse. Moishe remained on the ground until Shloimi found him, carried him home, and put him to bed for a few days. The two gangsters shared the same double-sized bed.

My father suffered dizzy spells from his trips into the

green grass with the tailor's assistant, but had a good appetite and slept soundly. Moishe suffered dizzy spells, slept poorly, pushed his plate away untouched. He suffered his headaches in silence. More than ever he disliked conversation. Shloimi did the talking. Now Shloimi held his brother's hand, because he sometimes fell, and the two gangsters strolled hand in hand, like lovers, on their missions of extortion. Moishe had a headache. My father gave him an orange from the cart to suck. Moishe had a thirst which never went away.

One day my father heard a suggestion from a neighborhood personage, the justice of the peace. "Enlist in the Army," he said, "and you will become a citizen. Also you will see Europe, because there is sure to be war."

"Is always war."

"This great land of ours will go again to the grand test, my lad." He paused before giving a sketch of the recent grand test against Pancho Villa. "Are you listening, lad? You have the look of a person who is not paying close attention. We judges sometimes call that Contempt of Court. But there is nothing on this earth, other than a proud scorn for Darwinism, which so unites a people as service in the Armed Forces . . . What, *what* are you dreaming about, Sam?"

"Citizens?" my father asked. Ben had heard the same rumor. It was an odd idea. To his knowledge he had never been a citizen.

He sold the cart and enlisted in the Army. They turned him down at the last moment because he couldn't find all his papers and they suspected him of being underage, although an orphan businessman during a long life in America. Ben was definitely underage. He bought back a larger cart, one with rubber wheels.

During this period of decision Moishe Spitz had temporarily let go of his brother Shloimi's hand and gone to stab the insurance agent who had knocked him on the head. Oddly enough, he remembered to take a knife with him. He stabbed him dead and was consequently waiting to be executed in the Ohio State penitentiary. My father arranged to visit him. A man owes this at least to his own extortionist. "Enlist in the Army," my father advised him.

"They won't take me," Moishe said mournfully. "I get these headaches."

They were going to electrocute him instead.

"Would you like some marzipan?" my father asked, extending the box to the guard. The guard bit one candy, chewed, nodded, index finger raised with judiciary authority. Then he lowered the finger into the box, closed about a handful, and allowed the rest to be passed to Moishe.

At about this time my father also decided to leave Canton, but for the big city, either Cleveland or Indianapolis. He said goodbye to his gangsters. Moishe was just eighteen when he was electrocuted. Shloimi, in despair, wept a whole night through. His brother would never know the joys of being grown-up in America. My father tried to comfort him by pointing out that a human life is valuable to the individual, from his own private point of view, but not particularly exceptional when you consider the history of the race in general. He said that in his own words. It was his philosophy. What he actually said was: "Tch-tch. It's terrible. Well, what can you do?"

Shloimi replied with little piping sounds. These were his sobs and tears. These high-pitched squeaks were an effort to explain himself to the world and to demand an explanation from fate. What Shloimi meant was: *Grief knows no general forms; my grief is unique.* He seemed inconsolable. Then he went to Detroit for a little vacation and to make new contacts for the insurance business.

4

As Shloimi moved on, so my father moved on; from Canton to Indianapolis to Cleveland, from pushcarts to a store. Like Shloimi, he discovered that it was only logical to be reasonable and only reasonable to look for the best possibilities in America. America confirmed the suspicion —good luck elsewhere, soon, pretty soon now, if you never let up. He kept busy.

He also learned to go out to seek in flesh and living spirit the visions that came to haunt him at midnight or in languorous Sunday morning dreams. He had doors to lock at the store, and a cooler for vegetables, and keys to jangle, and an empty room in a boardinghouse in which he sometimes sat with Ben and sometimes with an English book or a Yiddish newspaper, and sometimes sat alone with a haunting loneliness and desire. He roared out on his motorcycle in the rain when no one else dared try the tricky, slipping wheels. He almost knew what he was looking for.

My father met my mother at an ice-skating rink in Cleveland, Ohio, on an October night in 1923, shortly before I was conceived. Thinking perhaps about this, she says he had no taste in those days. He was uneducated. He was an uneducated greenhorn. He didn't care what people thought or she said to him. She said No and he didn't listen. She said No and he cocked his head to listen to something else. He was inventing his style—the one which signified his use of himself and what he was after. He spoke with a heavy accent, wore green shoes, rode a motorcycle. He was rude, quick, indifferent. Also he had the awfully rude habit of picking up girls at the ice-skating rink.

The last one he picked up, so far as history records it, was my mother. Though he had no taste, he liked the plump blond little green-eyed lady whose ankles needed strengthening before she could spend a whole evening on skates. He suggested that she take his arm and try something easy—a waltz, a two-step, or just going where he led her.

"Ohh, what's your name?"

"I said already—Gold."

"Pleased to meet you, I'm sure," she said politely.

"Some hot chocolate."

"Oh, oo, some cocoa would be tasty."

"Cocoa they haven't got, but chocolate I can arrange it."

Goodbye, little lady, you're going to get whatever he calls it.

He must have seemed a tough old-country character, pink-faced but not a boy, maroon-faced, wooing her with a heavy Yiddish accent, wooing her with arms and legs hardened from heaving crates of vegetables onto trucks, into coolers, off stands. For some reason he had learned to skate, and at that time could do tight, fast little figure-skating turns. Having no family sent him out a lot nights. To school, to the rink. To play cards. To try his luck in all ways. Probably he liked leading girls behind the organ— the organ at the rink that played "When It's Nighttime in Italy, It's Wednesday Over Here" as he led the girls round and around until they became so dizzy that he looked tall, elegant, and rich. He sold produce during the day; he leapt on his motorcycle in his green shoes and roared to the rink at night; he lived in a fury of using himself. After a starved boyhood in the old country, he found himself uncorked in the New World—full of food, blood hot, and the name of Gold for power and flash and the new tooth in his head. He smiled often to show the tooth. Then he met, took, and married my mother, some of whose people were rabbis. They were quiet ones and thought he looked like a brute, but a nice fellow; and perhaps he would be kind to her, as brutes often were in folklore.

Anyway, it was too late to do anything about it. He had

learned the words to "Just a Girl That Men Forget" and whispered them to her above their flashing skates. It was good practice in English. But he had tipped over his own life and hers and couldn't be bothered with mere commentary. The marriage papers were in order and my mother was already leaning back on her Enna Jettick heels in order to carry me more easily forward in her belly. Once he had bad taste; now he had her taste.

During these times when so many women are having children, I am reminded of an incident that occurred when my mother was pregnant with me and thus confused. My father's part in it was abstract and dark, like all the rites of fatherhood.

"Some women want peach ice cream, I heard of a woman wanting nothing but Kadota figs," my father complains. "My brother Morris's wife had him out at the fruit auction four o'clock, four-thirty in the morning, he should find cantaloupes in February!" Sometimes he howls with the memory. "But you, *you*—you had to go exploring, Mrs. Admiral Byrd, with your hat with the flower on it, with the feather on the flower . . ." As always, my mother smirks, since for her the event is now a mere ritual of words. Besides, the car was insured.

The bridge leading across the Cuyahoga River in Cleveland, Ohio, from the central business district toward Lakewood, the suburb where my parents had *the store*, passes over an area known as "the Flats." The valley of the river, once named by Indians, now serves the lake boat docks and the sailors prowling for their first drinks and first women after the long dull haul with cargoes of rusty ore, coal redeemed by rainbows of oil, or greased-down machinery. It is from here, in good times or war times, that the mills send up their red false dawn to the suburbs during the night. Buried in a bitter wet smoke, the joints of the neighborhood are forever sprayed with mitelike squiggles of black dust that squash under a finger, so that the waitresses and bartenders have quit complaining or even joking about it. You can tell they still notice by the way a man screws his finger into his nose with a sudden itch. It's not the place for an easy living.

A few jerry-built row houses remain, hovering near the mills; from some of the houses Slavic children stare out the windows, blinking for growth in a place where hardly a living plant clings. In time of prosperity, of course, the area throbs powerfully. The oily, acid-ridden river moves the barges; the fathers of the pouting, squint-eyed children work the furnaces. Not many decent folk pass through the lower depths of the Flats willingly—unless on business there—since sailors and foreign-born workmen constitute an unknown quantity, therefore a danger, whether they like it or not. Descending to them is a risk, an escape, the matter of desire and thus nightmare; as ominous as all this, it is not even a thing which needed to be forbidden.

Well, my mother had no business there. She was driving, thinking about something. She made a wrong turn. Her descent could perhaps be credited to my subtle crouching in her belly, invited but always a surprise, producing strange cravings. But did she crave dangerous visitations? Whatever it was, and despite her businesswoman, lady-driver peering over the wheel, some lower connection moved her to veer down the incline that leads to the Flats under the bridge, instead of hunting with the traffic across it to the parks and suburbs of the West Side. She sank below the bridge instead of sailing over it toward the sweet life with her first son folded and stirring within. Away from Lakewood and into the Flats. Down. There must have been an ease and languor in that soft descent. There was but one way to go, once she was on it—down and farther down. There must have been a sudden muffling of noise and strain.

Oh dear, who am I? she must have been thinking.

Down, down, down.

Once established on this slope, she seems to have coasted in fatalistic fashion until she finally pulled the brake when the two front wheels of the Peerless lapped familiarly over the edge of a moldering dock. Perhaps, if a flat-nosed Hungarian loiterer hadn't cursed her out and shouted, "Hey you, lady!" in an old-country accent similar to her father's, she might have slid peacefully, without protest, into the thickened water and metallic silt of the Cuyahoga River. So be it—so it almost was. Instead, the car stopped, teetering; my mother never turned, she never faltered; she floated to rest while the planks and pilings groaned. Then she scrambled out, wheezing, holding her belly for my benefit with one hand and patting her hair for the Hungarian's with the other. A rich breeze of garbage and industry steamed up from the idle waters. The Hungarian was now closer to her than oblivion.

"Hey lady, you crazy or something?"

"Me?"

"You, lady!"

Neither replying directly nor giving way to her tears, she answered severely, "I want my husband. Tell Sam right away."

"I said you crazy, you?"

By this time the children from the shanties nearby had given up their games to form a circle of intense admiration about the Peerless, my mother, and the exasperated Hungarian. A grass-roots social movement toward pushing the car back out of danger was stopped by her cries. "Don't touch that! Don't you dare touch it! What? No! You just wait for Sam. My husband's going to come right away—"

"It's gonna flop!"

"Sink!"

"You stay away!"

When she went to telephone my father, the Hungarian, defender of the will of a pregnant woman, stalwart admirer of a lady of passion, here called craziness, stationed himself with authority near the left rear wheel in order to prevent the children and the meddling adults from touching the car; he even momentarily intimidated the neighborhood cop. Opinion was divided, of course, between expressed schemes for pulling it back out of the yawning air and secret hopes. "Give it a little nudge!" one youth bawled cheerfully. No eyes met his. He enjoyed voicing his interest in seeing the Peerless swim or founder, according to its talents, but there was a rare solidarity on the side of non-catastrophe. The crowd gravely shoved; the Hungarian explained how he had seen it all, tried to warn the lady, what can a man do? At the center of the drama for a moment, his versions of the incident multiplied while the wax in his ears softened with sun and emotion.

"What can a man do when the lady she is peculiar? Be a gentleman—that's all."

My mother returned from telephoning. Married men sighed. The early customers of the café came blinking out into the street. Unmarried men sighed, too. Waiting, brooding plumply on the pilings and the greenish waters, my mother did not look at the automobile. It crouched in a submissive posture over the edge of the rotted, filmy pilings. Chewing over their own suggestions, the crowd goggled and goggled; a sailor hallooed above the rest: "She ain't bad, ain't bad at all. I'll drive her machine any time she asks me." His laughter died when no one helped. My mother did not move, articulating her aloofness, keeping the point, which was me, aimed discreetly away from the watchers.

Would the pilings of the dock yield under this sudden affront? How much vibration would it take to dislodge the wheels? Was it against the law to park like this? How do you know? They ought to put up a sign then. Passers-by bumped and gathered, unable to miss an opportunity for debate on a fine spring morning when the sun burst bravely through the haze.

Each opinion had value—there was no precedent.

"All she got to do is ask me," the sailor hawed, tireless.

"Where the devil's the tow truck?" demanded a lover of fires and other disasters. "You can count on 'em sure to tie up traffic, but when you really want 'em, no, then they're playing cards with the station-house boys. I know those boys all right."

"I'd just get in and drive right off"—the sailor tried once more—"but she sure got her rumble seat full already, that one."

It was worth being out this morning.

At last my father arrived, still wearing his apron from the store. Lord of this lady, he set up his standard with a trumpet flourish, blowing his nose ferociously and saying, "What's the matter with you, kotchka?" in a voice fierce enough to put the terror into my mother and shiver the spines of a sympathetic audience. But his wounded gaze found him little different from her lounging Hungarian adviser.

"So you have to yell the machine back up?" she asked. "Shame, Sam, shame. I got the morning sickness again."

"What's the matter with you?" he added more gently. An inexperienced man in the back room of the store was pinching and lining the strawberry pint boxes. And who was to prevent the clerks from filling their pockets? His impatience needed forgiveness from her, even in her hour of need. "Kotchka" means "duckling."

The Hungarian tried to explain, repenting his earlier harshness, that hers was a mistake which anyone could make. My father did not believe this. "What's the matter with you?" he demanded while the Peerless wobbled.

The sailor suggested that they tie a rope to the rear bumper and pull the automobile out of danger. Someone advised waiting for the police tow car, which should arrive at any moment. Another warned that the decayed edge of the dock might abruptly crumble. My father, an independent businessman, glared contemptuously at these meddlers and wiped his hands on his apron while my mother listened for the word. "What's the matter with you?" he repeated softly, merely considering and judging, murmuring it contemplatively this time, turning to measure the car and its predicament with a shrewd independent eye—that eye which was capable of challenging the A & P to do battle. My mother trembled with shame and love.

"All right, I'll drive it out," he announced.

A few splinters of applause in the springtime air of the Cuyahoga valley. "What?" demanded the duckling. It was her turn to be contemptuous. "You want to be a hero? Now it's your turn for crazy nuts?"

"Why not, Frieda?" he asked with a face of longing and sorrow.

"Sam, don't!" she cried. "Oh don't! I didn't mean it! I'm sorry, Sam! My stomach hurts me!"

Did he see this accident as flight from family, himself, and me?

Could he have been jealous of the Hungarian, the sailor, the strange crowd jeering while she never once smiled? She threatened him with her hands on her belly; he shook his head mournfully.

"I'll drive it out," he explained. Rather than ask the help of men whom he had never seen before, he decided to punish my mother by risking himself in a dramatic rectification of her error. No one ever even *heard* of turning into the Flats instead of going straight out to Lakewood where you belong, he thought sternly at her. "Stand clear," he said.

Opening the door stealthily so that no vibration could precipitate disaster, my father slid in behind the wheel. A hush descended over the Hungarian, the sailor, the crowd, and the children running in little circles at the edges of it. My mother, gasping, weakened by unspoken reproach, measured the brief allowance of wet splinters and blighted wood already under the front wheels.

She hadn't allowed him much.

He worked the starter. The Peerless motor made its truculent noise. He tightened the brakes and eased the gears into reverse. The brake too firm, he paused with a patient and masterful shrug of his heavy shoulders, full of wider considerations. The apron and the blue brawn of flesh at his arms distracted the watchers from the quick decision of his hands at the gearshift. He let out the brake slightly; with this motion, the clutch disengaged, and the gears slipping from reverse into neutral, the car jerked forward an inch or two. *Forward!* "Sam!" my mother cried. He came hurtling out the door, already angrily arguing, as the pilings cracked and splintered.

"Ah-hah, you see what you did?" he yelled. "It ain't enough you put the Peerless here, you had to—"

"But I didn't say anything! I didn't do anything, Sam. You—"

While they shouted at each other, the automobile ponderously slid, thus resolving their discussion on the level of tragic action while the crowd breathed *Ahhh* in chorus. With just a groaning noise and then a crunching one, it leaned gracefully over the oily water; it plopped in; it could not swim toward the opposite shore; it settled helplessly with a gurgle and rush into the ooze.

"Now wait a minute. Who started this, hah? It ain't some Mrs. Jones or other drove the Peerless where—"

"I suppose *I*—"

"—where she had no business, no, oh no!" He appealed to the crowd, Hungarian, sailor, and all. "Is that who it was? No, it had to be my Frieda."

"I suppose I practically just threw it away," my mother yelled. "I suppose I had to fix things all by myself, Mr. Show-off."

The children cheered while mud and bubbles swirled about the Peerless embedded in the Cuyahoga River.

Whenever this story is related now, my mother justifies her own part in the event by the fact that she was already profoundly busy with me, and my father winks at their children, my brothers and me, in order to tell us how deeply our mother's abstraction had confused him, withdrawn him from himself, on this occasion which demanded unambiguous action. Thus, over the years, I have learned to accept the accident as partly my fault, a commentary on the phrase *the sins of the fathers*. But in his response to my mother's mistake, my father also intended something beautiful, even sublime—he was a *chevalier sans peur et sans reproche* under his apron. He meant to bear on his own shoulders the disgrace for her false turn down under the bridge, just as she bore me on her belly. Chivalry is an idea; yet I too, once a mere idea after an evening's ice-skating, had already eaten the calcium from her teeth, the red from her blood, and the sleek from her hair. My father could sacrifice himself and the Peerless to my mother and me. No, it was not simple nerves or jealousy of the Hungarian.

"Is it my fault you drive like a crazy woman?" he asked.

"Genius then! Couldn't wait for the tow truck!"

"You had to come to work, like I need you in the store, people should talk I make you a slave?"

"Now *I* did it"—and she pointed to the Peerless, its blue top gently awash in the river. "Nudnik!"

"The High Level is so invisible you could hardly see it, I suppose, you had to take a ride down here. Woman!" he said, "you think a Peerless is a carp, it goes for a morning swim by the river?"

To this my mother smiled without answering. Surely my father sensed his own benevolence and his cunning, anticipating her disgrace if he had merely forgiven her. Two or three bored policemen's faces burrowed through the crowd.

Everyone watched, turning from the drowned car below the crippled dock to the fight between my father, gesticulating furiously, and my mother, stubborn, righteous, and scornful. The Hungarian, like most philanthropists not understanding all the issues, tried without success to mediate between the two of them. United in disaster, they turned coolly from him. "Kotch," my father said softly, holding her hand. Thus purged of pity and fear, as Aristotle remarks, my father called up his insurance man to find out how long he would have to wait until Metropolitan Auto & Life paid off.

Later the car was brought up, smelly and dripping; I think I was born the next week. Both events, I claim, were actions of my father's deliberation.

5

In Cleveland, some years after the trouble with the Spitz brothers in Canton, my father found himself with one son, a baby; then two sons, two babies; and then still another swelling in his duckling's belly; and who could tell when all this would ever stop? It just seems to go on and on, like sliding under a bridge.

Married to the High Level Bridge lady, he called her "duckling." He forgot the other lady with the green shoes (his). Canton seemed as far away as Kamenets-Podolsk. As a family man, he left his last motorcycle under old sheets in the garage. He sometimes missed those carefree evenings, zooming up the gentle hills outside Canton, looking for a patch of dry grass, but as always, he lived in the present. He might have missed his mother, too, but when you haven't got a mother? Kamenets gone. New York past. Canton over, and also Indianapolis. Cleveland here.

The sun and the moon and fresh fruits and vegetables are eternal. The produce of the season endures. A man can make do with eternal things.

Also a man must sometimes learn to make do with the pay-off. He grew accustomed to regular contributions toward keeping his truck from being tipped over. He occasionally arranged not to be beaten up. As part of his business expenses he included gifts to the police, who otherwise discovered or invented violations of the law, and to the fire and building departments; these gangsters spoke English clearly.

The market gangsters spoke with eastern European or southern European accents. My father learned to smile and pay. He had three sons. No, that was last year. He had four sons. That too was a ransom. How? It happened. He, like other businessmen, managed to bargain for the unbargainable—life and the right to live. With wives, with gangsters, with fate. They found a field of agreement. Balance was possible. Everyone is human. The gangsters knew the limits, too.

Then, in the middle thirties, a new style of gangster moved in. Where they had been waiting, no one knew, though certainly some jumped onto the piers from the fast motorboats which had carried Canadian whiskey into Toledo and Cleveland; and some scholars had tried their skill at distilling alcohol in the research laboratories of Canton, southern Ohio, and Kentucky. The end of Pro-

hibition made them nervous. They came blinking off their
launches, out of their red barns. They sought new careers.
Sometimes the dream comes true in America. Without
great delay their sincere desire to be predators was
crowned by success. Thus entered the racketeer.

For my father, "gangster" was a familiar word and object; the new racketeer was a menace. These men, pretending to be labor organizers, extorted dues and bribes
from employees and employer. They could ply their trade
openly under the disguise of a union. They learned that a
social structure beats individual enterprise two ways going.
They took tribute from workers under the name of dues;
they demanded payment from employers in order not to
call a strike. When they had trouble with the people, they
checked them in for new people. They paved the muddy
banks of the Cuyahoga with former friends set like jewels
in concrete. In turn, they sometimes looked out at the
world of men through holes in their skulls. They took
chances.

Exhibiting the natural conservatism of a man with
house, wife, family, a sheepskin jacket for going to the
market, and an extra suit for important occasions, my
father resisted the new style. Gangsters yes—racketeers
no. He was stubborn and told the police he had been
threatened. They told him to report back at once if
someone broke his arm or dropped a brick on his head.

"Yah," he said.

"You remember now," said the cop. "Say, Sam, my
kids sure loved that barrel of old no-good stuck-together
candy you sent over. Now it's all gone."

"Yah," said my father, "I think I got another."

He found a bushel of rock candy in the back room of the store, shrugged, dashed a glass of water into it, and told the driver to deliver it to Officer Cecil Bull.

One evening I had the mumps and lay alone in my room, aged ten, listening to the dance band from the Hotel Cleveland and wishing to be grown-up so that I could make sense of that tinkle of glass and laughter, those mechanical rhythms. I knew the child's perverse nostalgia for the future—for the saxophones and snare drums, the dancing, the absurd smiling, all the masquerades to come. I had heard about lust, and slightly feverish, developed an idea of what it might be. My face was as round as a turnip, and the purple swellings on my neck took the fun out of swallowing. I thought about style and sex, and also about the sadness of being a neglected horse; I had been reading *Black Beauty.* But I could not whinny. I itched. I could not swallow. Suddenly a rock came sailing through the closed window, shattering glass. I swallowed. Before I could whinny, my father was in the room, picking up the rock and cursing. Goddamn, goddamn, goddamn bastards. My mother swept up the glass. "Shush, talk nice, the kid," she said.

There was no note on the rock, but the message was clear. Ollie the Agent was communicating. The false union intended serious negotiation.

My father telephoned the police, who said, "Kids. Halloween is only two months away. Crazy kids."

"Officer Cecil," said my father, "listen, I sent you the candy."

"It was all stuck together anyhow, Sam, but my kids loved it. They broke it up with hammers. I tell you there's nothing I can handle. It's higher up. So you know what you got to do."

"Ach, I hate it."

"Well, they talk your language, Sam, From the old country, ain't they? Don't blame it on me. I didn't let in all the riffraff, Sammy."

My father put the earpiece back on the hook, sat for a while over the telephone, shouted at my brothers: "Nobody walks barefoot in this house! Use the vacuum first!" Then he sat awhile longer. My mother tiptoed around him. My three brothers stood in a row, six Buster Brown shoes watching him although he gave very little signal in return. Then he sighed and used the telephone again. No response. For a time there would be nobody home in the office. They were following a traditional ritual in the racketeer business. They were temporarily unavailable for consultation. My brothers were silent and frightened, I was excited, my mother was wild. When she came out of shock, she went into wildness. Someplace in the racketeer's manual it says you don't have to worry about the man; the woman gets wild, the children get nervous because their mother is wild, and the man can't stand the noise and strain, no matter what else he can stand.

Still, my father was stubborn. "They got no right," he said.

"Rights, rights!" my mother shouted. "With dead children you'll give them an argument?"

"Look, I tried to call them," my father said. "They don't

answer. Just don't go up to the races without I . . ." He lost his grasp of English. "I'm doing all I can, so don't ask me any more."

He sat up all night on the front porch, wearing his sheepskin jacket, a sentry on duty on Hathaway Avenue in Lakewood, Ohio.

Next day, still with the mumps I lay, and a boarded window. My father was sleeping on the couch. He had been awake all night; he had worked all day. A bottle filled with fluid sailed through the other window. The window broke; the bottle broke. "Foo, foo, fooey," said my father. It had a bad smell. He described it as a stink bomb, but it was homemade, home-created, and relatively mild. Still, no one could claim it smelled good.

He made another telephone call. It was the hour of arbitration. This time the racketeer's manual must have said: *Okay, discuss.* And who visited our house that night to perch with his plump white hands on his short thighs? Who came to squeak out threats and apologies and an incoherent rumble of promises? Who was the collection agent and negotiator for the racketeers? Answer: not Ollie the Agent, but an old friend. Shloimi Spitz, the gangster.

"Shloimi," said my father, "that was my boy in that room, he had the mumps, a shock like that could prevent from becoming a father."

"He's too young for monkey business," said Shloimi, who knew nothing of psychology or psychosomatic medicine except that a brick, a stone, or a bomb through the window made people reasonable. "What's a baby like that want to be a father?"

"Shloimi," said my father reproachfully, "I went to visit your brother on death row."

"Nu, so how long I got to be grateful?"

"A little bit anyway," said my father.

"All right, so I'm grateful. Now pay up your dues."

"Dues!"

"That's what we call them, dues. Dues me something."

"Oy," said my father. "You call that a joke? You call that dues?"

"You want to call them something else, that's your privilege, I invite you," said Shloimi, softened despite himself by the reminder of silent, dizzy Moishe, cut off in his prime by a jolt of electricity from the State of Ohio. "I'll tell you what, Sam, you're such an old friend, you can call them anything. How's that for an arrangement? Just so long as you pay."

"I guess I'll call them dues," my father said sullenly.

Shloimi smiled. In a movie he might have had some spectular gesture—his leitmotif—such as George Raft's flipping a quarter or Edward G. Robinson's delicious snarl. Instead, he merely smiled. But then, lo! He showed his gold teeth. He had a gold tooth gesture, too! "What's the matter with your kid?" he asked, taking notice of me.

"He's getting over the mumps."

"Okay, but why his mouth hang open like that?"

I shut my mouth, and Shloimi put his hand on my head. He tousled my hair. "Okay, nice kid," he said. "They didn't know they was putting the stink in his room. If they knew he was sick, they'd have said, 'Wait till the kid isn't sick.' I personally would say it."

My jaw was hanging again. My father wanted to kill, but did not. Shloimi Spitz said, "Okay, it's understood, everything's nice now. And how's my buddy Ben—Benny? How's he doing? How's our Benny doing?"

How Ben was doing: well, sometimes he helped in the store.

"Sam," my mother whispered, "it's four o'clock already."

"Don't I know? Why are my eyes wide open?"

"Do you want I should make you something? It's chilly outside. Poor Ben, he's waiting on the corner."

"Naw, they got the soup and pie at the market. I'll make sure he gets some soup. Shush, you sleep."

He was awake at dawn or before, splashing cold water on his face, no time to shave, throwing on his sheepskin coat with the silver-pronged crating-and-decrating hammer sticking out of his pocket; and a hand on my rump to propel me blinking back to bed—"Get! Schlof!"; and then he was off to the market to bid for fresh fruit, fresh vegetables, berries and tomatoes, and sweet damp lettuce. He drove through miles of two-family houses, filled with sleepers. Even the streetcars stood huddled in their barns at this hour. Occasionally a light snapped on and a face peeked out at him as the truck throbbed in idle gear at a stoplight. The face would see night, stars, mysterious rider on high perch; the face would hear gears, exhaust; my father rode against the dawn, piercing Cleveland in his Dodge truck.

Old-country, accented, a tradesman, this man rode like a stranger, even to his sons. The other boys' fathers were like their children in a familiar history, like sets of Chinese boxes, fitting into each other, leaning back into sweet America until they forgot that their grandparents or their great-grandparents had also been immigrants. Or their great-great-grandparents. But turkey at Thanksgiving, George never told a lie, Abe chopped wood, and some of us were all there first, ahead of the crowd. Or so it seemed to me then; I had the eyes of a stranger. When these fathers dealt with money, they received distant intermediaries, dividends, salary checks, allowances, ambassadors from cash. My father played with money directly in the form of silver and small bills; housewives poked, pinched, nibbled, squeezed up their eyes, brooded, swallowed, sniffed, licked, and handed over a few cents in exchange for a pint box of strawberries.

"They're fresh?"—coins still clinging to the bulbs of fingertips, magically defying gravity, magnetized.

"I guarantee, missus."

My father's words broke the magnetic current. The coins dropped into his hand. Commitment to these particular strawberries, including the half-eaten sample berry, caused sighs all around. No smiles, but buyer and seller were united in the ceremony of shopping. Missus dares her budget at the altar of food; the dark seller from foreign climes meets her challenge and swears by the gods that he is honest and true; a sweet demonstrator from downtown now asks her to sample the bouillon in a crinkly paper cup. ("Something hot for a man who Mister Coffee Nerves you know special offer genuine beef stock today only . . .")

Unseen appetite lights up inside.

Sip, sip.

Unseen appetite fades.

"I'll take the nice berries, Mr. Gold, and thank you for the sip, but I really didn't plan on any beef bouillon for today."

"I understand this, missus."

The demonstrator said: "For a few pennies a week, more delicious gravies, soups, broths, and wake-me-ups without nasty foreign ingredients dilute the blood cause sleepless nights, instead delicious hot beverage proteins for meals or in-between times—"

"I think missus got her shopping done already," my father said.

"In handy cube form!" cried the demonstrator as her hot plate shook.

"That's enough, Miss Herbox."

"Thank you, Mr. Gold," said the missus. "And maybe a pint of those lima beans too, they look so nice I won't even turn it over and burrow inside."

This was not mere money. It was a ritual of risk and communication. Gypsies and Jews brought danger, but bore secrets of fortune, sharpened cutlery, beans, and berries. This was cash.

When I received my allowance on Saturday night, very late, after the store was swept out and washed down and all the help was gone, except maybe Caruso and Myrna, who often hung around, it was not a matter of my due. The quarter lay cool in my hand like a weekly gift of love from my father. Slim. To be spent quickly on a movie, candy, ice cream. Sometimes he also tumbled loose coins between the cushions of the truck so I could find them when I cleaned it out. Next week we might be chased away or fleeing, as my father had fled from Kamenets-Podolsk. There could be fires, bombings, or mere drunken murder. Cash might give joy, but no security; love, but a flirting and fickle love, not protection against fate.

Caruso made the quarter disappear into the air, then found it in my ear. He made my other ear give change. Uncle Ben read the Latin on the coin and told me it was Indian talk. Myrna winked at my father. My mother cried out, in general, "Don't waste!" In case somebody was eating. The quarter flew about my magic circle, and returned to provide me with small instances of power in the form of laughter and pleasure. I recognized no other power, of course.

And yet, all about, the worn edges of the world admitted glints of leak, like the stars through a black velvet sky. I screamed with laughter, staying up late; and things were slipping away, slipping into being.

This was the time of the Depression, the Black Legion,

and the German-American Bund. Masked riders gathered in the countryside around Cleveland. A Legionnaire from Jackson, Michigan, screamed over the tail gate of a pickup: "Send 'em all back to Mount Sinai!" This gave me a start, since my brother Sid was born in Saint Luke's Hospital, but I had been born at Mount Sinai. Why me? Why not my brother? Father Coughlin, speaking with his rich caramel radio voice, stood up every Sunday afternoon in Royal Oak, Michigan, to drive the moneychangers from the temple. My father was certainly a moneychanger. His store was no temple, but it was a nice clean store.

The murder of the Jews had already begun in the great center of civilization across the sea. It was barely noticed. The Lakewood public schools exchanged students with schools in Germany. I sat stiffly through assemblies where the returned exchange students delivered reports on their year in the renovated Third Reich. "I didn't see any Jews being beaten. Of course, I didn't see any Jews, either." (Laughter.) Or solemn, precisely enunciating German children explained to us why the elimination of racial pollution was essential to German survival. Who could find an argument against purity? Even Ivory Soap suffered because it was only 99 and 44/100 per cent pure. Perhaps that 56/100 of a per cent was Semitic. Someday a bar of soap would sink in a bathtub, brought low by race mixing.

Not a rich man, my father dealt in marketing as if it were a commodity. His spirit responded to this abstract entity. He was a storekeeper; later he speculated in real estate. In both conditions he suffered great pleasure and success, and also reversals and loss. The same with gambling: he liked to play with money in the evening, abstractly, after playing particularly with money all the workday. When he won at cards, he smiled contentedly, showing his gold tooth. When he lost, he laughed uproariously, showing the tooth. Bargaining had abstract charms for him; gracefully he swung from the invisible sums in the air, head over heels into cash, risking his neck on a scaffolding of will and intention. It made no difference that he sometimes had to bargain with the crooked Quinn brothers or mean Phil Larkin. Caught by the fevers of speculation, he bought subdivided lots on the random raw edges of Cleveland. Surely the town would grow from its boundaries in these peculiar times, or maybe it wouldn't and the Quinns were blowing smoke at him. He could tell from looking at them that they had funny hearts, or perhaps half a funny heart each—they were twins—but he played real estate with them anyway. The game pleased him; he was like an elegant sportsman—a matter of form.

Myrna, Caruso, Ben, my mother, they were practical or longing people; they worried about survival. My father seemed to know in his bones that there is no survival and therefore there need be no fret about it. He was freed for play, for security, for insecurity. Money suggested the risks of art. He liked the game.

When he lost in the stock market, he said happily, "I had no business there. They're a bunch of crooks. What do I know about stocks? Somebody called me up on the telephone and told me, 'Buy,' so I bought, but I must have been soft in the head."

"Stupid!" said my mother.

"My very words," he answered softly, grinning, "what I was trying to say."

When the banks closed in 1933, my mother wept; my father ate raw turnips and chicken fat, and schemed at the kitchen table. My mother said, "We've lost everything." My father said, "We'll start again."

He enjoyed the sport of money as an artist enjoys the texture and potentialities of his medium. He liked to create something from nothing, but he did not rest on the seventh day. Near his eightieth year, when he had given up mystifying about his son the writer, he made this discovery as we sat in the steam room in Cleveland: "You're a lot like me."

"What you mean, Dad?"

"You got good feet. You're lazy and you like to work."

He would have said, if he could, that writing is like speculation, deploying the materials of life in an abstract formulation; it is the issue of an imagination which seeks to marry elements that have not ever before been joined together. Wood and flesh, steel and light, berry and branch. A woman's hip is a symbol of grace, of fecundity. Yes. And also a technique of presenting a berry to a shopper may bring power into the world, and represents that power. The Roman coin with a picture on it, signifying something, is far different from a brute slice of metal which lacks the imprinted dream of ancient rulers, Latin mottoes, the accumulated history of a nation. Intention changes everything. So does appetite. Silver is only silver, gold is only gold, until effort and history make them more than silver and gold; and in the magic of speculation, they become myth.

Thus the mystery casting its shadow over my father's life. Why did he seek to make his magic from these peculiar passions? My father's father did not. Ben did not. My father did.

Afflicted with glaucoma, suffering spells of fainting, eighty years old, he was still building his myth for the future, and no money in the bank could do it for him. Like an artist, he was only as good as his last deal, and he knew it. He found new energy and redoubled his efforts, spending himself ferociously in buying property, remodeling, floating loans, floating mortgages, building additions, juggling the economics of stores, apartment buildings, land, offices, houses, in a varied, fluctuating, and treacherous market. He dissected this fantasy of money like a schoolboy dissecting a worm. He seemed to find its nerve, for it wriggled as he wanted it to wriggle. His joy in the play of Cleveland negotiations was undiminished; the notion of security merely threatened him. Getting money or losing it was nearly irrelevant. It was what he painted on the medium of money that mattered—labor, relish, imagination, himself. Being able to act was what he loved at age eighty, and he acted.

At large family dinners my father sometimes liked to talk about food. He drank a shot before dinner, straight whiskey downed straight, and then stared the heavy table down, the turkey, the roast beef, the slippery steaks—and the diners, my mother, my brothers, and me—and wondered aloud how we could eat so much; or perhaps how he could have eaten so little when he was a child. "In the old country," he said, "meat once a week. If then. I don't think we had meat once a week."

Then he remarked that they ate lots of carp.

Then he remarked that often they couldn't even get carp to eat and had to make do with the heads of carp.

And then he said in great wonderment: "But carps' heads tasted better in those days."

He looked for confirmation at Ben, if Ben was there; or later, when Ben was not there, at the place where Ben had sat at our table.

The gold in the streets of America turned out to be Sam Gold, born something else. He trailed his greenhorn siblings from town to town across the American plain. All but one took this as the normal way to live. One, Ben —but was that really his name?—remained a child, no good at work, sulky, locked in and closed down, wanting to be elsewhere. Ben was the youngest, long at the breast, and his mother's favorite. She knew he would be her last baby.

My father had married. His brothers and sister boarded with him for a time, out of habit, but then found their own rooms; all but one brother found wives, the sister found a husband. Ben, the youngest, stayed on with my parents for several years as a boarder. "Until he gets used to things," my father said.

"So we'll have to get a place with an extra room," my mother said. "He can't sleep in the kitchen."

Families take shape, forming and re-forming like amoebae, and at last Ben had to find his own family. It was time to learn adult ways.

Ben moved out. He went from job to job. He worked for his brother. He tried other jobs. He fell in love. The girl disliked to be taken out in the truck, which smelled of lettuce and tomatoes, ripe fruit and wet scraps of paper bags. "Is that how much you care?" she asked him. "You don't even clean out the cab?"

"I come straight from work," he explained. "I took a good hot bath first, relax me."

"Well, in America a fellow tries to smell good—himself *and* his machine. Some people, for example, they don't smell like a pharmacy although they rightfully could."

Ben borrowed my father's motorcycle. He polished it up and bought springy black clips for his pants. The girl rode once on the jump seat, holding him by the belt, thrilling him, and he told my father, "It's good. She just has to get used to."

But he was wrong. The girl was not interested. "Too green for her," my mother said. The girl was a cute little dumpling from Canton who had nearly finished high school. Now she had come to Cleveland to take advantage of her education. She chose Ben's rival, a pharmacist—well, a man who owned a drugstore—well, it sold mostly candy and patent medicines, which almost makes it an *apteka*. Ben couldn't answer back to an almost drugstore. It wasn't his fault. But about this loss: he couldn't get used to.

Ben was forgiven his many failures because he was the baby. After my mother had put him up for several years, he lived away and came for meals; then he lived away, took his weekday meals away, but came for meals on Sunday. "Ben," said my mother, "you're always losing weight. You're like a rail. You got to eat every day three squares, not just when you're company."

"I ain't got a good appetite," Ben said. "It's natural with me, the bad appetite."

The eldest brother had quarreled with his father and made his way to America with the weight of decision on his shoulders. Thus he made the essential peace with his father, too. Carrying this burden, both the quarreling and the peacemaking, had forced him to become a man. That was what he owed the ghost of his father. He was able to manage Shloimi Spitz, the racketeer, and the sullen farmers, and temperamental Myrna, who liked to handle the cash register because this meant both that she was trusted (pride) and that she could steal a little (spending cash). He had enough energy to put up with crazy Caruso and my mother and his children. While busy in the life he chose, he had a sense that he had chosen it, and this gave him ease with it. He sailed to his own winds.

My uncle who had clung upside down to the slats of the cart, the nervous head-shaker Morris, was always one machine ahead of my father. A motorcycle when my father had a bicycle, a truck when my father used a motorcycle, a Chevy when my father had a Dodge pickup, a Pontiac, a Buick, a pink Imperial to carry his shaking head on its Sunday tours of the grandchildren. And my father saying tolerantly, "Well, he likes nice transportation. Personally, I go compact."

Esther, the girl in the family, married a salesman—steady. She learned to keep his accounts for him; she took an interest in selling. She read a book entitled *The Romance of Salesmanship* and thus was able to conclude, "You know what? Selling can be romantic." She knew that the secret of her husband was not to be discovered between the pages of this book, but it wasn't her fault. Perhaps he had lost it on the roads that led from one hardware store to the next, Rocky River, Elyria, Ashtabula, Lorain, Sandusky, Fremont, all the way to Toledo and back. But she made her deal and stuck with it.

As these normal processes continued, Ben just followed along. He was poor at transactions. America was not his doing; it was done to him. He had not finished with his childhood. He trailed from one brother to the other, to his sister, back to his eldest brother; he found a job, or a job was found him or given him or made him; he obeyed. He had not enough of a past in the Ukraine to make a future in Cleveland. Though the word "boredom" would not have occurred to any of these people, Ben had trouble getting himself through the day. He signified nothing to himself. He wanted neither automobile nor work nor wife, or he wanted them not enough, or he was removed from relish and hope, ambition and the conviction of his powers. He was still a child, but a grown-up child is not a real child; instead, he was childish. He played with me as a child plays with a child, and it made me uncomfortable, because he was not a child. He was not supposed to be a child. He laughed too much; he yelled too much when he roughhoused with me; he panted and grew red in the face. He kept glancing at my father for approval.

"Don't get the kid too excited," my mother said.

"What's the matter, he's just playing," my father said.

They were talking about Ben as if he were a child in their presence; as if he were a thing, absent by his unformed nature. Though my father defended him, he stopped roughhousing with me.

Busy with other things, absently, my parents worried about Ben. Well, in time he would learn—grow up and have a good appetite.

Noisy, brawling, weeping or alcoholic fathers must, to some extent, inoculate their children against the fearsome separations wrought by excitement. My father usually had things under control. He kept the lid on. I have seen him drunk once. On a Christmas Eve it was; he stamped into the house after the fruit store closed, wearing his sheepskin coat, snowy and wet and laughing in a way that frightened me. My mother kept trying to shush him (babies sleeping) and crowd him into bed. He reeled through the hall, and when his wild eye fell upon me, it made no connection. He was roaring, but what about?

Nothing. Just roaring. Perhaps his Chassidic father sometimes thus celebrated the God-given right to roar like a beast. Perhaps he roared for the unforgettable and the forgotten.

I hid behind a door and put my nose in the crack. I watched my father. If he pushed the door—less nose.

In silence I watched him, and in a terror of loneliness. To be present when a father laughs, and yet to be so alone! My wet nose was in jeopardy against the crack of the door. This was no Chassidic mystery. There was no ritual to grasp at; it was his festival, his alone, personal, excluding. He was thick and powerful in tufted yellowish sheepskin, and the crating hammer, with flat silvery prongs, stuck out of his pants pocket. There was also a bulge of holiday money—a good day's business. He had come from the party he gave in the back room for the young Italians who worked in his store. Probably Myrna, the bulging widow clerk, the heaviest thumb on any scale in town, the tightest corset, had led him to wildness. She always wanted him to let go, push and shove, be a truck driver with her. With her swollen lips and her hilarious shrieks of laughter, she had everything figured out her own sweet way. A tangle of widow's desire. My mother could settle that score later.

It was Christmas Eve; this was America; all down the streets of Lakewood, Ohio, children and parents put their lives together in momentary communion. Only in our house did the father celebrate without making his meaning clear.

Why did this come to be my model of isolation, separation?

I understood nothing. It had no connection. It was without reason. Even cruelty might have been easier—a Slavic father who came home drunk to beat his wife and children, or brought Myrna with him, or stayed away all night.

My father was happily exalted, shaking his sheepskin coat, but absent from us in his soul, lips wet and eyes gleaming. Ben was sitting unnoticed at the kitchen table. He had finished a plate of lamb chops. The little gnawed bones lay white on the table. He sat hiding in plain view over the food as my father crashed through the house. He came to find me behind the door, and without a word, patted my shoulder. Then he stood behind my mother as she said, "Sam. Go to bed, you'll sleep." Ben was a part of this scene, as he was a part of the next one. I stood stiffly, refusing to leave. I think it was before the banks closed. I was learning to read more than one word at a time. I had found the book my father carried with him from New York to Canton and elsewhere, and I had asked Ben to tell me about the gingerbread boy.

"Foolishness," he said. "I am, I am."

He stood silently behind my mother as she told my father: "Go to bed. Now go to bed, Sam."

I saw my father absent in another way a few months later. It was spring, and there was a continual drip of rain. On my way to school I watched the miserable hobos huddled on the slow Nickel Plate freights that ground through town on their way west or east toward deserted switchyards or lines of cops, those repetitive destinations in the wastes of the Depression. The sheepskin was in mothballs. The wild laughter had been put away. But there was a connection in loneliness.

My father's youngest brother was first ill, and there was silence in the house, and then he was in the hospital and dying. "What's wrong with Uncle Ben?" I asked my mother.

"He's dying." I must have looked puzzled, because she added: "He wants to live."

Ben, very quiet, was brought back to our house. He lay in my parents' bedroom. I came in from school and took off my rubbers without help. I heard him groaning and my mother—sometimes when *I* wanted her—spent a long time talking with him. She would let me look at him briefly from the doorway, but then she shut the door. Now he never spoke to me, although he used to scream with laughter, striving to rival Caruso, the singing produce man, the driver with the funny head. He read the Indian language on coins, unlike Caruso, who carelessly made them bloom from my miracle-filled, wax-filled ears. He lay in bed for what I seem to recall as months—hush, smells, worry. Perhaps it was only a day or two. Then a silent limousine came for him. He returned to the hospital.

"No hope," my mother told a neighbor. She also told her: "He drank lye.'

I overheard this, and promised never again to tell a lie if it could make you so sick. She looked at me in silence and only repeated, "He changed his mind. He wants to live."

My father left his motorcycle in the garage. He drove the truck to the store. I think Ben had been driving the truck before this happened.

"Now he wants to live," my mother said. "After he burned himself all out inside. It's late."

My father received the last news by telephone. He asked thick questions; not a word of it can I remember. He hung the earpiece back on its hook and fell into a chair at his accustomed place at the kitchen table; he put his head in his arms and wept with choking sobs. I first tried to stand near him to be noticed, but then grew frightened and pulled away. My mother, doing something with vegetables at the sink, was also weeping, but remained herself, with a hand on my head. She was running water over beet greens, washing out the sand. There were tomatoes, turnips, green onions, lettuce, stalks of Pascal celery in the sink, sending up fresh smells of wetness and earth. I was pushing into her skirts. She stroked my cheek.

Then I prowled about him as he wept, feeling courageous, as if the sight of my father broken-hearted was a danger which could somehow hurt me and I dared it to. Also I felt some primitive reverberation of his sorrow. This sense of his sorrow that night has increased very much with the years. Now that I have lived until the age he reached when his brother died, I begin to understand his heaviness, the yawning emptiness of regret in his body.

"Its a total loss," my mother said. "Sam?"

When my father did not stop his crying, my mother said, "Sam. The children."

He got up, went out, and I heard the screech of his

motorcycle in the spitting cinders of the driveway. Mother ran to the front of the house to stop him, but he was already careening down the street.

When he came back, a few hours later, the tears were gone. He said to my mother: "I'm selling that machine. It's too dangerous."

My brothers and I were in our pajamas, ready for bed. He was gazing at us with eyes which it is a part of everyone's voyage on earth to recognize, even in golden America. We cannot turn away; we find these eyes everywhere, and at last in the mirror.

Caruso the Truck Driver used to toss me up, up, up toward the ceiling of our house, toward the starry, impenetrable sky of Lakewood, Ohio, and that's how it was before bedtime on Fridays in 1934. The silence left behind by Ben receded; riot took its place. On those Friday nights my mother kept an improvised boardinghouse for the odd crew that worked weekends nearly around the clock in my father's store. Girls and men, they shucked corn on the back porch; they flirted with each other while dropping yellow silk in baskets and pots; they bedded down in all corners of the house after my mother's grand meals served on paper plates. Like explorers, they dropped to sleep wherever they found a congenial moment. Myrna paraded her billows of flesh back and forth to the bathroom, borrowed my father's robe for herself, and went about laughing with gross tenderness at everything anyone said.

Caruso, furious, knobbed at the shoulders with truck driver's muscle, flirted with no one, or perhaps only with my father. His sport with me was mostly to spend the strength not taken by work and song. Like most people, he was desperate to use himself up. Caruso, who was called Caruso because he was Italian and sang all the time, bellowed an aria from *Don Giovanni* or *The Pearl Fishers* and flung me high and higher until I begged for mercy from such excess of bliss and went to bed with dizzy dreams of flying. I might have become insomniac, but failed to learn this disease because I was too busy staying awake, straining my ears to make sense of the rustlings and sighs of secret love-making, the screams of laughter, and the drone of all-night talk which transformed my own home into a dense new society two nights a week. Work began at three in the morning during the spring and summer months; Caruso and my father and a boy rolled through the predawn streets toward the market to load up the truck with the earliest, choicest produce; by the time they rolled back from downtown Cleveland, top-heavy with crates of crisp greens, bursting reds, juice dripping from corners of crates, Caruso singing and my father planning, the others had got the store in order, the displays

ready, the doors cleared for the onrush of Depression bar-
gain-hunters. Then Caruso cleaned the truck and chopped
away with his lettuce knife, his celery knife, his arsenal of
flashing blades. And sang. And split squash and melons.
And sang.

Caruso was an orphan who adopted my father as his
father, myself as his younger brother, my mother as his
mother; but the relationship was altered by the fact that
he had been dropped on his head as an infant and preferred singing to thinking, that he was an employee of my
father, and that he was not blood son or blood brother to
our family. There is a limit to what non-relatives can be
forgiven. He first tested and then passed that limit. Beneath that well-oiled head of wavy hair over a peculiarly
round, dented skull, with the full nose and lips of a happy
man of song, strange reasonings came to birth. Caruso
blinked his pretty, heavily lashed eyes. A doll. When he
was at rest the eyes were pretty and girlish; most of the
time, since his teeth were bared to music or an amazed
enthusiasm, the eyes seemed to be squeezed shut. He often
brought news to astonish my father, and when not aston-
ishing him with recent events of the world, he sang out
the eternal news of lost, lost, O lost love, of the sun of
Venice, or of the glories of country and land far across
the sea, including hill and field, dark-eyed women, and
my mother mine (his mother his).

During one July evening the familiar guild was gathered on the back porch, gossiping, eating strawberries, and
drinking beer, which was recently made legal; they were
passing the late hours before bed, as usual, in the sly

adult intrigues of bedtime. I was sleepy, lingering on an orange crate, having been ordered to bed three times but not yet yelled or slapped to it. The adult world was worth a slap, maybe two. I would bear up within measure. Anyway, neither my mother nor my father much minded violating the rules about bedtime. Their slaps insulted but did not maim. The porch was screened, protecting the housebred flies from their menacing outdoor enemies; the flies buzzed, and like me, were slapped at, sometimes wounded; fireflies glittered beyond, a bare bulb hung above us; creak of swing and giggle of girl and sighs about the facts of life. The real stuff was openly available. That was an essential fact of life. It had bearing. Also Father Coughlin was a friend to the workingman. The screaming eagle of the NRA was a friend to the workingman. Roosevelt was a friend to the workingman. But if he had so many friends, why was the workingman in such bad shape?

"Well, I'll tell you," said my father, forgetting that he was the boss, "the working boy has got to put his foot down and not work so many hours. He robs other boys. Like that no jobs for everybody."

The help listening and nodding to this insight had come to work at six that morning, and after closing the door at nine, were now spending a few additional hours shelling lima beans. They would be back on the job at dawn.

"Father Coughlin," said Myrna, popping a pod, "will drive the moneychangers from the temple."

"Dot's a good idea," my father said in his guttural Yiddish accent. Personally, he preferred the synagogue for driving out the moneychangers, though he didn't attend services, not personally. Also he would prefer to drive out Shloimi Spitz, who took money and never gave change. But those who believed could certainly attend, with all his good wishes and respect. Likewise Caruso should sing.

At that moment a panting noise came up behind my father, and Caruso stood there, swaying with emotion, his eyes affrighted and the pretty lashes fluttering. "What happened?" demanded my father.

"Oh! oh! terrible!" gasped Caruso, exceptionally out of voice.

"What?"

"The truck!"

"What the truck?"

Caruso swallowed lumps and gobbles, fought for voice, fought for words, and finally explained, "Oh the truck, boss! Was just smoking a cigarette in the cab, Oh my God, was smoking a little and singing a little, and the cigarette fell down in the cushions—"

"The truck burned down?" my father asked.

But now Caruso could not be stopped. "You know, in the upholstery? the pillows in the cab? Well, so I just opened my mouth for the 'La cheeda da rem na mano' piece from *Don Giovanni*, you know, boss, that sad part . . ." And he went off into song until my father hit him hard in the belly with his elbow. "Oo, oh, oof," said Caruso.

"Tell me what happened to the truck!"

"Oh. Well, the cigarette fell down in the cushions. If I didn't of find it in the cushions there, the truck would of burned down, boss. It was terrible. Awful. My heart hurts me right here." He seized my father's hand and put it across his chest to feel the pounding.

There was a yelling and pounding of feet among the lima-bean shellers. Myrna shrieked with laughter. My father, chief of this gang, bore the responsibility to preserve order. He kept his head. "Okay, Caruso, so don't worry. Anyway, the truck is insured. I am insured for fire. So don't worry, you know it now?"

Everyone settled down to catch up with the lima beans after this interruption. Pop, pop, pop. Beans in pots, pods in hampers. Pop. The lima beans loved to be made slippery and nude.

A few minutes later, Caruso, who had been more silent than silence, got up and tiptoed away. His silence should have been interpreted for the rare event it was— responsive meditation.

Five minutes later he returned with a delighted grin on his face. "Boss?" he said. Caruso winked at my father. He would do anything for him. "Oh, boss? Hey, the truck's burning."

There was a red glow and slap of rivets in the vacant lot next door. The heated vacuum sucked itself through canvas. There was a whoosh of pause, and then the gas tank went, celebrating the twenty-second of July, 1934, and Caruso's homage to my father.

I believe it would be a mistake to call Caruso a psychopath. The implication of the word is that the person bearing that label is separated from reality, failing in sympathy and the gift of communicating with others. But Caruso, while he ignored the usual standards, was devoted to my father, devoted to me ("Up! up! up!"), and devoted to Italian opera and music with Italian words. The matter of the truck was explained to him with precision and emphasis; he learned his lesson and promised never again to burn down a truck on purpose. And also never to interpret my father's words, but simply to listen to what he said, and follow only the commands which had the specific grammatical form of an order. ("Clean the lettuce. Hose the back room. Deliver the onions to the Chinaman.") He would leave implications to others.

However, trucks still weighed heavily upon his mind. Caruso had a double-clutched head when it came to trucks. They meant freedom and power to him; his ideas raced noisily up inclines. Finally a man cannot live without implications. The new truck, a White Motors product, manufactured in Cleveland and purchased by my father out of patriotic loyalty to his adopted city in those troubled Depression days, smelled new and shiny, with a sexy freshness of paint, rubber, and various adhering oils and preservatives. The springs were stiff, proud, Calvinist, but they would settle down under vegetables. There's nothing like a few tons of asparagus, radishes, worms, weevils, cabbage, and other edibles to teach a truck a more liberal theology. Caruso lifted me into the cab and proudly conducted me around the block. He drove the truck to the produce market empty, and then returned heaped high. He also delivered orders to the lonely and telephoning rich in their Great Lakes Antique mansions with the captain's turrets along Lake Avenue. They gave him dimes; gloomy

butlers gave him dimes. And he transported the group of
boarders who slept under my mother's wing on Friday
nights.

You'd think all this useful labor would satisfy the most
ardent and tuneful lover of trucks.

It almost did, but almost has never sufficed for the
sensitive psychopath, the sociopath in good contact, or
the man bursting with love of the universe. Useful labor
is one thing; adventure and risk are another. Dimes do
not compensate.

One morning, instead of driving the truck to the market to pick up new-crop lettuce, Caruso just kept on
driving, across the High Level Bridge and east, going
eastward across the Cuyahoga River and out through night-
shrouded Cleveland. He never showed up. My father was
left at dawn with crates of produce on the pavements of
the West Side terminal; he smoked from the ears, and from
the eyes he looked every which way for Caruso. Caruso
had taken off. He had flown. He loved my father, but he
stole his truck, as a son might steal pennies from the
pockets of his father. Maybe his love was mixed with
baser elements.

Dad waited a day before deciding what to do. No
Caruso.

Silence in the cooler, silence in the back room, no
Caruso singing on the toilet in the basement. Still no
Caruso.

My mother called Aunt Sarah, her sister. She said call
the police. My mother called Aunt Anna, her other sister,
one of whose daughters was Elsie. She said call the cops.

My mother told my father: "Please, Sam, Officer Bull already."

Uncles Morton and Morris, Aunt Esther, Bessie, cousins Irwin and Bernie, the whole family checked in. Aunt Sarah, who had unlimited calls, telephoned almost hourly with new suggestions for recovery and revenge. Everyone rallied round the memory of the White Motors truck. They said: "What's the matter, you crazy?" They said: "What's the matter, you soft?" They said: "What's the matter, you let a Caruso like that get away with your machine? He's in Texas for sure. He's gone to Manitoba, across the line. They strip trucks like that in Chicago, Cicero. Oh boy, you are in for it now with the Mafia."

Myrna said: "I always knew he was a bad boy from the way he looks at me all the time. He sure does."

My father waited. No Caruso.

On the third day, reluctantly, he went to the police. He had earlier inquired about accidents: none. Now he reported Caruso lost, the truck lost with him. It would be hard to hide a shiny new red-cabbed White Motors truck with "Sam's Fruit & Vegetable, Free Delivery" stenciled on the door by Caruso's loving hands. (He was also an artist with a stencil set.) "I don't understand it," my father said, "can't understand," scratching his scalp before the sergeant's desk, unhappy at being there, since he knew that the police are the natural enemies of law and order and so what was he doing confiding his problems about the singing driver to them, to a cop? Their job was to receive turkeys at Christmas, occasionally a five-dollar bill if the sidewalk was littered; they had nothing to do with

Caruso and him. Littering and loitering were the things that made a cop wake up.

"It's hard," said the pleasant, broad-hammed sergeant, "for a red truck to get lost."

"Yes," said my father.

"Real hard to hide. No place to sell."

"Yes."

"Also hard for a wop to stay put, lost." The sergeant was smiling.

My father said, "He's an Eyetalian boy."

"No offense meant, Sam. Parm me, I'm sure. I'm Catholic meself and I know them wops like the back of me hand."

Together my father and the cop paused to examine the back of his hand. It was veiny, red, blue, ridged, hairy, scrubby, confused. Who really knows the back of his hand?

My father nevertheless accepted the apology. What he understood was that the sergeant was saying that everybody is classified, and not just by fingerprint; and my father was classified as a businessman and a Jew; and when the truck was found, the sergeant expected a reward. How this complicated set of signals was transmitted by the single word "wop" in this context is hard to explain logically, but nonetheless everyone understood the communication, even in those days before radar. They were trained to receive.

"Truck got lost," said the cop, beaming. He was tickled by my father's language.

"Yah."

"I'll put it on the wire—'lost Sammy's truck'?"

And it came to pass, due to the efficiency of the police and the visibility of the truck, that Caruso and the truck were found within twelve hours. Maybe Caruso simply ran out of gas. Maybe he wasn't really hiding. Why anyway did he roll into Erie, Pennsylvania? That is no resort to visit for a lover of music. It's just a red brick mill town on the road from Cleveland to Buffalo and noplace; it's just a spot on the map. Did he have a girl there? Did his singing soul lead him onto Route 6? No matter, it seemed. Caruso was in jail and the truck was in the pound. My father took the train to recognize one and claim the other.

He says that he came out of the train station, stood confused a moment, and then heard distinct reverberations of joyous, burgeoning song. With half the train ticket clutched in his fist, he followed tenor song through a block and a half of grimy Erie, Peeay. Men were selling apples in the street; there were still milk wagons drawn by horses; the bakery drivers had the look of men who ate what they did not sell.

Caruso's song increased in volume as my father trudged down the cobblestones leading to jail. Don Giovanni pleaded with Elvira, he sought understanding, he wanted love and forgiveness; and yet he was defiant, he challenged the Commandant to do his worst; and Caruso too found delight in both suffering and love.

My father found him from the street. He stood in a basement cell, with a barred half-window to the daylight. He was serenading the passing ankles of the women of Erie, Pennsylvania, who happened to find themselves passing the jail; there was a bruise above one eye and a cut on his scalp; he managed to grin and lift himself to the bars in an athletic gesture of greeting.

"Hiya, boss!"

"Hello, Caruso! Where's the truck?'"

"They put it in the pound, boss. Hey, howsabout you get me out of here?'"

"Why should I, Caruso? I lost a couple days at the market, I lost the price of the ticket, I lost time which is money. Who needs a train ride these days? Also the aggravation. So?'"

"La chee da rem na mano . . ." sang out the tenor. "I fell in love with Erie, Pennsylvania."

In the language of the time, Caruso was crazy. He was loco and buggy. He was a casualty of no particular disaster of the great Depression or the rise of Hitler or the mechanization of the West. He was just nuts, and after my father bailed him out, he just disappeared.

That was about thirty years ago. He was no more than twenty-five when he used to toss me up, up, up toward the sky, singing. Which means that he is now merely fifty-five years old, "a young man in the prime," as my father would describe him. Did he marry? Does he drive trucks? My nightmare is that he might be a bald short-order cook in a steamy diner in Erie, Pennsylvania, which once obscurely drew him with its magic. Is he burned out? Is he still singing? Caruso, you may have been below average for intelligence and social adjustment, but you get a superior rating for insistence upon music. You entered life like the rest of us. If there is no place for you, there is no place for many of the most worthy.

When my father took me with him to the Russian Bath and said, "Come sit by me—come!—sit!" but then sank into gambler's lust, hunched over cards all morning and afternoon, my unanswered love for him turned to gall within me. I had gotten rid of girls, my mob of brothers and cousins, my mother; Dad and I were stripped down to the naked weather of manliness, boyhood, and masculine loafing; business, the Depression, Hitler, and Father Coughlin were flung outside of Sunday; but now fifty-two more enemies were stacked up to do battle with me for my father—a deck of cards, worn and slick as money, and like money, smelling of pockets. I was merely jealous of my uncles, of his friends, of all the cardplayers; I hated the cards themselves, which my frowning father fingered so tenderly, caressing forth their deepest meaning, his lips pursed, his unshaven face creased with concentration, his eyes bright and withdrawn. I wanted to destroy the cards so that he could see *me* with those all-seeing, yellowish, crocodile eyes. I wandered in narrow pride and fury, my toes curling against slippery tile.

"Jack, tray, king," someone said, "so cut again." This gibbering chant was my enemy. But it was my father's pleasure, who embraced the risks of capricious fate in those hard years of the thirties. He was a lover of chanciness in a chancy time, and how could I, skinny and woeful, compete with lust and history? *Come sit with me while I play* did not ask enough of me, gave me too little. Often he thought out loud, asking his eldest son to sit with him while he puzzled over cards, market, or real estate:

"My building which half of it is already modernized, oh yeah, the other half is not in such good shape either. But I know where I'm at with it. Needs work."

"Why do you have to do it, Dad?"

"Work, I got to do it. A man is never secure. If a man is a man—never."

Taking his best hold, making sure in an unsure world— this was my father's deadly earnest game during those Depression days of hobos on freight trains, of the enraged debate about corn-burning and court-packing, a nation bewildered by sudden hunger and doubt. When I heard that the banks were closed and we were "poor," I asked my mother: "Can I wear corduroy pants if we're poor?" She was in mourning at the sink, cleaning the salad, and my father was saying as he awaited his dinner, "What means to be secure? No difference now. I got a young head, grown-up hands, which is I can make it again."

"Won't the bankers open up their hands a little bit?

Those thieves and bandits? Is it all gone? Will they pay a few cents on the dollar, would it hurt them?" my mother asked through her sobs.

"It was only paper," my father said, looking at his black stumps of fingernails and the horny, muscular, hairy backs of his hands, "which it is—only paper, so stop crying. Put a little lemon with the salad, will you?"

"You want I should peel the cucumbers?" she asked, the storm of tears running every which way across her face. "The nice cukes?"

"Slice, don't peel," he said gently.

Money was not to be trusted in those days; it did not reward a man with sweet heart talk as a plump artichoke did. My father pampered the heads of lettuce in the cooler by sprinkling them gently from a gardening can in the evening, and lettuce heads sipped gratefully and awaited his return in the morning; shocks of celery squeaked with delight when he girdled them round with blue rubber bands and put them on parade across crates in the window; but money? No answer. *Tingachug, tingachug* went its false noise in the cash register, but who knew from profit margins in those days? He was often paid at the store in "scrip," promises by bankrupt Cuyahoga County to hungry sewer workers, or I.O.U.'s from wolfish Black Legionnaires, or genuine Canadian Scotch with cherry pits floating in it (bootleggers eat too), or post-dated checks by little ladies in electric cars, who then asked: "Would you plug into me for an hour or two?"

"*What?*"

"The battery needs just a little juice to get me home, Mr. Gold, and since you have already proven yourself such a gentleman—"

"Chrisamighty. Drive around to the back and tell the man to get out the extension cord."

And relief checks. And church funds. And ahoy the touch from old friends recently out of business: "It's the A & P, it's the Depression, it's the racketeers they're all Italian—"

"What about Shloimi Spitz?"

"Okay, so not Shloimi, but I heard he's in with them. But it's my wife was nagging me so I couldn't sleep nights—"

"Next time get yourself an Eyetalian wife," my father said. "They're good to a man and hardworking. All right! I can spare you maybe twenty if you promise—"

"I'll swear on a stack of."

"Just promise, Dave."

"I'll return it in two weeks. I'm going for supervisor on the W. P. and A. I got a cousin he's very big in Columbus—"

"Columbus really excites him, yeah? And what about Dayton? Youngstown? Dave, listen, the smoke tickle your ears? Don't live in a dream. Take the job you can get, lots of my best friends sell brooms—that's business, too— and give it back to me when you got it."

"I'm sure to make supervisor, Sam, because I got a good head and I hate bending over, it makes me sneeze, and my cousin in Columbus . . ."

Ahoy and goodbye, there went the day's profit and my

corduroy pants. My father stood shaking his head, putting his hands for comfort on the firm chill back of a pet cabbage, because Dave would never make supervisor, I.O.U.'s and scrip are only promises to pay, and what is cash itself? Only an electric promise we allow ourselves to be plugged into, like love.

But some promises are kept! Especially the ones a man makes to himself! Therefore, dragging out the extension cord, he grew magically confident and boisterous as the Depression, like a mean-eyed cop, put its breath on our lives and looked for violations. The virtues of saving were in disrepute; my father thrived. He did not pity the poor very much, I suppose, since he felt their feet in his own galoshes when he rushed out to the market with Caruso's successor at three in the morning. From the sleeping house, filled with women and children and me, down the idle predawn streets, out through cold farmland and into the jabbering community of the market. The woodchucks stood up from their burrows and peeked beadily at him as he bargained in tomato patches; the overfed market rats swarmed within bins of frazzled lettuce while the farmers' wives, in sheepskins, sold nickel blueberry pies to go with nickel tin cups of soup. "Good, good," he said, huffing the soup in the morning fog, cooling it with his hot breath and a breakfast gulp of pie: "How much you want for a quarter carload of lettuce? Let it stand till this afternoon, you can't even make lettuce soup, coleslaw pie."

"I'll dump it on a restaurant."

"I'll give you cash for it. Five bucks."

"In money?"

"In bona fide cash."

"Sold!"

"Ah, your wife makes good soup," my father said, "good pie. Which she is a truly lovely lady."

"It's all stuff we can't sell, otherwise it rots," said the farmer.

The farmers were famished amid so much food; the people of the city went hungry; only the rats, spiders, woodchucks, silverfish, and swooping black dawn birds had no afterthoughts about the agonies of distribution in a time of waste and displeasure. Overhead, the market moon dimmed into day. All over the city of Cleveland, men who had no work sat up, switched on the light, remembered, groaned, and put out the light again. They had no work; they could try sleeping curved into the warmth of their wives' bodies. They twitched back into sleep. There was great weakness abroad in those days.

But my father wrestled the thickly evasive element of hope in the wind. He put both hands firmly upon the clouds. He would make his business work, he would make Sam's Market pay, he would squirt the juice out of spoiling tomatoes—"MAKE GOOD SOUP!"; he wallowed with fat lust in the appetite of insecurity, showing his gold tooth for luck. "Who knows if the berries will keep over Labor Day? Does anybody know? What if there's one bad berry sneaked in underneath? Well, put in the cooler. We'll see."

No fatalist, but a speculator, he did not examine each berry personally. He merely cast his eyes over the baskets and scared them. His crocodile gaze deterred mold, stopped rot, mitigated fruit rust, and also shamed the kleptomaniacs into stealing imitation vanilla instead of the real thing.

"What you gonna do? She's sick in the head and crazy." The elegant little lady with the electric car collected bottles of flavoring the way I had collected toy soldiers. The little nozzled bottles engaged in vanilla battles, extract wars, klepto surrenders and treaties, up and down her arms, in her lap and in her hat, and all through her muff. "So I add it to her bill," my father explained, putting his head close to mine, understanding psychology, knowing that dreams must be both compromised and fulfilled, "only I call it 'Service Charge' and like that she gets the vanilla free."

"She's a crook, shame on her, with that big house on the lake!" cried my mother.

My father let his gold tooth swing happily in mid-air. He chuckled.

"And that blue hair—*blue!*"

There went the tooth again. "Sometimes her daughter pays. Comes in and says: 'How much my mama hook on you this week, Mr. Gold?'"

"Uncle Sam! Didn't you hear Auntie?" Elsie demanded. "That's a crooked thing to do, stealing."

Elsie was one of my girl cousins who occasionally spent a week or two living at our house. When her mother had to go away to Mount Clemens for a rest cure, due to the difficulties of being alive, she would leave Elsie and the baby with my mother, along with instructions to try not to spoil them this time. My mother had wanted a daughter, and her sister felt angrily generous at lending us hers. Otherwise there were only sons. Another thing was Ben.

I think Ben had made my mother want to crowd the house with relatives.

"I got no morality to let people steal from me, huh Elsie? That what you think?" My father shook his head at the irate little knot of family perched around the table before him. "What do you think, son? Tell me, son."

I thought Dad had the right on his side because it was Sunday dinner and he was there. He was not always there. He was not always *there* even when he was there. But he was surely right.

"I got to check on the lights," he said, "I got to go down to the store. Don't wait up for me."

That was Sunday and sometimes Dad was there. Through the week, my brothers and cousins and I, the eldest, we all stayed late on the playground of Taft School in Lakewood, Ohio. Home was dark, silent, empty; our mother and father worked all day; the "girl," who earned four dollars a week in cash, plus room and board, was too busy with her policeman to bother much with us. The cop, whose amazing name was Patrolman Cecil Bull, left his Ford running outside while he recessed with an impatiently running motor upstairs in the attic with Linda-Lou. My girl cousins and I climbed the garage, not to watch Officer Bull and Linda-Lou, not to spy, not to peek, though we occasionally did happen to look; but really we climbed in order to practice jumping down without break-ing our arms. We did not dare break our arms during the busy season at the store, and since all seasons were crucial if not busy, we took care to leap out on the grass, ex-tending hands, buckling knees, and rolling with parachutist grunts to a stop near the tree where we had planted dead squirrels, pennies, and acorns, though nothing grew but birch and grass and the horror stories with which I poisoned my cousins' minds.

Linda-Lou leaned from the attic window, her hair undone, shouting, "If you don't stay off the garage I'll cut you up in ten pieces."

But then she was gone, captured from behind by Officer Bull, before I could say: "Head, two arms, two legs. torso, neck, nose, belly button—that makes nine. Hey what's the tenth piece, Linda-Lou?"

I have not told any adults on Linda-Lou until just now —how she abandoned us to arm-breaking in the middle of the thirties, in the middle of the latency period—how she made Me the Boy give my cousins our graham crackers after school—but I thought that Officer Bull was sure wasting the city's gas. Linda-Lou plays Hospital, nyah-nyah! ("Shush, you," said my cousin Elsie, "you want her to cut us up? Or pull down the shade so we can't see?") With fraternal gentleness I socked Elsie on the head with a rolled-up Shopping News.

Linda-Lou could cut me up in ten pieces, I thought smugly, but my girl cousin only in nine. "Now let me explain *that* to you, Elsie."

"Never mind. I got other interests in life. So shut up, just because you're so smart."

When we walked to the corner like an Indian scouting party—myself in the lead and the girls allied in irregular formation down the sidewalk, one of my brothers dragging a lollipop from tree to tree, stippled with loose birch bark after a long block—we found the slow freight which ran from Cleveland to Pittsburgh and Cleveland to Toledo. The Nickel Freight trains were covered with a crawling, clinging live weight, the weight of homeless men, and we watched them with puzzlement. My brother Sid sucked his lollipop dolorously. Like my father, were the men on the trains also not secure? And if insecure like him, why didn't they smile? Why so much shifting and why did they stare at us without expression from the tops of their boxcars? And finally, why were they so—so—*interesting* to us, like Buck Rogers, Dr. Dolittle, maps, gas stations, the backs of cereal boxes, and Patrolman Bull wiggling around upon Linda-Lou's hips in the attic? Other possibilities, other chances. "They want to go someplace, they're hungry," I explained to my cousins.

"That's not the way," said Elsie. "They could go to the Relief."

"They're looking for *work.*"

"They're bums."

"They're not—they're . . ."

"I suppose you know everything," she said resentfully.

"Not everything, but more than a girl. Okay, maybe some of them are explorers, that's what I'm going to be. No girls allowed."

We got home and washed where it showed in time for dinner. I was hungry because I ate no suckers (rots the teeth); an explorer needs fierce white teeth and lots of protein in case of emergencies. Mother hurried back from the store to make dinner; Dad would come in to wish us goodnight. Linda-Lou, with face rubbed raw by Officer Bull's beard, said that we had been good that afternoon and had not tried to jump off the garage. "*Really* good?" my mother insisted, wanting to be a good mother.

"Well, pretty good," said Linda-Lou, because she knew that she should be a "disciplinarian," a word which meant "strict, capable, careful, attentive, and they don't get away with shining flashlights on dead squirrels in the basement."

My father, who came in late, did not care about words. He valued things, money which buys things, the taste of chicken fat, radishes, fresh fruit, the pleasures of survival, and his chief clerk, named Myrna. "And you're not secure ever," he urged upon us hopefully. When the bank disaster came, his calm betrayed a secret delight that—like a novelist beginning a new tale or like a god—he could know once more the awful joy of drawing something out of what seems to be void. And he waged war with the A & P, which was beginning its mission to choke the independent merchants, and the Depression and the Black Legion and the Bund and Shloimi Spitz and the rest of the racketeers and the other facts of life in America in 1932 and 3 and 4 and 5, when I was eight and nine and ten and eleven years old, watchful, troubled, the eldest of his children, his first son. "Well, we've used up four thousand years of our time," he said, "and we haven't straightened things up yet. I figure there's no point in rushing. Suppose I even live to be say a hunnert. How much can I accomplish, son?"

I thought he could do a great deal.

"Thank you, boy. But the last nine-ten years got to

be discounted out. From ninety-four to a hunnert I'll probably be weak in the head. Say ninety-five."

It was hard to imagine him rocking at the window with a dirty beard like his grandfather's, that roar of laughter squeezed to a lemony titter. So I worried about the other things.

Sometimes he tried to explain to me about Roosevelt, script, the empty stores, and William Dudley Pelley and his Silver Shirts. He said: "Come for a walk." And we walked around the block, stately and silent, surveying a portion of the battlefield.

When the help came home on Friday evenings, they took a meal with us at nine o'clock, talked and drank, slept until two in the morning on couches and on mattresses spread on the floor, and then bolted breakfast coffee and flapjacks and were off to work, blinking in the fruit truck before the spring sun spilled out day against the sky. Huddled through the dawn and then shouting through the long commercial morning and afternoon. Then at last they separated late on Saturday night, when the store finally closed. They slept all day Sunday; my father alone among them had the strength to rise at noon for the news of disaster and the Katzenjammer Kids. It was his business; the business day was his risk—the others were salaried. In a sense, then, he had created Friday Night, as God ordained a day of rest and as the florists of America had created Mother's Day.

After Caruso disappeared from our lives, my favorite among the dormitory five was the poultryman, Red Schwartz, with his red, wrinkled, and hairy face like a peeled orange left in the sun, burly but soft-cheeked, rearing back to whinny at his own or my father's jokes. He made shadow roosters with his hands against the wall and then sent me sprawling into the air to celebrate his arrival and my bedtime. "Higher! higher!" I yelled, even if I touched the ceiling. "Like Caruso!"

There was also Andy, small, bleak, hay-fever-eyed, with a loose girlish titter and a hard girlish voice and muscles which he practiced rippling for the "Most Handsome Grocer" contest at the annual Association Picnic at Euclid Beach. In the morning he jerked up his head in an attitude of supplication in order to rinse his eyes with the Murine carried in his pocket, then resumed the day's defiant stare from a pinched old-maid's face, gathered about the flesh of nose which was wasted on his skimpy skull. I liked him least; respectful, envying, and contemptuous, he saw nothing but the boss's son when he looked at me. He ate mints because he had "mucosity."

This was the time when some went hungry and millions feared they might go hungry or ate with shame. A man with a job had a special, exposed, even dangerous status.

My father's paternal control of the store was a matter for enthusiastic gossip, and both he and his employees—proud of their ninety-hour week—referred to the union organizers as "the racketeer boys." When Andy reported that the boys were trying to talk to him, my father said, "Talk is cheap, which it is free. Did I stop you? Don't I know Shloimi from the old days?"

Ruby and Max, the newlyweds, squatted together to shell lima beans from a hamper on our back porch. Once Max put a bean in Ruby's ear and the remainder of the evening was devoted to getting it out. Ruby squealed, then whimpered; my mother exclaimed politely, "Oh! oh!"—her mouth barely kissing the air. Dr. Grunes, wrung from sleep at midnight, was climbing into his pants when a clever squiggle of my father's finger squirted the bean into the bin. Cheers for him! Kisses and tears! . . . Ruby took the joke like a little lady.

Most formidable of our guests was Myrna, my father's lieutenant in the store, that great sly creature who was as adept as a butcher in slipping her thumb against the scale, skilled in a thousand stunts of making overripe strawberries tempting and green tomatoes juicy, heroic in a boned brassière, the reason that a faithful coterie of CPA's and personnel managers volunteered to do their wives' shopping. She bulged, unimpeded by a white wrap-around apron with slithers of green piping. Two husbands had already died under her, and one had fled. "The coward!" she roared, holding her sides, and then winked: "I'm still hongry . . ."

The first time my father saw her, prow forward, he had said, "Look, the one in the middle's her head." She was hired. Her shrewd eye for figures and her fishwife's voice daunted all adversaries; heavy-footed in Enna Jettick work-shoes very like my mother's, she took possession. With Myrna there was none of the low forward thrust of a woman's head in dainty shivers of controlled anger; she emitted the bellow of passion proud of itself, her great flesh wallowing, and the portent of *woe! O woe!* Her appeal was limited. Most men look for little girls in whose ears they can put beans.

Red Schwartz, Andy, Max, Ruby, Myrna—the guest list at that regular Friday night supper—dined richly on foods taken from the store at the verge of spoiling, avocado pears with one bad spot and a hump of succulence, canned straw-berries with soiled labels, heaps of tomatoes and stacks of cucumbers and barrels of pickles and schools of cold fish; later came platters of fried liver and onions, the jeweled sauce running. (Once a leaking pipe washed the labels off hundreds of cans, and for two years we didn't know what we would eat until the cans were opened. A lesson in humility.) In talk accompanied by the musical splash of corrupt honeydew, all the sweeter for that, they finished their supper. The wine was a special bonus of my father's good feeling—cheap, red, sedimented, and strong, made with a loving lack of skill in Uncle Izzy's basement.

"Just don't get sick," my mother told them. "I don't mean you have to drink near-beer."

The guests worshiped the boss, each according to his own knack for piety. Myrna moved ambiguously across the room like the overfed female dog which trots down the street in June, its available rump drawing little circles for the fox-muzzled male. That was her ceremony. "I don't know your name," she had said upon first meeting my father, "but I think you're kind of cute." When she walked too fast or breathed too hard, her breasts popped like hungry twins from their damp rubber cradle. She was bigger than a man, but not too big for my father. Impatient, a worshiper of happenstance, smelling of honeydew, she snorted for exercise. She cleared her nose and looked into the handkerchief. She was free and easy. My mother allowed accident to the opening of a can or the composition of a vegetable soup; this was a species of economy; in general, she liked to plan ahead. But all, all was free to Myrna's appetite; extravagance, her only rule, did not surprise her. Her great defect seems to have been the failure to be surprised, which made an evolution toward humanity difficult and slow.

On this particular June evening of which I speak, they sat about the back porch after dinner, shelling lima beans to keep their hands busy. Ruby and Max, snapping the pods in unison, wiggled next to each other under the glare of the mosquito-repellent lamp. An occasional curious fly whanged against the porch screens and then bounced off to whang again, while Myrna said for the third time to my father, "What's this I hear about you scaring away the other bids at the auction yesterday?"

"*Scared* them away," emphasized Andy, a licker of

boots who stole his personal groceries each week—it's only natural, Dad said—and thought my father didn't know.

"Polite"—my father's freewheeling grin. "They knew I wanted the Pascal, they were polite."

"Scared them," Andy insisted admiringly at my father's hairy left ear.

Abruptly Dad slapped his thigh, this time with impatience, not with relish, remembering Myrna's dismissal of Andy: *A bathtub-dirtier.*

"They just ran," Red remarked, not a bootlicker but feeling the competitive stir.

My father turned his Tartar eyes toward Red Schwartz, a man whom he respected. "Maybe Square Deal Foods and Abe from Ansel Road just didn't need any Pascal," he said, letting the ambiguity of all profound statements imply that the real crunchers of celery came to Sam's Fruit & Vegetable. "Abe from East-Side-Abe didn't even show up."

While they drained their glasses, my mother had her first chance to whisper the question for the end of each day: "How much?" Even when she spread the bills and checks on a pink chenille bedspread and officiated at the ritual counting, she asked this question of my father: *How much?*

"The usual," I seem to hear him saying, or I see and smell his gesture, a sweaty shrug in summer and a warm wet one in winter off the yellowing tufts of his jacket as he stamped free of the snow. He revived an old joke: "A ruble and a half," sure that even my mother would know he was kidding. Rubles did not come in halves.

"What's a dollar come from: I mean the woid," Andy asked suddenly, imagining what he had overheard. An argument followed. Everyone had ideas.

"The right pocket! the right pocket!" Myrna roared, using any excuse to release her storm of laughter, shedding a cloud of Kresge's finest perfume. "The right pocket, that's where!"

My father leaned an ear, cracking lima-bean pods between one black-nailed thumb and his long juice-stained index finger. "It's a German word. *Taler,*" he announced at last.

"No! . . . O no!" they all protested, but it was so. He smiled the sad wise smile of the man who values pure knowledge above his sentiments. As the eldest son, I was allowed to sit awhile, wearing the shirt in which I slept during the summer, its collar, once frayed against my father's neck, now slipping about my shoulders; I listened to the grownups. They discussed Max's ardor on his wedding night, the amorous couple abstaining, Myrna's monumental laughter and my father's hawing and Red Schwartz' steady chug-chug and mother's giggling and Andy's heehee's all flattering the newlyweds. The summer flies and the moths and color-blind mosquitoes which ignored the lamp contributed to the conversation, sometimes alighting to sip of the wine or, stretching, to sting its oily red surface.

From love, the talk swung naturally to food and business: for example, how to pack strawberries into a pint box to make them look better and more plentiful than they actually were, insulated from the bottom with a slanting lining of paper, shaken until sheathed like individual rosy ideals in a cushion of air, each one floating alone in the aristocracy of the expensive, the richest on top. In business the shifting tensions of competition offered even the apprentice after-school fruit clerk a chance to express his creative strivings. The operation of packing a strawberry pint box demanded daring, dexterity, an acute eye and sense of balance, and an equilibrium between thumb-on-the-scale greediness and a dismal Sunday school morality. Those like Myrna or Red Schwartz gave a great deal for twenty-four fifty a week, and also took.

My father unraveled the clues to his philosophy for a survival of the spirit in a fruit store on Saturday afternoon. When the talk came to chickens, he made a brave speech on the back porch to prove that his sense of justice survived even a vital deceit in the store. Mrs. Chicken-Picker's fowl has its firm yellow flesh patted and praised, held high for inspection; it travels downstairs to its gutting; there, a busy butcherboy slaps it to one side and sends up another which is already poised in readiness. Well, the butchers can't spend the busy days scraping innards. They prepare in advance for the Saturday rush, so that the same chicken might commute in the dumb-waiter from the basement and back a hundred times on the Saturday before the Fourth, being tirelessly replaced and then purchased from the display case by a hundred women who pride themselves on their ability to judge a springer.

"What else can you do?" he inquired of his student philosophers on the back porch protected only by screens from a restless universe.

"What else?" breathed Myrna.

"Hire more help? Charge more for the exact same birds?"

"What else?" Myrna breathed expiringly.

"So," he said. "You got the answer. Which it is easy to see. The strawberries are good, a good buy all the same." He had thrown down the gauntlet. Now he would pick it up. "And chickens! Why, the chickens are the talk of the town! Every Monday they come back"—he meant the women—"and they tell me, 'I sure know how to pick 'em, Sam. I can get a good chicken out of you, Sam,' they tell me. And they're right, those chickens are all Grade-Triple-A-one, gizzards as clean as mine, fresh pupicks. Those ain't soupers, those ain't restaurant birds. Those ain't no hanky-pank roosters, those chickens! I'll singe the pinfeathers and roast the worst of them myself any day you name, the whole city can come, I don't care if you stuff it with parsley, *my* chickens."

So saying, he tiddlywinked a bean down Myrna's bosom, the bean slippery and chill, everyone loosened in laughter by his speech and by the bean now at her navel. She celebrated more loudly than the rest, turning the joke back at my father. Encouraged, a few moments later he performed the same trick on my mother; the bean got stuck; she extracted it with two dainty fingers and said wearily, "Sam, it's not funny." This statement, true but careless of skill, unconscious of its portent, manifested a fatal flaw. The trial by lima bean had set into motion forces large enough to bring down empires and close fruit stores.

"I'm sorry," my father admitted soberly. "I know it ain't funny, ain't it?"

"No," my mother repeated.

Myrna munched a pod as she studied past rumpled chins the path between her breasts. She thought it was funny, but waited to make her move. Sleepily the party unwound. An inconclusive debate on the origin of tangerines—"What I mean, who invented it?" Andy asked—was marred by my father's silence.

"Shloimi didn't. He invents nothing," he said suddenly. "Time for sleep."

We have to work out the rest of this story from scantier data. The women, Mother, Ruby, and wakeful Myrna, cleaned the wooden platters on which liver and onions had been served, only their breath mingling. Mattresses, beds, and couches were assigned—Red in the room with me, Ruby on the parlor couch and Max discreetly on a mattress there, Andy in the kitchen; Myrna insisted on making a place for herself on the back porch and refused an extra cover. They climbed away separately, as appointed, heavy with work, food, and talk. They had only a few hours. "Gotta sleep fast tonight," Red remarked. "We all work together, we can add up eight hours."

Many soft palates vibrated; I dreamed inconsequently. My mother's body rolled into the sag of her bridal mattress. My father (let us say) went to offer Myrna a quilt; perhaps repose could chill even this woman. He found her breathing juicily, uncovered amid the smell of pods and spilled wine, a mountain sleeping. She awakened. She might have remembered his name: "Sam!" She may have remarked on the humor of a bean pod down her bosom. I suspect that she made some irrefutable physical gesture to which he responded with the instinctive rush of a powerful and thrifty workman; but perhaps it began with a sly joke about the two tiddlywinked beans. Both elements, hospitality and instinct, culminated in a few moments of my father's dozing while Myrna subsided heedlessly in the morality of pleasure.

Now we come to the sad part. Andy, jealous of my father, jealous of Myrna, an idealist in pure jealousy, lay alert and blinking in kitchen gloom. He heard enough—not much was needed—to stimulate him to sacrifice his interests to his ideals. He arose, peeked into the porch on tiptoe, descended quickly, padded across the floor toward the bathroom, paused at the door leading to my parents' room, and sneezed.

He listened, the cartilage of his ear pale in a spear of moonlight. He took a breath. My mother damply slept on. He put his nose to the crack in the door and sneezed so hard that his forehead rapped the knob like a cleaver and the door creaked open! *Tchew!* Serving his jealousy, he sneezed. A man so eaten by envy that he could sacrifice his job in a deed of heroic malice, emotion freckling the skin which flared back from his nostrils, Andy sneezed. He listened while he sneezed. He peeped through reddened eyes; the skinny head bobbed on its stalk. He sneezed like a librarian behind whispering children; he sneezed like a goat whose nose has been tickled. Tchew! Patiently he snuffed out my mother's dream. He stood before her door and sneezed, put his nose to the crack and sneezed, sneezed with inspiration. He sneezed, too, because his blood was thin. Such unselfish jealousy is always a surprise, as is the white worm which can sometimes be found in the cleanest, greenest Ohio Valley pod. Ah-*tchew*!

"What's the matter with you, you crazy barefooted?— you sick?" my mother demanded, barely awake, coming to the door in her nightgown. "I'll ask Sam for the mentho-lator."

"I think my blood is too anemic," Andy said.

She patted her hair net. She moved past him and went looking for Dad.

She found him. Poor Dad! She woke him up.

Even if she had been granted an aptitude for discretion she would have awakened him; he could catch a cold like that, all tossed over a strange woman like that. Before she screamed, before she howled, before she brought them all running and the lights flashing in the house, she murmured one intimate word for his ears alone: "Bad. Bad." All the banks had failed at once. We milled like stunned depositors about the mattress where Myrna and Dad lay.

My mother wailed, the long line of her upper eyelid taut and thick above the pupil. "Bad, bad one!" Myrna, who was hungry, contemplated her watchfully. My father lay with the sheet pulled over him until we went away.

Later he got dressed. "What you doing in the toilet so long?" he asked.

My mother's voice came through the door, the sound muffled by running water: "Eating my heart out." But the men went to market as usual; the women opened the store. My father stayed home all day, making his arrangements with my mother. Peace. Peace. More scars.

Troubled as I was with him, he lay more troubled than I in the close embrace of family. I was an American and spoke the language of Taft School, not his irregularly accented one. Life was too easy for me—all I had to do was grow up. But for some reason like the flooding of stars through the Milky Way or the compulsion of carrots to sprout green lace in the dark (rationality does not explain it, though the lace makes seeds), he found himself at age over forty laboring like a deck sailor (a whirling sun, a bursting carrot) on behalf of a wife, a sulk of sons, some no-good in-laws, nieces, nephews, and why? He valued pure risk and freedom too much not to wonder what had made him a husband and father. Why this bondage? Why, for example, didn't he turn over quick cash in colored shacks, as Phil Larkin did, the real estate kid? Phil was not married, not kind, no fun at all, had a bad stomach, and wore red eruptions with white spots on his neck—but why not? Flowers on the neck were a small price to pay for the simplified life. And why not take fast money in unimproved lots, as the twin Quinn brothers did, looking alike, practicing their cunning and getting rich together? They finished each other's sentences. When a person talked to them, they gazed into each other's eyes. When one Quinn said, "Tough," the other Quinn said, "Titty." They each held up half of their half of a conversation.

Larkin, Quinn, and other Quinn cut the risks by limiting what they cared for. And Shloimi Spitz, he too had found a direct and easy way: *You give. I take.* Only Sam Gold seemed to be tied into so many obligations, doing family and work and money and the future in complicated style.

Perhaps he figured it out while slicing raw turnips into a bowl, stirring chicken fat over it, but there was a stub root of question left over which no man can ever quite figure out to its end. *What wrapped me in? Could I have followed another way?* He ate buttered radishes for a nice change the next day, and went on figuring.

Consequently, despite all the chanciness of his life in family, at the wholesale market, in the front and back rooms of the store (including the basement where Myrna crooked her little finger), he was not sufficiently inoculated by the odds against Luck. There have been frequent difficult years since Solomon, so we must all be gamblers to bet on a good one next time. Next best to a good year for humanity is the private season a man creates by work

and love, making things and loafing, and my father had
at least a passion for work; but still he could not work all
day, every day. Hell, even Solomon had to relax after a
hard morning dividing babies in half. He was confused by
family (what means this "Parents Day in Your Elementary
School"?), by wife (a woman should be loyal, but does
loyalty define a woman?), even by the store because a
man needs more than to sort tomatoes and crack open
cases of baby food and haul lettuce in and out of the
cooler; therefore his passion for cards grew more ardent.
He gambled at the produce market and he gambled on our
Sunday picnics and he gambled wherever he found an old
pal with a deck in his pocket. "Hey Sam, you like a little
game?"

"Sit down, sit down."

And they might pull up a couple of orange crates in
the back of the store if everything was going okay up
front. Let the kleptos klepto a little bit, a man has got to
take his pleasure, a little bit. What's a few extra bottles of
vanilla extract if you're going to live to a hundred? "Watch,
watch," my father asked me, but I hated it. He urged me to
watch him, but he did not care; he excluded me as only
the gambler or the passionate lover can exclude the rest
of the world. He could hear the blue fuzz growing on an
orange, and bring it light and air, nurse it back to health,
but he could not hear the hatesong strummed on my jealous
heart by a shuffled deck when he turned from me to it. The
slap of cards, the click of coins, the contemplative grunts
of the players gave him too much pleasure—ungave me
him. My baleful eyes strove to corrode the neat columns

of nickels, dimes, and quarters, spread like the ruins of
the Parthenon in the arena of Sam's Market, shared only by
my father and his friends sitting on their orange crates in
the back room. Adults had pleasures! And each joy seemed
to be subtracted from my proper due. I did not dare
dislike the store, which stood between the misery of the
Nickel Plate freights and a family in the Depression, but
I could dare to hate rummy and poker and pinochle,
which stood between my father and me when I wanted
him to throw me a ball or take me fishing, as the "American" fathers did. "Don't go away, watch," he said as he
felt my evil face upon him. "Here's a quarter, which you
hold the money. Here, watch, you'll learn the game."

Didn't I know what a bribe was?

"Here, son, you be my banker. Keep the quarter. Sit
already, *sit*, you're making me nervous."

Yes, I knew what a bribe was. But maybe after a
while—

I learned the game, I took the quarter, I sat. But I
was wrong to wait. This was not like Myrna; he would
not tire of it. A woman weighing nearly two hundred
pounds talks babytalk; it's cute; speculations follow. Then
a man thinks of loyalty, his own back porch, and the
wife who listened so carefully and stroked his head when
he made his confession that he felt sad and lonely sometimes, what the Americans call blue, and he needed someone to love him. And so fare thee well to Myrna and her
bellyshaking ways. But cards? No. The more a man plays,
the more he wants to play, unless his reddening eyes
blank out and he topples from the orange crate. Hardly

likely before the age of ninety-six. Before he tired of cards
I was sleeping on the grass (picnic) or across a stack
of Libby's canned peaches (back of the store), dreaming
disasters to this father who so sweetly, fluently, smilingly
departed. He departed from me into the game. There were
Italian fathers at the picnic grounds who drank wine and
wrestled with their sons while mama mia to all of them
rolled the spaghetti; there were men who worked for my
father, squirreled away cans of meat in their pockets when
they thought he wasn't looking, and went on picnics with
us; and they hung about their babies with feminine, adoring gaze. But my father was playing cards.

I didn't mind work and Myrna: that's fatality. But
rummy, poker, blackjack, and pinochle gave me my
model for all the craven yearning of unrequited love. He
was busy in isolation. Having wished him ruin, I then
performed magic—hopping on one foot without falling
while spelling "Kate Smith" backwards, counting to five
hundred by threes—until, at last, my father turned to his
oldest child and said, "Let's do something, son."

Here is the model of the gleeful yearning of requited
love! He spoke, he smiled, he winked, he joined me in my
spaceship rocketing through Kate Smith backwards!

Often, however, before my magic could take effect,
Mother was after him. She had small complaints, such as
Myrna, who was too good a clerk to be let go, but had
lured him into the basement to discuss the problems of a
healthy widow. Such as: What to do about the screens in
the fall? Where could a former wife practice her vocabulary of babytalk? What do you think of a man who drives

up in a roadster, marries a girl, but has a weak heart he keeps from everyone? Well, even Solomon would take his time over that one, and my father concentrated hard on Myrna until he clarified the basic truth: You can leave the screens up all winter. If they rust, buy new ones or learn to swat the flies.

By that time Mother had hurt feelings. And she did not let him forget it, because though she was loyal, she was also verbal. He was guilty of spilling something like love into Myrna. Mother's heart, she explained in her own way, was breaking.

"Can I help it if I'm a workingman?" he roared, plunging into thickets of partial relevance. (Verdict: Guilty As Nagged.) "If I need my strength to live and so I got a lot of it? Look, see that fist? How many crates I smashed open with it, how many fights I had on the market with the anti-Semittin, how many bushels of potatoes I lifted with my bare hands?"

"How many, Sam?" my mother asked, suddenly curious.

"I can't afford to get sleepy. I got responsibilities. You think life asks me questions? It gives me answers, that's all, and who told Linda-Lou she could keep her Cossack here all night? I need a big cop jumping around on the ceiling all night when I got to sleep fast, get my eight hours in five? If you prick me, I'll bleed. And if you make googoo eyes at me—"

"You'll what, American?" demanded my mother.

"So enough nagging! Genug! I heard enough already!"

Brooding beneath lidded eyes, Mother turned away with her argument brilliantly organized in her head.

He had no answer to her dream argument, but life is not a dream, and when she started to inject an appetizer of pickled reality into it, he answered back, loud. He could not count on the pickled, creamed, smoked, deviled, and diced forms, but when it came to reality, he had the main course on his side.

"And besides, I never started. I stopped already," he said contritely, with eyes like my mother's—hooded by dreaming of that fair fat Myrna spread like a teeming bin of fruit across the level stacks of canned goods in the basement of the store, her apron parted, her skirt pulled up, my father discussing.

Mother and Dad looked at each other. He put out his arms. They kissed. For the moment, history cleared out of their eyes and there was only the pure embrace of separate hopes, opposing dreams, and a joined intention. But the language was different. And the hopes. And dreams. And the way of traveling through the four thousand and more years of reality.

And then they kissed again. They smiled upon each other from the small space between, and my father's gold tooth shone like a mote in the air. And then they went to the back of the house to kiss a third time.

Naturally, though they could abolish history in the clasp of love, they could not get rid of Aunt Anna. History accepts fact, but Anna demanded explanations. When she was not leaving her daughters in our house, she was leaving her criticism. When she was not depressed, she was worse—depressing. She planted her ankles, all five of them, in front of the stove and said, "Nu?"

Mother felt that "Sam's trouble—he got too much energy—his trouble—"

"What? What trouble? When? Why are you letting the kasha get so brown? *What is Sam's trouble?*" asked omnipresent, omniscient, omni-ankled and many-nosed Aunt Anna, for whom everyone behaved or else. (Or else what? She frowned. The garden became a desert. The kasha got too brown.)

Mother dropped the pan into the sink and said, "He got too much energy."

Aunt Anna became all beak. "You mean Myrna, that Divorcee, how he's been carrying on?"

"She's only a widow. He don't any more. He promised."

Anna sniffed.

"He keeps his promises, Anna. Why are you sniffing?"

Aunt Anna snorted. "Acts like a dee-vor-see to me. Where does he take her? On the cans?"

"You got a cold tongue, Anna."

"On the cans in the basement of the store? On the baby food? On the peas and carrots?"

"He handles only Libby's succotash, the very best U.S. Grade A-One," my mother said proudly. "At least he took her on the cans, he didn't spend our money on hotel rooms."

"Or he could go to her house," Aunt Anna pointed out, still sniffing.

Mother was scandalized. "Her house? The neighbors should see his truck? What's the matter, you crazy?"

"Well," said Justice Brandeis my aunt, "he's a shtunk sometimes, if you ask me, but maybe he's a good provider."

"He's a good man," said my mother, "a good provider. And he keeps a clean scalp—you know he shampoos twice a week? And a good heart—a good heart, Anna."

Sniff, snuffle, snort.

"Just he gets nervous sometimes, his way. A nervous type sometimes. You want some kasha and mushrooms?"

"It's too brown," said my aunt, "it makes me drip, my nose runs, and I got to go home and make Morris his supper. He don't like the kasha so brown. He goes crazy missing me if I'm not there. That man, hm, snt, koff, he *can't do anything without me.*"

"He's a trial to you," my mother commented.

"Hm," said Aunt Anna. "Well, don't let it aggravate you. They say aggravation is bad for the teeth, and what happened to all the calcium already? You're a young woman, Frieda."

"Four children."

"Who asked you to be a old-country mama?"

"Sam never *asked* me, Anna."

"Byebye," said my aunt, obscurely bested.

My mother stood over the stove, stirring with a wooden spoon and letting her tears fall upon the too-brown kasha. She had fought Anna to a draw, but still there were those tears left over. Four children and all that calcium weren't enough for him? He needed Myrna too? Is all of life just sacrifice and bitter memories?

Oh-oh! Here's Pop, who likes to salt the kasha himself. Dry the face quick!

12

Dad tiptoed into my room and rested his hand lightly upon my cheek. I flew straight up out of my dream. It was seven o'clock on a Sunday morning in November and he lifted a finger to his mouth. *Shh.* He was wearing pants and an undershirt, needed a shave, grinned and winked at me. He was whispering. "Son, you want to do something?"

I was dressed and unwashed with the speed of one of his best kleptomaniacs getting a bottle of vanilla extract into general circulation. Yes, I wanted to do something.

What we did on these occasions of doing something together was to go to the Russian Bath on Sunday morning, before the rest of the family mobilized for breakfast, sneaking down the driveway in the old Peerless before my cousins or brothers could whine about being left out, conspiring against mother and babies, just the two of us men. On Sunday mornings, when the suburb of Lakewood showed its Depression mothers in veils and its daughters in tulle, congested before the Christian Science church, the Catholic churches, the various churches, we drove miles into Cleveland, to West Sixth Street, just above the industrial flats, Republic Steel and Glidden paints, where the Bath drew its clientele of old-country loiterers. Our Peerless, shot through with smells of apples, lettuce, and grapes, rattled down Clifton Boulevard, along Lake Erie with its mansions and captain's towers, across the keeled-over city which was frozen by autumn rain and bank failures, miseries and hopelessness. Even on Sunday there were families lined up for giveaway baskets; Hungarian and Slavic men gathered on street corners to beat their arms against their overcoats and assess the blame and curse the memory of Hoover and the foolish message from no-body which had brought them to this frosty America. The breath issued from their mouths in short angry white puffs, like Indian smoke signals without the fire.

"You know why we're called Gold?" my father asked me on my eleventh birthday. "At Immigration they couldn't pronounce my real name. I thought: Call myself by the meaning of America. Gold in the streets! Me I picked it!" Furious, conned, delighted laughter: "Gold! Hah!"

He meant Smith or Jones, I now realize; he meant to be known as an American and to create himself pure, out of the streets of this country, Sam Gold the Smith-Jones American, with no history, heaven, or hell but his desire and hope for the earth of Cleveland and the truck farms nearby.

"Voogaltair," he said, "remember it. That was my name. Teach it to your kits—I was wrong. A kit should know his real name. *Woo-gal-tair.*"

But when they ask, "Who's there?" how could I answer, "Voogaltair"? Gold was the only name I ever needed to answer with. My father had chosen it as he chose me, and I would not worry it too much. As Sir Toby Belch said, "Care's an enemy to life," and he also had a funny name. Let Gold be your good friend, America; peace be with you, be with you peace.

We rattled through these Sunday streets to sweat it out—pestilence of boyhood, pestilence of fatherhood— at the Cuyahoga Russki Shvitz on West Sixth Street, near the Public Square of Cleveland, just below the Russian Orthodox church where an ancient, bearded, hunch-backed priest prayed under onion domes, a gift from the last Czar, for relief from plague, famine, earthquake, volcano, alcoholism, and the perils of civil war. And doubt. And despair. And the insecurity of that and all times surrounding the Cuyahoga Russki Shvitz (Indian, Russian, and Yiddish words, in that order). *Gospodi pomilui. Gospodi pomilui!* Sometimes we could feel the old priest's ferocious double bass vibrating in the looser bones of our heads as we walked up the steps past the sign which said TOWELS SOAP ETCETERA ONE PRICE TO ALL. My father always paused, cocked an ear toward the church, and said the same thing: "Nice. I heard Chaliapin once. A great man." The priest was chanting, flashing his garments, swinging chains and incense while his flock received their blessing. Overdressed, packed together, they stood with reddened eyes early on Sunday morning and wept for dread, for beauty. My father sighed and nudged me along.

"Let's get into the steam room—get this wool off our backs, what do you say?"

Lord save us, Lord save us! We fled inside from the perils of civil strife.

"Sam," my mother had remarked a few nights before, "the dentist says he'll try some more fillings—then it's a bridge."

"Okay."

"Expensive job for first-class bridge dentistry."

"Okay, you got to have teeth."

"They say it's aggravation rots the teeth."

"Who said?"

"Scientists. Anna."

He filled himself with air like a lizard at stormtime, and then let it out with a hiss, generously not exploding. "And Anna the Scientist says I aggravate you, yes?"

"Well, it's just my teeth are no good. Facts is facts."

My father picked up the paper and put his head behind it. "I'm sorry," he said, "I invented Hitler, the bank closings, the racketeers, I organized the Depression and the Black Legion, I'm sorry I—"

"*Sam?*" Timidly, tenderly, brokenly.

Muffled from behind the paper, distant and worn out, thus hiding his face, he said, "Myrna was a big mistake. I'm sorry. She made me crazy in the store nights, Frieda— *the boy's listening.*"

"What does he understand?" my mother assured him as I snaked my tongue through my teeth, looking for aggravations. I wiggled like a fish not caught but hypnotized onto the hook.

My father heaved a sigh up from his pockets. "Here, kotchka, read the paper anyway."

"It aggravates me," said my mother.

Supersophisticated, I had understood all and explained it to my cousin Elsie. "Maybe she has this mad passion for the dentist?" Elsie asked.

"Aw, Ma wouldn't do that."

"But I think she's beautiful, very lovely," said Elsie, "you know? For an old lady?"

"Don't tell the kids."

She looked at me as if I were crazy. Do you think a girl ten years old, going on thirteen, American-born, with a Cleveland accent—the West Side of town, Lakewood, in fact—didn't know enough to keep her blab flapped down? She was contemptuous of my aggravating male lack of consideration, and turned on me in chill snubbery. All right. Okay. But then how did the whole neighborhood find out about Ma and the dentist? I was sick of Elsie.

Freed of women on the steps of the Bath, in the shadow of the Czar's onion domes, with the priest's double bass swelling resonantly between his flock and the perils of life in Cleveland, my father asked me, "You got the deck?"

"You said you wouldn't play cards today."

"You're right! Hokay! And if I got to play, Saul Landau always brings a deck."

What a joy to exclude women—my mother and cousins —from the naked and sweating world of the baths! Among the nations of men finally at age eleven, I was my father's son, his eldest, lounging at my ease within a maze of room devoted to skin pleasure, lung relish, intense getting-out-the-kinks and dozing and hilarity on rusty chairs.

"Looks just like you, Sam!"

"Why shouldn't he? But he'll be taller—eats American food."

Swaddled by towels, these giants, folds of belly and folds of terry cloth, stood about on hot tiles in solemn contemplation of me. A hero with a changemaker on his belt—Saul Landau the news vendor—took off his great weight of belt; truck drivers and carpenters with Glidden-paint caps flung them into their lockers, union buttons clicking against metal; businessmen strolled elegantly on their bunions, heaved off their shoes, examined their corns and bruises—"too much standing, kid"—and went into the steam room with a pumice to give their dead flesh the slip. Guy Mallin handed Joe Rini a towel. Joe Rini gave it back. He already had two towels and a sheet. Frazzled bozos with clogged pores, backwatering sinuses, and fishy scalps came to renew their youth. Spindly shanks and flopping thighs looked for grace and unburdening by steam, salt, switching, stretching, alcohol, and massage. Distracted gaze, constipation, and kidney stones, galled by experience and worn down by the Depression and nagged a little at home, picked up fresh towels and soap, sat amid geysers of steam on the highest and hottest shelf they could bear, sighed and groaned, brushed teeth with finger, went from hot into steam room, steam room into hot into showers, back and forth, till thoroughly cleansed. Then shower again. Then the towels in a heap with abundant dirty towels, and fresh white ones, white as fur, for final sitting, gossiping, cardplaying, or dozing.

Closed-in, smiling, skin-proud men, freed of family and love, at least for the moment, amiable and hulking on stools, toweled heavily, one was named Saul, another Izzie, another something else; needed no name or occupation in this place. They were relieved and loved to sigh. Though they talked with each other, the talk was an expression of their general sensual blitheness, not a means of communication and only slightly an expression of more than this pleasure: a sigh, a grunt, a stretch, a yawn; a scratch of toes, a gargle, a relieved rumble of gut. "I got good feet for my age," my father said, "not a callus, look!"

"I see," Saul Landau mournfully observed, and grudgingly added, "I stand on them all day."

"So I don't stand?"

"And naturally they get sore, the newspaper business."

"It's in my family. My son got good feet. My nieces, they got bad feet, like my wife's side of the family. And they got it without standing—maybe just from telephoning, using the telephone all the time, Elsie got calluses on the bunions."

"All right, Sam, maybe your side of the family is good for feet."

My father called me over with an imperative hooking gesture. "Show Saul Landau your bottoms." I must have looked surprised. "Of your feet, mug. Here"—and he grabbed and he kept me hopping.

The near-sighted news vendor bent and squinted at my big toes, between the toes, the ankle, instep, and heel, and then straightened up. "Sam," he said, "I got to hand it to you."

My father smiled. "I wouldn't make it up," he remarked contentedly, showing that tooth which sang like a bird in his head, and then became kind all at once. "But Saul, I hear your boy is good in school. My Frieda heard it from your Ida."

Izzie Rabinowitz, frowning and vain, bent nearly double on a stool, put his tongue sideways and breathed through his mouth in short absorbed wheezes, plucking out the gray ones among his pubic hairs. "Ouch! ouch! outch!" he sighed, successful at last, and straightened up. It was also a trial to have deviant vision. "Not as young as I used to be," he remarked, summing up the experience.

"So now you feel younger?" my father asked. "All one color? Red?"

Izzie shrugged. "You got to please the ladies, youth they like."

"*They like,*" said my father, knowing that this was not what they valued. "Pluck, pal, but there is other ways to step up strong."

"What you mean by that?"

"Bifocals. Hair dye. Chutzpah, what you think?" ("Chutzpah" means "hubris," that mad pride which led so many Greeks into trouble by assuring them that twenty-twenty vision and pubic hair all of one color do not make the man.) Izzie Rabinowitz bowed his head and turned "with quiet dignity" to wash his feet with a long-handled brush.

Stately giants in repose, the men at the Bath ate, drank,

sweated, steamed, and bathed, lounging swathed in towels like monuments waiting to be dedicated or sitting thinkerishly on stools. And their buttocks! Some of them were stringy and lean; some ripe, pale, and knobby as basement roots, paired sweet potatoes; but mostly they had fine fat ones, storing up a history of corned beef, rye bread, pickles, and hot mustard, yearning for Sunday. Their buttocks were striations of meat, flesh like aging oak with concentric rings which each stood for the years, patience, climbing, tension, and romping joys of thickly buttocked men; and on Sunday morning at the baths, the release of gut was pure pleasure—all the time in the universe when they desired to squat, and the Sunday paper to pass the time between spasms of relief, and showers and soap for perfect cleanliness afterwards, and then abandon in the pool, doing a slow breast stroke, blowing water. Ah, a man hurries all week, clipping short his rightful rump joy while the telephone shrills outside, while his children or his wife bangs or hollers at the door; but on Sunday, Sunday at the Russian Bath! Rows of private booths! No pants to tangle in ankles and keep off the floor! Freedom of knees and unfinicky noses! And most of all, time, blessed time! The noble brow of Izzie Rabinowitz took its rest, and Saul Landau the news vendor's capacious paunch against which so many nickels had tinkled, and Guy Mallin's fierce jut and sprinkle of hair—belly, back, behind, and tangle of ribald commercial eyebrows. And my father, more muscular than the others, with thick hocks and thick control beneath the pink salt-bruised flesh, moved in the center of my vision.

The steam room was the sanctum sanctorum, of course, the holy of holies for halvah and chalah eaters, the best palace of delight, an impregnable citadel of tile. There were also equipment and appurtenances beautiful in their hot, wet, logical simplicity. Wooden shelves were arranged in tiers along the walls, each level hotter than the one below: a man climbed, dangled, accepted what he could bear. There were nozzles, hoses, radiators, and if you wanted more steam, you turned the water on the radiator and it flew forth like bee droplets, buzzing and fighting in the air. Occasionally one of the Ukranian attendants, naked but for his handle-bar mustache, brought in a bucket of pine water and dashed it against the radiator, and a pouf of piney steam broke into our lungs. Men lay blinking on their shelves, gasping with pleasure, or stood yelling confidences at each other in the sea roar, and just waited for the good to come to them. Towels, soap, water, hot water, hotter water, gravelly salt for rubbing, chatter, laughter, and hairy companionship in the strain and ease of this invented weather—they dreamed of it during their bitter week of the Depression autumn in Cleveland.

"Harry Hopkins says—"

"You mean Harry Ickes."

"It's Harold, and I mean General Johnson too, so listen!"

"Why should I, Sam? Let's get some more steam!"

The boarded the cloud of steam like amiably quarrelsome fat angels, bellowing at each other for joy in lung power amid the roar of fantastic plumbing. Beneath us, the tangled pipes gave their all, and beneath the pipes, another Ukrainian heaped enough coal into the furnace to send us skimming across Lake Erie to Canada, parting and drying up the waters to our stern. Skinny and prideful, I moved underfoot in the steam room like a drenched rat, learning the ways of men. Just as a few years later a uniform would reduce me—or raise me—to being a man exactly like all other men, except courageous or cowardly, evasive or direct, foolish in life or getting through, so the uniform of nakedness removed all these men from the pride, disgrace, and works of their days. In my child's eyes they were very much alike—swollen sex, hanging gourds, purplish veins, creased bellies—and to them I was different: a child. "Sam's kid! Lookit the kid, little Sam, he's learning the steam room! Sam Gold's boy! You making out, kid, with all you got is that pinkie of yours?"

I hid myself in shame and giggled. I was only a child, agreed for the sake of peace, but I was the only child whose father trusted him here. And Dad said I was no bother to him, not too much anyway, as briskly, grunting, enjoying, he rubbed salt into his velvety pelt until the skin beneath flamed pink, glowed. And therefore I was a gladiator. I sloshed through the drain that lay at dead center of the tiled steam room, and then climbed the hot and hotter wooden shelves along the wall. Dad pushed me out when he thought I might get dizzy, and once when I felt abruptly soft and faint, he carried me into the locker room and made me drink salt water. Hot and sulky, I tasted blood on my tongue. I thought I looked like a man and smiled at my father.

"You okay, son? It can happen to anybody."

"I want to go back."

"No, no, no, it ain't no dare, the steam room. Next Sunday some more, son."

I was learning to take heat, and though white and hairless, to have an appetite for foaming steam. I waited for Dad while he returned to wash down the salt crystals from his inflamed chest and flanks.

In the back rooms, beyond the arena where these businessmen took their ration of steam and salt, there were dark cubicles where mysterious muscled recluses provided the pleasures of massage to a different, younger group of plump *Amerikantsi*. These dandies and sissies composed another society. We never more than nodded to them at the entrance. They never paused to listen to the Russian priest's chant. They had never heard the voice of Chaliapin, Lord save them.

"Now," my father said on this particular Sunday morning of which I speak, "you okay? So I'll play a little cards maybe."

"But breakfast!" I wailed.

"But breakfast, sure—*after* breakfast." He lay his heavy

arm across my shoulders. "Which it is we wouldn't have breakfast first?"

In a room like a huge restaurant kitchen reigned the smiling and sweating Ukrainian cook, wearing nothing but white duck pants and a mat of skin hardened by flying fat, healed-over blisters, calluses, more flying fat. He cooked at an open coal stove and handed platters of breakfast meats to the happily depleted men after their immersion in vapor. These were not men who did exercises: their lives gave them plenty; but having reclined amid the waters and hallooed at each other and rubbed salt onto their flesh, they then emerged, hung with towels, to eat hearty of liver and onions or steak and onions, served on worn, grooved wooden platters with pink juices running in the grooves. Ravenous, hilarious, clean-lightened of their burdens, they said, "Have some more smothered onions, kid."

"I got my own," I said.

"He got his own," said my father, "leave him alone."

"He's just a pinkie off you, Sam!" cried the news vendor. "Haw, haw."

"I got me a nice pinkie," my father said, touching my head, and I blushed with gratitude and love. Escaped from the women of our house and the world, escaped from small children, we were father and son alone in a man's place, stripped to our skin, tender with each other in our inexperienced ways while the world spun its strange course outside. There was no justice, Shloimi Spitz was extorting his toll, Germany was burning with hatred, the Black Legion was mumbling its curses in the countryside about

Cleveland, but here on West Sixth Street we could eat liver rare, plus smothered onions, and smile handsomely at each other. Since he was a fat king, I was a skinny prince. As much as I knew how at that age, I blessed my father.

"More onions? More liver? Better than home, hey, kid?"

"Yes."

"Just seems that way! Something about sweating! Salt and liver taste good, and those onions!"

And something about home, too, I now believe I then thought.

Having eaten, the men flung away their forks and knives, left the dripping platters, and went to the card tables. Sex bulged under their swaths of towels, their swaddles of terry cloth. They talked business and politics, they sighed, they said, "Ai-yeah, what can you do?" Then they settled down to cards.

I wandered disconsolately, found by my father, then losing him to the game. After the joy of steam and food, I was dismally abandoned. I felt as dull-eyed as the hobos on the Nickel Plate, going noplace between Toledo and Cleveland. I had traveled this way before, many times, each time predicting another destination. Another road away, and toward the same isolation. I stood by his side, not looking at the cards, forgotten as he sank once more into the game. I knew too much to nag him for attention. I stood there hopelessly, knowing it was useless, but with a child's cunning, seeking to shame him by my loitering. He shook his head and pursed his lips and was rid of me. I went wandering again through the corridors and locker rooms and back to the empty kitchen. Where we had steamed, there was only a smell and strangers. Where we had eaten, there was only dishwashing and cold grease. I was alone.

Even one of my cousins, even my mother, would have been welcome company to me now, at eleven o'clock on a Sunday morning in the Russian Bath. This was defeat: to be lonely in my father's presence, thinking of a woman and of girls.

An hour passed. I thought of getting dressed and going to sit outside, but the frosty morning had given way to a rainy gray November afternoon. I poked my head into the back corridor where the *Amerikantsi* went for their massage, but the cook found me and grabbed my ear. "Hey! That not for you!" he said. "Your papa know you poke nose back here?"

"My father's playing cards."

"Go be with your father, Little Sam."

Pouting and dismal and dim, I obeyed orders. Maybe this time he'll be finished, I thought, and swore to myself, as I had many times before at this hour: *I won't come back here again.* But each time, each Sunday morning, I remembered the fresh, secret early morning ride in the Peerless, the steam room and the pine vapors and the jokes, my father's pride in me, the liver and onions and wooden platters; and I knew that each time I would be teased once more by hope against betrayal by the cards which took my father from me.

I wandered back, stepping only on the cracks.

The game was different; I saw it at once as I entered the room. The four players were looking at each other's hands and chortling. The men were different, the towels had fallen agape, and their faces were flushed. They were not dealing; they were sharing the cards. I came up quietly, and just as during the game, they did not see me. I stood by my father and looked at the pack of photographs spread about on the table.

There were pictures of women, women and men, women and whips and men, women and leather thongs and shoes and men, women stooping and grinning and very false-serious. It seems to me that I must have known what all this meant without any thought at all; I had learned on the playground and in the alleys; but I had never thought to connect my father with such matters. I stood for a moment in stricken shame.

Someone said, "Hey Sam! Your boy's here!"

With that word I burst into rage. Naked, I threw myself on the table and it collapsed beneath my weight; shrieking, I grabbed the cards in my fists and flung them about; I did a dance of craziness, a screaming tantrum of protest against so much betrayal, until suddenly my face took my father's slap and I fell sobbing to the tile floor. He picked me up in his arms. The other men had turned away. The cards lay soggy and abandoned on the wet tiles, no one finding joy in them now.

Cradled in my father's arms, my skinny, convulsed legs dangling, I suddenly saw his face, heavy and white, come into focus above me. He was weeping. "Kit," he said. "Son. Son."

I tried to flood out the tears once more so that I would not have to see his face. But only dry sobs; and as I lay in his arms, we gazed into each other's eyes.

"You don't understand now," he said. "Which it is not so terrible, son. It's just—nothing is enough like it already is for most men. You know about Myrna too. Nothing is enough."

Cigar smoke rising from the group of men huddled together against the wall on the other side of the room. They were murmuring and smoking.

"Son?" my father asked, as if this were a question.

"Let me down," I said. He paused, and then swung me easily to the floor. I felt the tiles on my feet. He waited for me to make the next move.

"Son?"

The cards still floated in the puddles and stains on the floor. There was a smell of wetness and cigars. All these men who gathered on Sunday morning in the Russian Bath for a quiet time together stood silent, waiting for me to rise to pity for their loneliness—me, at age eleven.

No, I could not feel pity. But abruptly my eyes swam in a flood of the knowledge which rises from pain, released from my prison of self-regard (many times released, many times imprisoned).

"Son, would you like to do something now?" my father asked.

"Yes. Let's go home."

The company of men is not enough, I think I meant to say; let us now turn toward women.

We went out into the gray November afternoon, my father holding my hand, and he paused to listen for the service from the Russian Orthodox church. Silence. He shook his head. "Guess they've stopped already," he said.

"Hurry up, we got to get you where it's warm. I'll bet your pores are still open."

14

Now back to ice-skating again. My father, who worked in a smiling rage all day and much of the night, who did not *understand* children in the American style, as did the parents of my friends, who did not really know how to play with a child once the time of tickling and dandling was past, liked to ice-skate and was determined that I would see what he saw in it. He decided to teach me. After I learned, he continued to go ice-skating with me on Sundays at the City Ice and Fuel Rink, or at Lakewood Park when the firemen watered the baseball diamond, or at Rocky River Park when it froze over nicely. He was a good skater, slightly stiff on his feet compared with a child, but steady and tireless and continually smiling with his red face frozen and his hair tufted with bits of snow. He hated to stop for hot chocolate; he liked to skate—when you skate, you should skate.

As I grew self-conscious I thought, Now everyone will know my father has an accent. I was in love with other skaters, of course. They would like me less if they saw with their own blue eyes, heard with their own shell-like ears, just how Jewish my father was. He called to me on the rink, "You want some cookies? You want to rest a little?" Pattie, Donna, Lucille—they took in the news that v's and w's can be confused.

But on the other hand, he liked to skate, and I liked to skate, and we liked to skate in each other's company.

Round and round we went, and sometimes my father tried little figure-skating turns that he had learned long ago, perhaps to impress my mother or some girl before her. Afterwards he liked a bowl of soup. He took it noisily off the spoon. He told me to order anything I wanted, just finish what I ordered. "Your mother used to skate," he said, "but now she don't. Ankles."

"Yeah."

"Which I suppose it is normal if a lady don't keep up the practice—"

"Yeah."

He tried to tell me his troubles with the racketeer Shloimi Spitz, but I was not interested. He noticed my absent gaze and took it for boredom. It was boredom, too, but also love of Pattie Donahue.

One day at school I was teased by some kids about my father. He was foreign, strange, walked differently, talked differently, did different things—bad, they thought. This happened more than once, but there was one particular day. Snow, mud, a boy yelling at me, distended folds of snout: "Parkyakarkus! Parkyakarkus!"

This may have been the first time in my life that I formulated a most necessary thought: The hell with them, they don't know Greek from Jew, but I know what I want.

Suddenly I wished I knew more about Shloimi Spitz. Next time I would try to listen.

In 1935 my father had two mighty enemies. Against one of them he struggled all the long fruit-and-vegetable day, hoisting the crates and loading a top-heavy truck in early morning, at dawn, in his wet boots, then meeting the customers until evening in a store built narrow and dark in the alleyway between a bakery and a Peerless showroom. Against the other enemy he fought all night, tossing and groaning in his sleep, fierce with that strange nightmare which allows an angry man to be pursued without ever retreating.

His daytime foe was one shared by most other Americans—the Great Depression. The adversary of his nights was that beast clanking and roaring in the streets of fantastic Deutschland. "Hitler!" he said at breakfast, shaking the sleep from his head. "I'm almost ashamed to be human. The other strawberries don't like the rotten strawberry, they blush rotten red if you don't pluck him out—"

"Have another cup of Wheatena for the strength in

it," chanted my mother, grieving with him like a good wife because of the need for strength on a troubled planet.

"Sorry, no time—look at the clock!" He hadn't meant to complain; it was the only earth he knew. "The lettuce is in already, and the Pascal comes with it." And standing up, jacketed, shod in Army-Navy boots, he drained his coffee, dropped the cup in the sink, and was off to the market downtown near the Flats of Cleveland. Before light on a winter morning, he fought the battered reconditioned motor of his truck, cursed, lifted the hood, wiped the wires and plugs. Mother opened the kitchen window to watch. Then fits and coughs, then action. Mother watched him go, and waved. *Action*—his pockets filled with knives, hammers, dollars, a deck of cards, and funny pictures to show his friends in the chill damp of a January morning. Down the suburban streets, up the suburban highway he rattled; and through the sleeping city where the street lights abruptly died in the dawn; and only rare bedroom lamps and kitchen noises greeted him on his way.

But the West Side Market was a city in full life. Carloads of vegetables steamed with the haggle and babble of selling under corrugated zinc roofs and no roofs at all. Desperate eaters, standing near the great tureens of soup, could not remember whether this was their second or their third breakfast. My father paced the aisles of lettuce and tender peas, the green corridors of spinach, deep into silent back parlors of early fruit off the railway cars. Private, at one with food, he sniffed gratefully, at his ease, homely, taking the pleasures of business on his tongue and in his deep-breathing lungs. He went to the produce market as to worship—putting Hitler and bank holidays behind him in the glory of America's bounty. He squeezed a plum until the wine spurted. He wiped his eyes.

Joe Rini surprised him in his shadowy lair. "What you doing here, Sam?"

"Same as you! Good, eh?"

"But can we sell it? I still got last week's plums left over."

My father shrugged, the sheepskin ruffling against a crate. "They get soggy in the cooler. What else can we do?"

"Nothing—and these look like prime. Here, let me taste."

"Taste, go on. Me, I'd like to buy."

The fruitmen rivaled, of course, for the favor of the farmers, who were of another breed, not washing in those days as a protest against the cost of living. Their best produce many times rotted in the fields, and the farmers often suffered terrible bellyaches from the hopeless eating of an unbought crop. Even striated beefsteak tomatoes, warmed by sun and dusted with salt, can be too many! The farmers suffered from mortgages, skin diseases, unrepaired fences, chronically pregnant wives. Regularly removed from their lonely land to confront a crazy urban cackle, and perhaps returning without the profit of seed and fertilizer, they too passed cards among themselves.

The immigrant Italian and Jewish fruitmen, with their occasional Greek and Negro colleagues, exchanged printed jokes and dirty pictures. They first competed and argued, then huddled for soup and coffee and gossip, sharing each other's hard times in the pleasure and intimacy of these early mornings. They left dawn with regret, jamming their trucks into gritty day.

The farmers' wives, bundled and red and unfragrant as men, dipped up the last coffee and watched without a word. Drops of fat cream whirled round like crazy fishlets in the tin cups. The farmers too had their whispered consultations, but these never ended in a burst of laughter as they got the point. Their little cards were other dreams, dreams of riding and hunting, gothic fantasies of ritual, celebration, and chastisement. The Black Legion haunted the countryside around Cleveland. It made contact with the Klan in Parma and the Bund in Lakewood, and there were histories of drilling in open fields, the youngsters standing guard with broomsticks. Their cards made them members together for sacred order and vengeance. Cousins who rarely came out saw each other on Sunday after church to listen to screaming harangues from the platforms of pickups. During the dark winter of 1935, some farmers discovered that they had the call—or at least as much a one as the man in blue serge sent down from Black Legion headquarters in a warehouse in Jackson, Michigan.

Al Flavin was a farmer with whom my father had dealt for almost ten years. They had never been friends, but my father gave as good a price as anyone and Flavin took good care of his lettuce; they met in commerce. An angry man who had sometimes wrestled at country fairs, a giant with magnificent hairy paws, he began to know glory for the first time since abandoning his boyish victories on sweaty canvas. Men listened to him. He became a Commander or a Knight or a Dragon, whatever the Black Legion name for it was. He could not pay off the loan on his greenhouse, but he could gather the Legionnaires in before-dawn consultations at the edge of town.

It must have made Al feel distant from himself to discuss the meeting, give the mystic handshake, crushing the wrists of men less mighty than he, climb into a truck with a load strapped on, and then drive meekly off to do business with Sam Gold.

"All right, make it eleven crates for ten," my father said.

"Ten crates," Al repeated stubbornly.

"Eleven. Or ten and my last price."

"No. Ten crates. My price."

"Al, listen to me," my father said. "You *know* I can't buy it your way. Joe Rini will undersell me, he'll throw circulars on all the porches, and then where will I be? You got to make sense in business."

"You heard me."

"What's the matter, you don't feel good today, Al? Something hurting?"

"Joe Rini don't buy from me. I bring in first-quality stuff."

"I know, I *know*, that's why I stand here and argue with you. I *want* your stuff, Al. I like it."

My father rocked, smiling. Al Flavin stood behind his barricade of lettuce. Patience, patience—the soul is tried on earth. At last they were agreed, someplace between demand and offer, and then, joining in the traditional after-math of successful negotiation, the two of them completed their deal by hoisting the produce into my father's truck. Hot and sighing when this was done, the cash changing hands, usually they came to a moment of benevolent treaty, and the plump fruitman would light up with the burly, brooding farmer. Al Flavin was busy behind his squeezed-shut eyes trying to remember who he was, who other people were.

"Okay, Al," my father said, "have a cigar."

Now he remembered. He felt his card and sorted my father out: "*Kike!*"

"Wh-wh-wh," said my father.

Flavin's shoulder caught my father and half spun him around as the man stamped off in the flapping galoshes which he wore almost into summer. My father stammered, wh-wh-wh, meaning *What?* and *Why?* First amazed, then stooped and solemn, pouting with thought. It was well past dawn now, but suddenly the nightmare toppled onto his daytime dream, and he was standing in the sad, crooked streets of old Kamenets.

My father stopped dealing with Al Flavin. This did not put an end to it. He heard Flavin's word every market-day morning, first whispered, then called after him, twice a week. The single note grated on his nerves. The market is supposed to be a pleasure. My mother made him promise not to fight. Flavin, huge, profligate with his wrestler's flesh, yearning to brawl, would crush him in his paws. It was policy. Flavin was a Commander. He hoped to con-

vert the waverers by rolling with Sam Gold in the running
wash of the market gutters.

"I'd get him with the peen of my hammer first!" my
father yelled.

"Sam, Sam, we don't want trouble."

"I'll break his head with the claw!"

Mother petted him, stroked him. "Think of your bus-
ness. You got a family, Sam, you got to count them."

"I'll kill him, Frieda."

"Shush, you're making noise, the neighbors. You got
to count me, too. No trouble, please for your kids' sake."

"No, no, no." His eyes were red with sleepless thinking.
There was an angry scratch in the tender eye-flesh. He
breathed as if he were struggling for air. "No, you're right,
Frieda. But if he touches me one more time—"

That time came, however, on a morning during the
dog days of July, when even at early market hours the
men panted and sweated under the bloody-eyed sun before
it reared up onto the exhausted city. Ice trickled through
the crates of lettuce, rustling, and evaporated on cement
still hot from the day before. The overfed market rats loped
along on seared paws. Flavin sprang from behind a
heap of crates, pretending to be in a hurry, and struck my
father with his knee at the belly, so that he lost his balance
and stumbled like a drunk. He grunted. He tried but could
not quite sob out his breath. It was caught, trapped, ex-
terminated someplace within, and he lay sprawled on
the soft market refuse while the little world of pain in
his belly spun faster than the earth's turning, and only a
moment later, when the hurtling agony at the center of

his being slowed down to weakness, and the weakness to a sour sickness that drained into his mouth, did he remember again who he was. It's an assault against life that brings this gnawing, liver-eating agony upon a man gasping for his breath with his head against a crate of lettuce. The blood shrieked like eagles in his ears. It's a wish of murder —extermination. It's a terrible pain that make a man forget he is Sam Gold.

Flavin roared, pushed the laughter forward with all his weight, and stood with his huge arms welcoming. Once taciturn, he had learned the trick of oratory: "Looks drunk, don't he? Ain't he a rummy? Never did run into a rummy kike before, did you ever, boys?"

An offering of laughter. The rest would gather when the rich noise of brawling crashed out. Flavin was in boots, kicking free of a broken crate, ready.

Sam Gold pained badly in the gut. He climbed up dizzily and shook his head clear. He felt for the silver-pronged crating hammer in his back pocket. Flavin crouched, his long jaw twitching with desire. The buttons of his pants were stretched and a tab of his shirt came out of his fly. Flavin could wait another moment to make himself real. The usual hubbub of commercial dispute hid them now; the life of the market swirled unknowing about the two men, food rising in great towers and vaults above them, around them, and only a couple of farmers watched. Joe Rini, terrified, blowing saliva, also watched.

My father had promised my mother.

He loved life and the right and *to win*.

Flavin might kill him.

My father walked away rapidly, hunched, turning red
for shame and white for planning, and grabbed Joe Rini
by the sleeve and took him with him. "Joe, Joe," he said,
"I got to talk to you. I know you got friends. I got to talk
to them too."

"What you got to say, Sam?"

"Oh maybe I could kill him, but then again maybe
not. Which it wouldn't be so good if he gave me a beating.
Those other Cossacks would feel too nice about it. Or
worse. A bad example. No good in that. So . . ."

Eagerly Rini talked into the void. "So you know how
they drink. They're drunkards. So don't raise your blood
pressure." My father's eye made him stop. Rini agreed. My
father decided slowly:

"The way things are going on the market now, Joe,
it won't be safe for any of us soon."

"What you thinking, Sam?" Rini asked.

He was thinking, but in his own words: precedent,
morale, example. This was a political question, to be
answered in the impure, compromising way of politics.
A passionate answer—Sam Gold's face bloodied, a crowd
secretly smiling over Sam Gold's fallen body, an inflamed
Al Flavin finding his dream of power fulfilled—this was
the worst possibility which my father's furious body had
almost given him. The philosophical thing to do was to
master that hot inner twitch, and then, only then, to think
out how to discourage the Cossack mob.

Job and Noah had patience; yet Job was permitted his
anger. Not an educated man, my father knew that the
patriarchs had even spoken for passion on earth, properly

used. And he knew no other place for justice except here below, on earth, where he hoped to have more children.

He breathed deeply once, twice, again, that's better, and then thanked God for giving him a sense of responsibility. He thanked the Lord of Creation that his healthy, willing, complaining wife had come to mind. Wistfully he thanked the Almighty for prudence—and also for his friend Joe Rini. He said to Joe Rini: "You're going to help me now."

That very night Joe found the three young friends whom he had in mind and brought them to the house. My father wanted to meet them: "Make your acquaintance, I'm sure." How formal we become under embarrassment. For fifty dollars he could buy a beating with any refinements he named. Except nothing vicious, of course —what do you think, they were queers? They were mere administrators.

"No, *no!*" my mother cried. "So then he'll kill you next, and what's the good? We can't afford it."

"We can't afford not to," my father said stonily. "We're going to do what the Frenchies won't do. When he makes his noise, we march into the Rhineland and stop it good. You don't have to listen to that noise. You stop it the best way you can. You stop it. You *stop* it."

"Sam, O Sam, it's dangerous, it's fifty dollars."

"It's the cost of living, Frieda."

Joe Rini's friends, three young chaps with slicked-down hair, nervous hands, and old jokes, were very sociable. They jiggled and dandled and played beanbag with me as if I were a baby, although I felt as serious as any adult. They took time over the business because my father likes business. Also he wanted to be certain. He did not like this business, and that made him slow and cautious. Mother served liver *with,* the rich slabs covered by curly, glistening onions. How can businessmen discuss matters without keeping up their strength? Mugs of strong black coffee, too.

"For fifty dollars, Mr. Gold," said the leader of the group, "we can maybe kill him for you. It's no extra. We'll be working anyway. His truck has got to stop for a light on the edge of town, and there we are."

"No, no," my father said. "Put him in the hospital, that's all."

"Mr. Rini says he used to work in the commission house with you. He says you're buddies from way back. It's no trouble at all."

"No!" my father said. "The man has a wife and kids, just like me. His big boy is too dumb to run a farm by himself—"

"We got smart kids," my mother interrupted, smiling, politely patting with a napkin, pleased by their appetites. "My big boy, he gets such marks from his teacher—"

"Frieda, shush. Go call up somebody on the telephone if you got to talk. Listen."

The businessmen shrugged apologetically, being brought up in a tradition which favors mothers, and turned regretfully back to hear out my father and his scrupling. They were unaccustomed to fine distinctions, but they came of devoted families; they enjoyed a mother's pride. "So don't do that what you said there," my father repeated.

"I just want him to learn a little, have time to think a little. The hospital."

"Okay," the leader of the trio said reluctantly, "you're the boss. You get a hold of us if you change your mind, will you? To you the price remains the same."

"The hospital," my father repeated, making them promise.

"Let us worry about the details, Mr. Gold. Fifty goes a long way these days."

My father arose angrily, sending his cup ringing against a platter. *"I said the hospital!"*

"The hospital, hospital," they intoned mournfully, and filed out.

The next morning Flavin did not show up at the market. It was so easy to follow him from the country in a flivver, stop with him at a red light, get rid of the cigarettes, and pile quickly onto his truck. So instead of Flavin, a weary, hardworking young thug appeared and nodded to Dad, saying that they had been careful, just as he said. But it would have been no extra trouble, in fact, the reverse.

My father was undelighted. By his veiled eyes he signaled regret at the weight of the world: he was obliged to send Flavin down to defeat without earning the kiss of victory. Life had provided him—as it does everyone—with one more little blemish on the ideal of brave perfection. He found it a necessary business, nothing more, a merely rational victory, and he foresaw the possibility of being ambushed in his turn by a man who might not bother to think of his wife and children. Nevertheless, reason consoled him.

Another man might have done nothing against his enemy, because he believed vengeance the worst of sins. He might be a good Christian; he might be a coward. Another man would simply have killed him or hired him killed. That seemed simple, and it might seem easy to some. Another man might have stayed home and brooded till his wife shamed him into desperate combat. These were all ways some men might have replied to the disaster of assault.

Reason consoled my father. Perhaps he had not taken the right way, but he found his own way.

Still, he did not like it very much and he was unconsoled by reason. Reason did not help when he cut himself off from his father; reason did not help when Ben cut himself out of life; reason was only a way of trying to make the incoherent coherent, and it never did all the job. It washed over grief, but it left grief intact. It shrunk grief into a tiny matted lump in the belly, but it left the shame and grief where they lay.

"Okay! Which it is what I had to do," he told my mother. "Okay! I don't want to hear about it."

"Sam, what if he does to you? Where will I and the kids be? Where will *you* be if you're dead?"

He grinned. Coming back to his world. "Well, it's a risk," he said, although he had just said he would not speak any more about it. "But in this life you have to take chances and defend yourself like you can." He frowned angrily. "I don't always like how I can, Frieda."

She was frightened by his face. She waited to see if he had something he wanted to tell her.

"And now let me answer your question: If I'm dead, I'm noplace."

He sent Flavin a five-dollar bouquet of flowers, followed the next morning by a two-dollar plant with thick wet leaves and a decorative sprinkle of spangles. Joe Rini approved. A friend who went to see Flavin in the hospital reported that they were the only flowers he received.

The moral which my father drew was one which he wanted to teach England and France in 1935 and after. Still strong and capable, Flavin came quietly to work in his bandages about ten days later. He sold tomatoes to my father, and they haggled like gentlemen over the price. They mistered each other warily. There was further talk of the Black Legion, but not a gesture from Flavin. In a few years even the talk passed.

Sometimes my father thought that he might be beaten up, but it never happened, although once he was robbed. That was not Flavin's work.

Flavin had taken instruction well, administered according to Aristotelian principles, with moderation, by a man whose fundamental passionate mildness led him to a reasonable strictness: the hospital for Flavin, nothing worse. Nightmares go on, but they have answers—albeit risky, rational, incomplete, and not ideally valorous. Poor Flavin, unused to surprises—he was discouraged.

A few days later Shloimi Spitz telephoned to ask: "Sam, why didn't you let me know? I could of done a better job for no charge—included already."

"You get what you pay for," my father said.

"You don't like me. Aw, you don't like me," said the racketeer extortionist. "And we done business together so long already."

"Monkey business. Foo," said my father.

"I could of crippled him good. My pleasure," said Shloimi. "I protect you good, don't I, Sam?"

"Like clockwork regular," my father said.

"You don't like me," said Shloimi. He waited. When there was no answer, he put the telephone down. My father said he had a bad taste in his mouth. All this monkey business cost too much.

"Fifty dollars," said my mother.

"No. A bad, bad taste. A bad, bad time. Frieda. I should have figured out another way."

But my mother was consoled. Dad made another fifty dollars to replace the ones spent in good works in a bad time.

16

My father, his horny hands black with sulphur, lit a cigar with a brief, modest, but spectacular one-handed gesture, his thumbnail crr-racking across the blue-headed kitchen match; when he described his first job in America, selling water to the men building skyscrapers, teetering across the girders for fifteen cents a pail, green flecks fumed and sailed in his yellowish Tartar eyes; he peeled an artichoke with both hands simultaneously, the leaves flying toward his mouth, crossing at the napkin politely tucked at the master juggler's collar, until with a groan that was the trumpet of all satisfaction he attained the heart; he—but he was a man of capabilities, such feats apart.

As my mother said of him before they married, "He's well off. Lots of personality." Older than the other women of her family, she used the word "well off" in a primitive sense, to signify a general relationship with the world, not subtracting from the term all but its usual financial refrain: "Well off very, he's a Buick . . ." But she took the word from Aunt Sarah and Aunt Anna; it's important that the vocabulary derives from economic security, to be extended outward only by an exceptional act of vitality. We—my brothers, those frequently lent girl cousins, and I —could never eat enough for her. "Don't aggravate me. Eat. Eat," she would say.

"We already ate," I pointed out.

"But look at your father!"

He was eating. He ate with silent respect for food, a great deal, and not out of gluttony but with appreciation for his own labor in it. He knew the cost. In each spoonful of soup carried with music to his mouth I heard the winds whistling through the branches of the *knaedloch* trees; I saw the farmers' trucks, laden with chopped liver, musing in his crocodile eyes. "Eat," he pronounced at intervals, easing his love for us, "eat, eat."

We ate with a hunger in our bellies or in a filial loyalty while his own hunger lay in the heart. Perpetually he was digging in, losing and winning. Hunched in the coat which came as a gift from Mother and Pitkin's with the no-overhead, the silvery-pronged crate hammer arming his back pocket, tools and keys clanking, he climbed into the cab of his truck before dawn on market days, his wife's lips still parted against their single pillow. Joined with the other fruitmen in Solly's Market Tearoom, he checked off a list measured in gross over a breakfast of steak and eggs. Perhaps at the earlier moment of supper, while we heedlessly digested, carloads of artichokes were coming in at the food terminal for the Thursday morning auction. He would get the best for Sam's Fruit & Vegetable: *The Best is the Best Buy.*

"Always," my mother piously breathed after him. She was proud of his slogan. "He made it up himself one day I remember it, he was by the cooler sorting asparagus. Lots of personality, loads," she informed Aunt Anna and Aunt Sarah. "Eat," she said to me. "The nice oven-baked potato."

I once asked the address of the poor hungry man in China who would be glad to finish my potato. "I'll send it to him with Mr. Connelly the mailman," I suggested.

"I need your back talk like I need my own brother Morton's agar-agar oil for his constipation. Morris. The same name like your uncle. Your father's brother. A whole tablespoon," she said, "I need it."

Repenting of my sarcasm, I never believed in the poor hungry man, although I had recently become convinced of China as a part of Geography.

My father was making more serious demands on me. They were closer to my own nerve, and therefore harder. I was rushing toward trouble with my father.

My father had the knowledge of things—how to hoist an orange crate in a movement like a dance, how to tell an honest farmer from one who will hide his bad Pascal or iceberg under bravado and a show of good ones, how to tell Shloimi Spitz the joke that would keep him from raising the union dues when he had it in mind, whom to trust in the fleet meetings of money at a fruit auction; this is already a great deal. Only once was he famously tricked, and by Uncle Morton from Pittsburg Road (Morris né Moishe), a man who installed automatic sprinkling pipes in his lawn ("For show! for the neighbors!" my mother communicated, outraged) but spent his Sundays tightening the faucets and complaining that his daughters filled the bathtub too full. ("How clean can a girl get? What's so clean about using up all the hot water and making the gas company rich?")

Well, this brother-in-law, exalted by cupidity, suggested a partnership in the property in order to eliminate my father's competition at an auction: Should brothers, or as-good-as-brothers, bid each other up like cats and dogs? *No* was the human answer, just like Homo sapiens. Near blood was thicker than almost water.

Afterwards, the deal secured, my father approached, tendering a hand-rolled cigar fraternally-in-law and saying,

"Nu Mort, now about the partnership, which I think we should let Henry there in the Republic Building, not that Hank from 105th Street, Henry a reliable man Hazleton Hotels uses him, draw up the papers—"

"Partners! hah!" Villainous Uncle Morton, performing for some secret inner croak of applause, permitting himself laughter at such innocence. "I'm partners me only with my wife"—and they haven't spoken since, nor have his daughters and I, cousins all.

But this was real estate, not food, which in those days was the true sphere of my father's power; besides, such an error brings scope and savor to a legend of paternal infallibility. He could say, or let my mother say while above the broad cheekbones his eyes glittered like two long plump lima beans on sidewalk display in the sun: "The only time Sam got it but good, it was that time with the Woodward property, his own brother-in-law, my own brother, they run a house in the Heights and two cars—they need it?—a Buick sure and a Chevy for that wife of his and the kids, may his breath turn sour in his old age—"

And his daughters' breath, too. Breathing toward him. Amen.

As my mother talked, my father measured us from under a vast biblical forehead which had sojourned in Kamenets-Podolsk; it was a forehead that escaped the scars of reprisal for a tradesman's life customarily given a man who needed labor in the open air. He wrestled out this frozen compression, these knotty ravages, at the cost of an overquickening in the work of the store, wielding cases with a plunging violence and mounting trucks like a burly fruit-store tomcat. Overhappiness too is a threat, Zarathustra said. The yellow flecks of his long narrow eyes fumed in contemplation. His sons were strange animals, born in America.

Question-shaped, my belly in advance of my thoughts, I had unnoticed by all but myself become skinny, pimply, shrewd, and poetic. I trained myself to wake at dawn, not for work like my father or to drink formula like my youngest brother, but because of the possibility that Pattie Donahue might feel my presence and stir in response to it; I believed in telepathy, tuning in on no messages because no one sent me any. I searched her face during Miss Baxter's Reading and The Library How To Use It, for a sign of complicity (received no answer); I never spoke to her, for reasons of shyness and reasons of magic. She had aquarium eyes, profoundly green, profoundly empty, and a mouth like a two-cent Bull's Eye candy, and pale transparent fingers, swift, busy, and shifty as fins. She powdered her nose in public, no longer picking it (not nice for a growing lovely girl); she touched her ears to make sure of their presence on the beach of her head; patiently she plucked the angora from her mittens off the front of her cardigan, with this gesture of pale-boned fingers exploring herself and me. I exorcised her into a poem—tried to. Together only abstractly, we were linked by both imagining atrocious ways to wish her well.

I let her swim again in my memory. She considered the future by judging it with the deliberate active forgetfulness of a fish floating asleep under ice: power through patience. Pattie Donahue wanted more than love, more than strength; she wanted mastery in denial, divinity in refusal of her own blood. Up the ladder to godhood or down to fishliness? That was her one risk in life. Seaweed is good for you! Lots of iodine! She had a repertory of head-tuckings, wiggles, peeps, curtsies, suckings, winks, herself charmed by herself; she was crippled for eternity, condemned to increase by parthenogenesis. She could not laugh with her body because her body could never move to another's, sway as it might under the seas of her ambition. Bemused and pious, she granted herself an adoring hand, fingers straddling to squeeze her sweater at the root of milk and psychology. Recall that princess who could undress before a slave because she did not regard him as a human being? We are all sometimes slaves. And afterwards we write purple passages.

Slavishly, with empurpled passages, I kneeled for her chamois penwiper where it fell behind her desk in Music and Singing.

"Oh, thank you," she said.

"Never mind, never mind"—me melting like March ice in a spring pool of timidity and chagrin.

"Oh, don't stop me, Herbert Gold. Thank you indeed. My mother says I need practice how to be gracious. Please let me do thank you. Oh, thank you, Herbie . . ."

This too is a sort of excess!—and I let her take me under the green grasp of her greedy eyes. The fishy princess pouted, ducked, abstractly reached; I worshiped this body shivering and glistening under bracelets like scale. I saw her as age. Age during that time signifies secret power, secret passion, and the death which follows age is known only as the death which follows love. Girls, born queens, are always older than boys, ten-thousand-eyed drones, living for love, empty-headed, precariously house-broken. "Oh, thank you really," said Princess Pattie Dona-hue, her royal sardine, queen of the hive.

She was gracious on me.

One day, the talk of the Horace Greeley Junior High playground, a pride for events beyond the time took her; she wore a shiny black brassière. Her first, our first to-gether. It hung in lank splendor beneath the faintly dis-tended yarn of her sweater and the morning's accretion of pink angora. She plucked, she pinched; in my poems I never found a rhyme for Donahue. Desire for a girl with nipples like tapioca spots! She went out, it was alleged, with high school seniors.

It was at this era of sudden sweat and pubic rancor that the issue of working in the store afternoons, or at least Saturdays, became prominent. "To help out," my father said.

"To learn the value of a dollar," my mother said.

"To know what's what in life," my father said.

"To learn the value of a dollar," my mother said.

"To find out which it's like something to be a man," my father said.

"To learn the value of a dollar," my mother said.

"To see how people—"

"To learn the value—"

"To help—"

"To learn—"

There always remained another word to propose on the subject. "I have homework to do?" I asked, making this a question because the whole world knew I did no home-work.

"Your cousin Bernie works in his father's store," my mother said. "He's learning the value."

"Your cousin Irwin works in his father's store," my father said. "Very mature kit, grown-up. Knows what's what."

No fonder of my cousins, Sarah's, Anna's, Morris's, Esther's children—impartially unfond—I began to work in the store. At first there were compensations besides learning the value and knowing what's what. For example, I quickly suspected the potentialities of stacking Jell-O. Its six deli-cious box colors made possible the exploration of a curi-osity about baroque structure in counter displays. I gave over to fantasy in exercises of pure form; I brought art to Dried Desserts (end of the first aisle), evolving from a gothic striving and simplicity to a rococo exuberance, rasp-berry mounting lemon in commercial embrace. The Jell-O man beamed and said I had talent. He promised me an autographed photograph of Jack Benny from his sample case, the signature printed as good as original, the *same identical thing*. I stood off, narrow-eyed, architectural, three loose boxes in each hand. While orange buttresses flew and lime vaulted over naves of cherry, my father grew impatient. "Is that all you got on your mind, the playboy?" It was not all, but he was right: there is a limit to what one can do with Jell-O. And what finally happened to my dream of a celestial engineering? Bananas were sliced into it.

I knew that my friends were playing touch football in

the street, or perhaps, if it was late afternoon, amorously lobbing rocks onto Pattie Donahue's front porch. Pity the man with an unemployed throwing arm! Aproned and earth-bound despite my Buster Brown aviator shoes, I stood in exile among the creak of shopping baskets and a cash register clang, such matters unmusical where a rumor of roller skates on a girl's sidewalk pledges passion eternal and a well-placed rock portends an invitation to Rosalie Fallon's second annual traditional Halloween party; these are suburban verities which held firm even in the pre-history before Mayor Cassidy's first reign, when I had begun my studies of how to pee in an enameled pot. A marksman now, I turned sullen despite my skill, sour as a strawberry plucked too early; my father knew the need of strawberries to ripen wild in the sun, unfingered by ambitious farmwives. I was a bad crop, green through, lazy for spite.

"Stop slouching," my mother said. "Stand up like a mensh. Sarah's Bernie *likes* the store. He stays and works even when his father says go home, here's a quarter."

I learned contempt for my cousins, the submissive ones, who worked so that they could spend dimes like grownups instead of nickels in the Chippewa Lake slot machines. No amount of labor could harden their gluey hands. Irwin had flat feet, a mustache at fourteen because his mother did not tell him to shave, the habit of standing too close when he talked, and, as luck would have it, a talent for projecting his bad breath with such accuracy that any customer's sales resistance must have died in the first whiff. Later he learned to brush his tongue, shave his armpits, sprinkle himself with Johnson's Baby Powder, and rinse his mouth with spearmint mouthwash. Anything for a client. He gave up his soul, a pulpy one at that, which resided in the crevices of his teeth.

Bernie, Narcissus Gaynesbargh the Go-getter, developed an artist's pure love for illness, hospitals, and operations. He saved up enough—"All by his lonesome," bragged Aunt Sarah—for an operation which joined his ears more cunningly to his head. "Clark Gable can let himself go, he's a big man already, but not my Bernie," his mother proudly recounted. "Today he looks a million—stand frontways, Bernie! And how tall is your Herbert?"

Bernie had enough left over in his account to have his piles removed during the after-Christmas slow spell. *Carpe Diem:* he obeyed our junior high motto, constantly improving himself, a medically made man, an expert on vitamin pills, eye exercises, and local anesthesia. He was also judicially made; let us not omit the subtle alterations in the orthography of his name. Imagine the legal nightmare in which a Ginsberg-into-Gaynesbargh signifies more rebirth than immolation! The suicide was a complete success. Neither his ears nor his ancestors stuck out, although the stitching showed.

"*They* will marry nice rich girls from New York City, you'll see," my mother threatened me. Later both took Marital Engineering courses, one at Miami University and the other at Cornell, and it paid, because Bernie married a nice rich shoe business from Hartford, and Irwin married a wholesale Divan & Studio Couch, a steady thing.

"But," as my mother said, "you can't measure happiness in dollars and cents. There are things more important especially with the taxes these days. A sweet little wife, a nice little family, a good income . . ."

"Have a piece Sanders." Aunt Sarah consoled her with the Continental assortment. "I got it by Sanders Chocolates when I went downtown to look for my new Person Lamb yesterday. Purse-and-lamb, I mean. Who knows maybe I'll settle for a Shirt Beaver, the season's almost over."

Not even Aunt Sarah could distract my mother when philosophy came over her. "You could marry in a low element, maybe he wouldn't really be rich only pretending, living high, that kind of a click—"

"My Irwin, hm, hm, you should know he sent me a this year's pillow direct from the factory to me," Aunt Sarah remarked by the way. "He don't have to put birds in his vest to swell up his chest, my Irwin. He looks big to me."

"Don't tell me, I know," Mother groaned. "Some people are real-type big shots, some people have to make look big to themselves with escalator heels and Scotch shoelaces, who ever heard?"

"My Irwin—"

"What, you crazy? He's a nice steady boy your Irwin, clean-cut, a neat dresser. I'm mentioning it so happens one of those fast clicks, oh, oh."

"Ho," breathed Aunt Sarah.

"Don't I remember?"

They communed in silence over the family shame. They clopped the bitter memory from their outraged palates. They drew the lesson from what befell poor Cousin

Bessie, who returned from a vacation—she had a nice job with the government, too—with pierced ears and coral earrings, a pair of chartreuse silk slacks, and a new man to replace the one who broke his head. "My new husband," she announced, indicating a plump individual with oily sunburned pouches under his eyes, Novelty-style shoelaces, and a sky-blue Kalifornia Kravate with a silver-lightning pin, the tie tucked into a Hickok Kowboy-type belt: "Roland, he's in the wholesale business in Los Angeles."

"Wholesale what?" Mother had asked, suspicious already.

"Just wholesale," Cousin Bessie said equably. Roland smiled to show the gap in his teeth bridged by invisible platinum. His little woman spoke for him: "He has the biggest outlet in Los Angeles."

"Ellay," he corrected her.

Later, after Uncle Moish from Indian River Drive discovered that this Roland was a bad-type thief off the legit, not a dealer in factory-to-you eliminate-the-middleman low costs, they helped Bessie out again. She promised to be more careful next season. She was pushing thirty-five, although the family loyally counted only the last twenty-seven of them; she had combed the summertime mountains and the wintertime seaside since she buried Lester. Mother took three deep breaths and announced, addressing her in the ceremonial third person while Bessie wept wholesale tears: "Next time she should vacate a week ten days in Atlantic City on the Atlantic, the sun, the salt water taffy, she should meet a nice steady New York-type fella, she still got her health why not? Knock on wood.

Just he shouldn't have the biggest outlet in Ellay."

Still my cousins were generally nice, steady and successful even at that early time. I was recalcitrant, a failure in affairs.

"The whole world knows. Aunt Anna and Aunt Sarah know, it should happen to me I try to be a good mama to you. The whole city knows."

Aunt Sarah encouraged my mother in her own way. " '*Mama*,' my Bernie tells me"—and her eyes moistened over such devotion—" 'Mama,' he says, 'you look like sugar in the urine again. What did I tell you about those two-dollar Sanders assortments?' . . . So thoughtful," she concluded, folding her arms across a high stalwart bone of her *garment*, leaning back, and waiting for my mother to tell something good about me. I couldn't even read an oral thermometer. After a while she sighed for pity, yawned for contentment, and added soothingly, "Your Herbert working nice in the store these days maybe? Just tell him about my Bernie, he'll learn, you got to encourage."

"I look in the looking glass I ask myself why, I get no answer. A son of mine, why? A thirteen-years-old lump," she encouraged.

It wasn't laziness. That's a maternal answer. I would have worked in other ways, and did; if I could have remained at some comprehensible task, delivering orders perhaps, building shelves, loading the truck, or manipulating the stock in the basement, I might have attained a fulfillment equal in its way to Counsin Bernie's avarice for operations. The constant pouring of commands from a triumphant father shivered and shattered my sense for work; he wanted me by his side, proud of an eldest son, any eldest son. For good reasons of his own—he had been poor, he wanted me to see what he had done for himself and for us all—he urged me to learn the pleasure of a direct delicious manipulation of money, its worn old touch of cloth, its warmth of hands and pockets, its smell of sex and work, its color of economy or death in our world, signed in those days by Andrew W. Mellon. "Here! it says right here. Read it yourself. That's the secretary of the treasurer of the United States of America, U. S. A., used to be, his own autograph."

"Oh, for God's sake. Sam, you can notice such things?" —my mother discovering new depths, she a modest economist, my father not.

"Notice, notice," he admitted virtuously. Money was poetry, a symbol of life and power on one side, economy and death for him with the White House on the other, but only a symbol—how could I understand such metaphysics in that epoch of despair with girls and ambitions of purity? My agile Tartar-eyed father made the distinction by enjoying both the earning and the spending, finding his truth higgledy-piggledy in an exploit of strapping a load-and-a-healthy-half on his 1928 White Motors truck or in giving himself to a snack of artichoke with Kraft's dressing, the heart his end but the money-colored leaves loved for what they were.

He wanted me to clerk, to *wait on trade*, then, to be an aproned catalyst toward the final term. How could I take money from Mrs. Donahue, whose daughter no one but

Tom Moss knew I loved, while Pattie herself teased her mouth with an end of lipstick without glancing at me in my feminizing wrap-around? My languishing yip should have betrayed me: "That'll be just three sixty-five, please," recited as I had been taught. It did not betray me; no one saw. The money joined money in the new Serv-a-Slip cash register. *O love me, Pattie! look!*—and I feared that she would. I gave the cash to Myrna, the cashier, my father's deputy, while he bargained with the Wheaties jobber for bonus Eversharps and an electric fan-flame, wood-glow fireplace.

"Okay, Little Sam, you're picking up now. I'll tell your pa. Just keep the hands out of the pockets when you're making a sale. Say thank you to the customer." Myrna had a cracked and ridged tongue, meaty mounds, fissures, yellowish scale—she was betrothed to dyspepsia. These wounds came of a continual talking confused with a continual eating. No one knew a remedy. My mother had robbed her of the remedy she prescribed for herself. She suffered unsilently, chewing Baseball Gum. "I said take hands out of pockets that's a boy. I said say thank you to the nice customer."

"Thank you, Mrs. Donahue," I mumbled miserably.

I carried Mrs. Donahue's order to her Hudson. Pattie moved ahead, her rump twitching like a snapdragon delicately pinched. I fled as she fumbled with her purse for a tip. The next Monday, inspecting my approach from her station at the side entrance to Horace Greeley Junior High, without taking her eyes off mine she bent significantly to whisper into her friend Rosalie Fallon's ear. To stifle their laughter the two of them made paws of their silly adored hands at their mouths. This gesture insured politeness and (reward for a suburban virtue) the secret renewal of laughter when the grocery boy had passed. Sober and unblinking. Pattie nonchalantly rubbed her edible kneecap.

"Don't call me Little Sam," I told Myrna once more without hope. "Call me my name."

"Okay . . . Little Sam," she said, humorously chewing.

Sometimes I carried a book to work, wearing it piously between my shirt and my chest, and then hid with it and a cigarette in the basement among the cases of Libby's Whole Sliced Pineapple and Hinz-zuzz Pork and Beans with Tomato Sauce. The whitewashed walls sweated; the storeroom smelled of dampness, rat poison, cardboard packing cases, and a broken bottle of soy sauce. Here I was happy, the complicated atmosphere making me dizzy as I perched corrupt with one of Andy's Wing butts on a peak of pineapple under the dusty 40-watt bulb. Sometimes I put down the Poe (I had memorized "Ulalume" without being able to pronounce it) and moodily considered my childhood, before Pattie Donahue and before my parents had decided I was a man, when I had sometimes visited this range of cans and bottles to leap like a goat among them in my innocence. I practiced a tragic sigh, inhaling soy.

Always my father roared down the stairway to discover me. "YOU THINK YOU CAN KID ME, HAH? The A & P can't even kid me, I got a list of your tricks—"

I stood up with no answer, understanding that he would forever find me, silent in my chagrin. I could not explain to him the disgrace of working in a store in a neighborhood where boys had important unexplainable things to do, secret clubs and fatal loafing, while their fathers managed offices for Standard Machines or handled law cases for insurance companies downtown. I wanted him to commute instead of work, like the others; I could not tell either of us the reason for my stubborn reluctance to follow him to the market. I felt a justice in his despair with me. A coward, I hid each time.

"Your mother says today you'll be good, I say I'll find you sneaking off with a book."

I studied his boots on the cement and deeply assented. He had looked in the back room to see if I was filling orders, giving me the benefit of a doubt and profligate hope which is still my debt.

"Nu, what do you say for yourself? I'm going crazy upstairs, it's a big one-cent sale, the Saturday help's no good these days . . . Hah?"

I said nothing.

"Why not tell me another lie, you'll be good like you promised I should be happy?"

I stared, Poe sweaty in my hands.

"So why don't you at least say you had to go to the toilet, the men's room?"—a treble note of exasperation hidden in his bass, wanting an excuse for me, loving his oldest.

I refused this. I was overmoral for a moment, going on thirteen, as he was overhappy; I despised anything but extreme commitments, surrender to his world or defiance of it.

"What's the matter, you constipated? You got stomach

trouble?"—pretending that I had given us this excuse, unable to bear our misery together.

He watched the tears silently fill my eyes.

He relented; he appealed to me, trying to preserve his anger by shouting; he betrayed his helplessness by heavily sitting down beside me on the canned pineapple. "What's the matter, you hungry, you want your mother should make you a tomato and baloney sandwich with Kraft's Miracle Whip dressing?"

"I want to go upstairs and help out," I whispered at last.

Reconciled, unable to preserve animus, he bumped against me up the narrow steps. Instead of letting me sink into the crowd of customers reaching with their lists and their clippings of advertisements at the counters, he ordered me to go to lunch with him, knowing that I liked this. To take the Business Men's special with Dad in a restaurant was one of the compensations; choosing food is the act of a god—only gods and businessmen don't have mothers to tell them what to eat, filling their plates with it. It was a pure joy although a bad restaurant; we had to go there because Guy Mallin owed my father two hundred dollars, which he never paid and we couldn't eat through by the time he left his wife and ran off to Montreal with Stella, the waitress, and a week's receipts. (When this happened Dad tried, although he knew little about the restaurant business, to help out poor Mrs. Mallin, who had no children but only a thyroid condition to give her an interest in life.) Both of us would have preferred an egg roll and hamburger steak at Louie's, the Chinaman across the street, and our unity on restaurants—winking across the table as fast-talking Guy Mallin approached—cleared the hatred of civilizations between father and son. I should insist on this: the storm confined itself to its direct object, my laziness, rising like an east wind to its peak on the busy day, Saturday or before holidays, then falling away. "You learn with meet people," he only said. "You learn with know their ways."

After we finished our lunch I hid in the basement of the store to read Edgar Allan Poe.

As the months went by, the ruses deepened and the anger swam like some exiled bull carp in the deepest pools of the natures of my mother, my father, and me. Pattie Donahue had definitively given up roller-skating in the street, and not only on bricked Pittsburg Road but also on the mellifluous asphalt of Chesterton Avenue. She definitely meant it about wearing a brassière. We were freshmen in junior high, seventh graders learning dignity from a Social Dancing teacher added to the curriculum by the Board of Education which decided that Grace and Poise (formerly Comportment) were as essential as geography

and algebra to the Young Men & Women of Tomorrow, be
they bond salesmen like their fathers or *homemakers* like
their mothers. The Real Estate Taxpayers League issued a
protest against educational frills; pioneering virtues that
made our country great, assessment already excessive, it
argued. Artichokes, bulky and hard to handle, were coming into season again.

Shamefully I pretended to be sleeping Saturday mornings when my father had gotten up at three or earlier.
Mother was more violent, my father more deeply hurt; the
denial, after all, was of him. She nagged constantly; yet
on Saturdays when I stayed motionless slugabed, her pride
in sleep—"It's very healthy"—protected me there. Later,
my father telephoning to ask if I had arisen yet, he fell
silent before her report, pressing the receiver to his ear
amid the mob of shoppers importunate about fork-tongued
Myrna's dais, and he darkly said nothing while Mother repeated, infuriated with me but stubborn in her allegiance
to health: "Let the kid sleep just one more morning, kids
need sleep. It's good for them."

"Is he tired?"

"Let him sleep, Sam, please."

Having vacuumed, she herself got ready to go to the
store for *relief*. Out of some relic of pride I could not bring
myself to feign until she would safely leave me among my
angry bedclothes in the occult reproach of a house. "I'm up,"
I fatally admitted. What did they know about an American
boy's dreams in bed on a Saturday morning? I reached for
a paltry revenge in wearing yesterday's socks. She edified
me in a steady torrent on the streetcar to the store:

"No good! big lump! lazy good-for-nothing! You're thirteen already and look at you!"

"Twelve," I corrected her.

" 'Please, Daddy, I want to work in the store like a big man,' Bernie always says. Aunt Sarah says. Such a go-getter! But what do you say?—look ma the dog wet the rug I'm twelve years old. Aunt Sarah says I should stop aggravating myself. Please give a look my waricose weins from standing up." She had forgotten that the effect of threatening to telephone Aunt Sarah when I was *bad* had been dissipated years ago with the advent of Unlimited Calls. Sometimes I had even offered to dial the number for her.

"A big lump like you he should give me a rest, take the load off your feet Ma like Bernie, not trouble trouble all the time."

"Why it is you always say I'm thirteen when it's something you want me to do and you know I'm twelve?" I asked, a savant without rimless glasses. "And when I want to do something I can't because I'm not old enough, I'm only eleven? My birthday is July the thirtieth at six o'clock in the morning."

"I remember," she said morosely. "And a fine night I had with you in Mount Sinai all night too, they almost had to use force-its. Doctor said my bones were so delicate close together . . . Thirteen, going on now. Even Uncle Morton knows about you, I'm so ashamed in the family, why I told Aunt Anna I'll never hold my head high again, at least Morton he got daughters they keep themselves clean at least not so much aggravation, all right so worry a tiny bit they should marry nice, but not heartache a no-good like you day in day out—"

Outside the streetcar the first autumn leaves were burning in piles on the street, sending up an odor redolent of freedom in the open air. My brothers, being younger, were free of my burdens. They could stay at home and play and envy me my burdens. My friends flamboyantly loitered on the Saturday streets, chalk in their mouths, their hearts unfettered. Pattie Donahue was perhaps walking alone in Rocky River Park, just waiting for me telepathically to find her.

The store opened about us with the intense plushy smell of old vegetables. Myrna was comforting Mrs. Simmons, a childless widow whose husband had been manager of the Guarantee Trust, Rocky River branch; she generally admitted herself among us with the distant face of someone who disliked the smell of the inside of her own nose, but now she claimed to have seen a spider in a hand of bananas. "It probably wasn't a deadly poisonous banana spider," Myrna said. "Did it have a lot of legs? Furry ones from Costo Rico?"

"A South American banana spider! oh!" Mrs. Simmons, realizing that the creature was a foreign element, rolled her eyes in search of a pleasant place to faint.

"Probably not deadly poisonous though. Probably just a sleepy little old banana spider from the deadly jungles of Hatey." Mrs. Simmons fainted. That is, considering her dignity and the aristocratic unpaid bills in the drawer with Myrna's sandwiches, she *swooned.* "Anyway, no one else saw it, the thousand-legger bug, the horrible deadly spider," Myrna mused on, rubbing Mrs. Simmons' wrists without taking off her Ovaltine Birthstone & Good Luck Ring.

"Ouch, you're scratching," said Mrs. Simmons.

My father, harried but always expecting the best, greeted me with an order. Stack the oranges, wait on Mrs. Simmons, put on your apron, what's the matter with you? . . . Could I confess the chief reason for my tardiness, a hope that telepathic pressure concentrated among my bed-clothes might compel Mrs. Donahue, Pattie's mother, to buy her Ohio State hot-house tomatoes and Swansdown ready-mix no-sift cake flour before my surrender to penance in a wrap-around? *Develop Your Will Increase Your Power. Sample Booklet Fool Your Friends. 25¢ Coin or Stamps.* No, I could not. My father's will already developed, he spoke a language in which existed no vocabulary to explain that among the people with whom he chose to bring me up, it was more important to run end in a pickup touch foot-ball game, spinning craftily about the young trees planted by the Our Street Beautiful committee, than to fill orders in sour old orange crates on Saturday afternoons. We all paid, in our various ways, a price for those trees and for the privilege of overhead doors on our garages and colonial-style magazine racks for our *Saturday Evening Posts*. He did not draw the consequences of his ambition for me. If he judged our neighborhood to be better than that of his childhood, then our neighborhood would judge his world. In a develop-your-will (Fool Your Friends) like my father's, the only lack was the will to find my will-less longing. He worked! Mother worked! Like dogs!

They were right, but they could not see through to my rightness, forgetting a child's hunger to belong. "Ulalume" might have been for the ages, but Rosalie Fallon and Pattie tongued their malicious pencils and wrote my fate in their Slam Books. He knew he was a foreigner, my father did; I had to discover it in pain, shame before my parents, and self-judging. "I earned my own living when I was thirteen, and proud of it," he had said.

"Your father earned his own living when he was twelve," Mother remarked contentedly in explanation, "and he is proud of it. *Proud* of it."

"Thirteen he said," I said.

"Proud he said," she said.

He studied me in sorrow and silence, figuring with his short, black-nailed, thick-knuckled hands reaching for the crating hammer in his back pocket. I was just a kid. I even looked like him. Myrna said so. Caruso used to say so. Even Guy Mallin said I was a chip off the. "Hey kid? You want a Business Men's plate with chocolate ice cream instead of the green peas with butter sauce? It should be easy to figure . . . Gravy on that there ice cream haw-haw, yessir, hey kid? Gravy!" Guy Mallin roared. "A real chip if I ever saw one, Sam. I'm telling you listen to me now. Your eyes. Your chin. His mother's, a sweet little woman you got there, nose. Yessir. Your hair. Off the old block there, Sam. Good material, hey? It won't be long before it's *Sam & Son,* what-do-you-say? I'm telling you now Sam you heard what I said remember I said it."

"Maybe things are different these days," he told me. "You ain't like I was."

My father had the gift of listening to the artichokes at the top of a load in such a way—they informed him in a language which only he and the artichokes spoke—that he always knew when their brothers at the bottom were defective, defeated, edged with rust or shriveled from a stingy soil. Silent in their hampers, they communicated by the violence of love, all knowing their role on this occasion as opportunities, each thick-leafed one, for a sociable debating between farmer and merchant, green, crisp, candid, and nutritive after a pleasant journeying into the hands of women. They accepted the gift of himself which my father made, their shoots curly for him, their unbaked hearts shy in a bra of ticklish felt. Buy us! sell us!—they asked nothing more. Artichokes understood my father, and his sympathy for vegetables arose to meet theirs for him. Devotion—he gave this freely. He accepted too, being stuck with thorns.

Unfortunately I, even in those days, was not an artichoke—perhaps not so rewarding, my heart not luscious with a dab of Miracle Whip, stunted in fact, even hornier, full of bad character and a brooding plant rust. "Lots of personality," my mother had said, feebly defending me when I had tried to evade shelling lima beans for the store with the rest of the family on Friday nights. "Everyone says he takes after your side, Sam. Anna says, Sarah says."

"Since I was thirteen! I got scars on my back, the bucket cut me, the greenhorn I didn't get a pad cloth. Look at Irwin, look at Bernie born the same week like you in Mount Sinai, you was the first so I got your mother a semiprivate. A healthy kit like you, which he sleeps all morning Saturday."

"Since he was twelve years old a greenhorn," Mother mournfully intoned. "Who ever heard of it?"

Pattie Donahue plucked at her sweater and pouted with kissproof lipstick (maybe) over teeth lucky to serve her. Lewis Snyder, the sheik, told stories about Rosalie Fallon and Pattie. Tom Moss told me. "The liar," we agreed, ferociously believing him.

Such matters flowed in time; the store remained outside time, its claim ripening through the spines but as incredible to me as a heartless artichoke to my father. The store gulped me down. I evaded, I squirmed, I stubbornly bent, receded, and persisted like heartburn, taking all shapes but in fact knowing only itself, which has no shape and a mysterious matter.

"You don't want, what kind of a reason is that?" my mother demanded, fertile in argument. "No reason, that's what kind."

I couldn't explain to myself or to them, much less to Aunt Sarah or to Aunt Anna, to Myrna, Guy Mallin, or Cousin Bernie the Smarty. Let him marry a nice rich girl from New York Queens in the clothing business, I don't care, I sacrilegiously insisted. My single purpose was love for Pattie Donahue, whose father carried a portfolio to work in his hairless pink little hands; she would love only the elaborate loungers, the conspicuous consumers—a little Veblenite she was! You Americans all long for the useless, the hymen no proper end; it feathers no beds, it fleshes no bellies—this Mother and Dad might have pointed out if they had argued their philosophy. I sensed, too, that my father's agility and strength and devotion moving among the objects all his in the store were a threat to me, the more dangerous because—one of his few fatal thoughts outside the moment—he was beginning to see Sam's Fruit & Vegetable in terms of immortality for both of us. Why else should he struggle with the racketeers, the klepto-maniacs, the help, the farmers, the A & P? The Depression, the government, the daily weariness, the slow rot and the spoilage? For his children. For me. For the future. He asked only a sign of recognition for this gift.

I refused his gift daily now. Even the Jell-O counter fell into ruins. My ultimate denial lay outside morality, essential to character. My father was overhappy, overmoral. I crouched like a troll under a mushroom in the cellar, a troll who read "Ulalume" and murmured, "Pattie Dona-hue!" with dilated eyes in the shadow of a shipment from Procter & Gamble. Poor Dad!

We can measure his desolation. He left his struggle and joyous head-on combat with farmers, jobbers, sales-men, Saturday help, policemen, wilting lettuce, and pears which remained green until they rotted, competitors, the chain stores, the landlord, debtors, creditors, the delivery truck, the account books, the government, insects, rodents, spoilage, wastage, heat, cold, the margin of profit, draw items, push merchandise, merchandise which he could not get, premiums, samplers, one-cent giveaways, Christmas trees on January second and Easter candy in May, chil-dren who skated through a display of jars of olives (the olives lined up one by one in bottles shaped like a straw, optically illusive, expensive all the same), Mr. Jenkins who insisted on Aunt Mary's pancake mix and would not be content with Aunt Jemima's or any other Aunt's because he wanted to honor in this way his poor dead old Aunt Mary his mother's sister, Mrs. Rawlings the klepto lover of vanilla extract, the charity ladies and the lottery girls, the kids selling advertisements in their parochial-school bulletins, the beggars who claimed to have had a store just like his in Phoenix, Arizona, until they hit a run of bad luck back in '29 (he was unanimously elected to a directory circulated by a syndicate of beggars, Phoenix and Miami Beach Chapter), the faithful customers who tried to convert him to their religions, Mrs. Colonel Greenough who came with tears to tell him that her husband forbade her to shop at Sam's Fruit & Vegetable any longer because the colonel himself had given him three months to read a book on technocracy and he had not yet complied (she bought a farewell bouquet of cauliflower before she left), the high school teacher who wanted to pay an overdue bill in the privacy of her chamber, the judges asking support both moral and ah financial in the coming primaries, the tax collectors, the bill collectors, the garbage collectors, the health inspectors, the housing inspectors, the zoning inspectors, electricians, refrigerator repairmen, insurance which only covered fires begun by safety matches when his fire had resulted from a cigar butt, illness among his clerks, jealousies, rivalries, romances, extended lunch hours, female troubles which (a gentleman) he could not publicly doubt, inventories, lentil soup in cans labeled liver pâté, children who descended like locusts to remove all the tops from the Ralston boxes to send away as a mark of esteem for Tom Mix, the electric cash register playing Chopin in a short circuit, Ruby who had B.O., Max who left his hair among the macaroons, Myrna who showed too much of her bosom in order to encourage Mr. Tramme to take an extra cantaloupe, and other problems which I'll not mention because I want to avoid making a list.

But I must not forget Shloimi Spitz, who sold protection and collected his payoff on Saturdays and a little extra on holidays.

My father abandoned his direct response to these issues in order to *use psychology* on me. He appealed in subtle ways. He tried to *get me interested.* His Tartar eyes were made to squint for laughter and appetite, not cunning. My heart contracts with sadness for him now, sadness and regret. He came to me on the porch one Sunday afternoon, his great arms slack at his sides, saying, "Say!" in the way of a good fellow, and asked me to write a paragraph for his weekly advertisement in the neighborhood throwaway. I responded, too, working hard at a composition modeled on "The Raven," sharpening three pencils into oblivion before I finished. Proudly I announced to Tom Moss the prospect of publication in the *West Side Advertiser.*

The work never appeared. Trochees had no place next to bargains in Crisco. The Crisco people paid half and supplied the engraving; the Spry people, not to be caught napping at the shortening, offered to pay sixty per cent and sent my mother a portable sun lamp for her sinuses. My poems fit poorly into their co-operative advertising budgets.

Living by Poe and Pattie, I would only confuse the fans of Procter & Gamble. Psychology failed; my father came as an alien to such maneuvers. Nevermore!

Another Sunday he admitted to me the possibility of other businesses. He treated me like a man. He opened his heart. "I bought some lots from the Quinn boys, you know, the real estate Quinns, and you know how much money I made?"

"How much?"

He started to laugh. "With the taxes," he said, restraining his delight. "With the interest on the money which I took a loan from the bank," he said. "With the expenses. Well, I think I lost three quarters of my money I put into it."

"That's terrible."

"Oh no," he said happily. "Lots of my friends, they lost everything in real estate. I hear even Shloimi got stung, that smeller, good for him. I was very lucky. The Quinn boys left me my galoshes to walk around in, they didn't attach my wife, they was good to me. I came out okay. Listen, it's Depression. And what do I know about real estate?"

"What?"

"Beans. I was paying for a little education. I can't complain, the store is good. Lots of dentists and doctors lost their stomachs, they got so sick in real estate. Several big professionals downtown jumped out the window with their stomachs. But I'm okay. I got a education plus a good laugh when I think about how stupid I was. But you know? I just can't get it through my head the Quinn boys are smarter'n me."

"They're not, Dad, they're not!"

"That's what I been thinking. I been waiting to figure that all the way. I come to that conclusion, son. So someday I might have to try that game again." He spoke with awe. "It comes and goes so fast, with just a little thinking. With you are right or you are wrong—so fast! I like that speed about it. It stands to reason I'm smarter'n the Quinn boys. Are you listening, son?"

I wasn't listening, but I heard. I didn't hear, but I was listening. He looked at me uncertainly. Was I boy or man?

Probably neither. Ingrate. Fool. American monster. If I could have Pattie and the rest of the smoke in my head, I didn't care what happened in the world. If I could try to possess the whole world, I didn't care what happened to my mother and father.

One day I sneaked out of the store at four-thirty, made my own dinner of Laub's rye, Blue Moon pimento cheese with those taste-delightful little chopped-up pieces of real pimento, Krunchy peanut butter (kan't remember the brand), and Thursday's spoiled milk; then I went to an Edward G. Robinson with Tom Moss. The three of us stood off the coppers for a reel and a half, and when they finally got Edward G. the camera noticed a paper boat which sailed down the gutter in the symbolic rain. "Just like The Strange Case of Monsieur Whatsizname," I pedantically reminded Tom. We fought back our tears, magnificent to THE END, ate a dime's worth of evergreen mints, and went divvies on a *Spicy Detective* to read under the Jantzen's Swimsuit for That Lee-*uscious* Look billboard on the way home. I told him about Pattie and he told me about Rosalie Fallon. Our patient listening to each other was more than politesse; we learned through it although the histories remained classically similar, unmodified in months except for the time Rosalie kicked Tom in the shins when he complimented her by rubbing one of the last March snowballs in her face. He rolled up his pantleg to show me the wound once more. I accused him of preserving it with salt. He denied this. He accused me of envy. I lowered my eyes. Tom was a lady-killer, he was; I'll never understand how he did it.

"Well, good night Tom. Good luck with Rosalie."

"Well, good night Herb. I'll ask Lewis Snyder about Pattie. He took Donna Thompson out on a date and maybe she knows something. He'll tell me if I ask him because I know something on him."

Good night . . . Good night . . . In that midworld of childish seriousness and the first adult frivolity of passion, Tom and I needed the sense of banding together, our sufferings held in common while our sense of them remained untouchable, pariahs of glandular enthusiasm in a structure built of economy. He gave me the *Spicy* to hide in the garage. I had often dreamed of moving through an atmosphere of glue, invisibly held from my family's home in an empty night. Empty? Full of unknown excess. Now I whistled, leaving Tom Moss an hour before midnight, forgetting that I had last seen my parents seven hours earlier when my father had said, "Wait on trade!" and I had crept out the back door where Andy was boxing strawberries and beet greens were blackening in the sun.

The door to our house was locked. The windows were dark. There was no key under the mat.

I was locked out.

The crickets suddenly deafened me, like in the movies. I thought I knew, then, how Edward G. felt when the boys went over to the South Side mob, but found a basement window open, crawled through the coal chute, and significantly murmured Pattie's name out of the side of my mouth. Ulalume Donahue, Killer Gold's moll . . . I'd have flipped a quarter with disdain except that it was too dark and I had no quarter. *Dad!* I thought. I worried about the gas stove upstairs. Maybe they were all dead and so I should bang on the door until they let me in to sleep in my own bed. What if there were rats in the basement? Big ones like in the Paris sewers with Gene Valgene? The washing machine opened its mouth at me in the darkness. *Mother!* I thought. If the water pipes broke and I got drowned they'd be sorry. They'd be sorry someday when I spit blood into my monogrammed handkerchief from sleeping all alone in a damp basement. They would be sorry. I was sorry. *Mother and Dad!* I thought.

Without taking off my shoes I slept on the extra kitchen table in the basement, amid dirty laundry (my pillow) and old hatreds (my dreams).

18

Even this passed. The next Saturday I was as faithful as Irwin, as true as Bernie with his eyes like spoiled oysters. I tasted during one evening the delights of approval, staying up with Mother and Dad while we discussed the day's business, counted the receipts, and discussed the pros and cons of tangle displays against neat pyramids of cans or fruit. I spoke for tangle displays, Mother for order; Dad listened to us both, sipping his tea with little Ahs through his lump of sugar, and reserved decision. He tried to lasso my head as he used to in a ring of cigar smoke. "It's too big," he complained. "Just like mine, a size seven seven-eights. So look who needs a hat! You want a Stetson?"

We had a long late supper, and before going to bed he slipped me three dollar bills in a secret conspiratorial gesture while Mother stacked the dishes.

"I saw! I saw!" she cried out, her eyes peeping bright in the mirror over the sink. We all giggled together.

Dad slapped her rump, yawned, and said, "Nothing like a good day's work, hey?" in his imitation of Guy Mallin.

"Sam, you crazy?" At peace with each other we parted.

"And don't forget whose birthday is next month," my mother said. "Yours. You'll be thirteen, kiddel."

She had it right this time. It was a real truce; I knew its joys. But had anything been altered? As aphoristic Aunt Anna might say, "A leopard coat can't change its spots."

A few days afterward I received a letter. The envelope carried my name on the outside, together with the smart-alecky title "Master," all printed in green ink. I studied it, marveling, my first mail since the revolutionary discovery of INCREASE YOUR WILL POWER FOOL YOUR FRIENDS, and for that I had sent away a coupon and a quarter. I sniffed it. I licked the ink and made a smear of what our art teacher called *graded area*. I tasted my name in green, finding it more artistic than black but approximately as lucid. At last I decided to open the letter.

It was an invitation from Mr. B. Franklyn Wilkerson to go on a Nature Walk a week from Saturday. Mr. Wilkerson, who taught General Science to the seventh grade, had worked out a plan to augment his income during the summer vacation by conveying flower names and leaf shapes to suburban scholars. Small, swarthy, with three daughters and thin black hair artfully spaced and glued into place to cover his scalp, Mr. Wilkerson recited Science (general) with his neck petrified for fear a sudden breeze or emotion might betray his baldness. Zealous, he devoted himself to general-science textbooks, turning the pages slowly to avoid drafts. A real scientist would have perforated the pages to keep from disturbing the air. He was but a general scientist, however, combining, as he thought, the virtues of the practical and the theoretical in Elevating the Young, an intellectual sort whose pink resentful mouth and clenched neck made the expression of someone who had just swallowed a banana sideways.

The first walk, a free trial, would take place on a Saturday, and the Saturday before the Fourth, the third-busiest day of the year in the store. I decided not to go.

Tom Moss was going. Lewis Snyder, who had dates alone with girls, was going. I learned that several of them, including Rosalie Fallon and Pattie Donahue, would be botanically present. I decided to go.

We met, everyone carrying lunch but me, at eleven-thirty. Mother didn't know about it; I had run away from the store, taking my cap from under the cash register and, for some last scruple, telling Myrna to tell my father that I had gone. "Where?"—but I disappeared without answering, subtle as a hungry tomcat unable to hide its rut, sneaking around corners with its yellow eyes scheming. Lewis Snyder had a scout canteen filled with near-beer left over after repeal. I suspected him of planning to offer Pattie some.

Pedantic, amorous, shifty-eyed general scientists, we followed Mr. Wilkerson into the Rocky River reservation. He wore a checkered golf cap, its band black with Sta-Neet, and showed how he had taught his wife to wrap his lunch—cellophane insulated the deviled eggs each from each. "Practical. Sanitary germfree. Vitamins spoil in the open air," he advised us.

Tom Moss, my friend the skeptic, whispered to me that he thought it was supposed to be *good* for you to be

out in the fresh air, and then went to step on Rosalie
Fallon's heels.

We penetrated the woods, already hungry. "Now right
here on your left children we find an interesting phenome-
non page one hundred and forty-eight in Brenner's figure
sixteen that orange growth over there with the black spots
now that's a wild spermaphore," Mr. Wilkerson remarked.
"Ess. Pee. Ee. Arrh—"

"Looks like a toadstool to me," I said.

"Spermaphore. Silver spoons unreliable poor quality
silver these days no workmanship. Damp places. Twenty-
four on a picnic without a general scientist. Could have
told them. Whole party dead in eight to ten hours. Horrible. Too bad. Ess, pee, ee—"

A voice occurred behind me, whispering, "Hello, there."
It was Pattie. "Toadstools are very poisonous"—she leaned
sociably. "Do you like, are you fond of mushrooms?"

I soared into paradise at her feet. "My mother cooks
spermaphores with meat loaf," I said, "and stuffed pep-
pers."

"Oh"—a gasp of scandal. "She does not! You'll all be
dead . . . Does she?"

"Yes," I lied, death-defying—what could be a better
beginning between lovers? All lies come true in the world
of supple twelve-year-old facts. It was cool here across
the city from the store. Birds soon to be falsely named
cocked their heads in the trees and lectured us. Someplace
customers swarmed amid the imperatives of telephones,
and the distance between my father and me widened

past even the nine-month doubt separating an instant of giving from the birth of a son. Fatherhood, a metaphysical idea, was being taken from Dad as Mrs. Rawlings slipped her daily bottle of vanilla extract into her muff, no one to distract her, and as Mr. Wilkerson bravely broke the perfidious spermaphore with a five-foot stick, no academician he, a man of general action in science. Rosalie Fallon gave her pressed-lip assent and moral outrage against hypocritical silver spoons while my thoughts fled back from the store to recall prepared speeches of passion for Miss Donahue, known by Killer Me and Edward G. as Ulalume or The Lost Lenore.

"Oh-h-h," she was saying.

"Look the bug," I replied.

She pretended to be scared; not. I knew. Death and complicity—love is not a biological gesture in suburban children, O Mr. Wilkerson! I had forgotten my speeches and Ulalume.

Despite this meeting I again felt deserted, lunchless at lunchtime. Tom Moss pretended not to notice: excuse him his hunger. "Where's yours?" Pattie asked, her mouth full.

"Don't have any. My mother didn't. Not hungry anyway."

Girls always have enough to give. Suburban girls (economical) always have enough to invest. Sweetly she murmured, "You can have one of my bacon and tomatomotto sandwiches and a bite of cottage cheese with the canopy, please do." Smiling, licking her lipstick, her eyes calculating under the modest, fluttering, venereal lids, she whispered intimately: "And a cookie the one with the candied cherry in the middle, please do, really."

"Oh!" I protested.

Take, take, my mother would have said.

"Really, I don't mind, please do," said dainty Miss Patricia Donahue.

I did.

Later, when we bid farewell to sporting, big-toothed, intellectual (generally scientific) Mr. Wilkerson, and thanked him for a lovely nice afternoon, and promised to ask our parents to fork over five smackeroos for a Program of Nature Walks, Pattie Donahue allowed it to be known that I was walking her home. Under the circumstances even Lewis Snyder had to count it a date with a girl; the evidence whelmed, overwhelmed. I obeyed the protocol. We had a Coke and then an ice cream stick. That Snyder must have been eating his heart out, at least aggravated. All right then—I soliloquied with Tom Moss *qua* Conscience & Scorekeeper—half credit then for a daytime date.

At this age my father had already seen the wonder-working rabbi. He was crossing borders at night to find freedom in America. He had found it for me too.

"Did you get a free one?" I asked.

She read her ice cream stick. "No," she said.

"Neither did I. Don't believe in luck anyway"—and I expounded my philosophy of will power concentrate your way to fame and/or fortune. Just like a wonder-working rabbi from Lakewood, Ohio. I tried to recite "Ulalume" but forgot it.

My mother's arches were hurting in her Enna Jetticks, but she avoided my father so that he would not order her home. Andy was making off to the vegetable cooler with a bagful of macaroons. Basketwood splintered under orders; customers fidgeted untended; my father wiped his forehead with a paper towel from the pine forests of Maine, leaving crumbs of lint, and mourned his losses: Where was his son?

"I never knew you were so smart," said Pattie Donahue.

We had fallen silent, sitting on the front steps of her house in the shadow of a bush where her mother could not see us. Up the street someone was hosing his car, an incontinent sound, in preparation for a Fourth of July trip. The afternoon was over. Pattie Donahue, an economical creature, an Indian giver, took back her gift in a way which expressed her genius. Business acumen. Operating costs and turnover. Appraising me with her turtle-round eyes, shrewd to calculate the value of an investment, she first created a bear market by sighing, Ohh, rustling her dress, and accidentally touching my arm with her transparent turquoise-veined hands. Cologned and dusted with powder, she breathed on me.

"Yes!" I spilled out, naked in summer smells. "Do you like me, Pattie? I like you."

"Sure I like you"—disappointment and a pout that it had been so easy. Even economy becomes sport with such a housekeeper. "Sure I like you but you're too fat."

"Fat?" I repeated stupidly.

Her laughter tinkled in the July calm by the watered bush. "Fat I mean skinny. I mean you're just a *grocery* boy, you. You just grub around a certain store I could name all the Saturdays *I* ever heard about, except I suppose today—"

She was a sly old creature, that Pattie Donahue. The lips: *grocery boy*. The frozen iris: the same. Her laughter caroled forth, free, enterprising, resolute, the investment paying off in a Saturday afternoon dividend of power. Not all men are men, her laughter told her. This is a profit forever, my face told her.

"Oh but—oh but—oh but," I said.

She put her little hand to her mouth and delicately closed it. Tee-hee. She looked at me, unblinking. My father, knowing he was a foreigner, could have accepted this in the perspective of history. I had to discover a fact without a past; it leapt out at me like some fierce fish from the glittering shale of Pattie Donahue's economical eyes.

I stood up. "Thank you for the sandwich and the cookie," I said. (The cookie with a preserved cherry on it.)

"Oh, me, no," she said.

"I was hungry."

"Oh, you're welcome really," she said. "Thank you for the Coke. Thank you for the ice cream."

"Goodbye, Pattie."

"It was nice," she said, "truly very nice."

19

I prowled, growing up fast that afternoon. I climbed the fat hump of a mailbox, and hands hanging in front, or elbows on knees and fists in cheeks, I watched the traffic on Clifton Boulevard. Into town, out of town. To work, toward home. The burnt metal smell of streetcars. Black Fords with NRA stickers. All adult, all organized.

When I had seen enough, I climbed down. Continued on my way. Rounded the block. I did not choose the sentimental places, the tree by the lake, the woods where the river on which we skated in winter spread out suddenly like a sheet. I began to understand how the lost Lenore really got mislaid, without a dark conversational bird, without a tomb, without even a long metrical sigh. I circled the territory like an explorer lost in my snowy wastes. A blizzard inside, Lakewood around me. A heavy July sun lowered and thickened above.

I climbed back atop the mailbox, my new home. I perched on the box like an animal in a dream.

But I was no animal in no dream. I was wide awake, me, itchy, straddling a mailbox. Once someone mailed a book between my legs. I did not stop to wonder if it was some quaint and curious volume; a book, I thought. I studied the houses squatting like fat-necked bullfrogs along the boulevard, puzzled over the nay-saying mouths and step of the emerging strollers, celebrated and grieved over the crystallizing structure of my judgment (my complexes), no longer contained by sad and pretty words— grieved.

The sun went down. A blizzard still whirling in my head. Cold sun blinding me.

Long after dark I finally went home. My parents were in the kitchen, talking in low voices, the relieved hawing of Saturday nights absent today. Entering at the street, I went directly to my room and lay down on the bed. I made none of the dramatic flourishes of locking the door or pushing the footstool in front of it.

"Herbert!"

Doltish, I wondered if this was what it felt like to be an adult. True that for weeks I had been awakening mornings with my bite clamped, my jaw aching, and my tongue plunged against my teeth.

"Herbert!"—Mother's voice. I went. Mother stood by the kitchen table. Dad sat without looking at me, his head lowered, his hands about a bowl of soup. "You should come when I called you," she said.

"I did come."

"When I called you I said. Not whenever you please." She looked at my father and waited for him to speak. He did not. We all waited for him, the challenged one, amid the summer smell of flypaper in the kitchen and the buzzing of the wily flies.

Resentfully I broke the stillness: "I went on a nature walk."

"What?—what? A nature *what?*"

"I learned what's a toadstool and the names of birds. A nature walk. Mr. Wilkerson general science from junior high, he—"

"And what about Mr. and Mrs. Slave-their-heads-off, I suppose your parents by the store?" my mother asked. The sarcasm gave me hope; it was, after all, only dialectic again. How soon hope returns! We dwell in it even after the exile to which Pattie Donahue's laughter and nibbling teeth send us.

Turning to my father, whose head bent over the table in a way I only remembered afterward—his brother had died and Mother said he was crying because he was sad and I didn't believe her because daddies don't cry, not my father—I appealed to him with a manly challenge: "Almost everyone I know went on the nature walk."

He did not look up.

"It's educational. Mr. Wilkerson says. Tom Moss was there. Almost everyone in our Grade Seven-B, Seven-A was there—"

"Lookit my waricose from standing up all day working like a horse eating my heart out," Mother said. "You should take a load off my feet, not I should carry you like a baby you're going on fourteen."

"Thirteen," I said.

"Going on anyway," she insisted, *"going* on. That's

what it means. Big lummox. Look at my waricose go on, look, lookit."

She could not know—my cruelty at twelve years, soon thirteen!—that my only concern was for surgery on the distended veins, as other women had, instead of wearing the lumpy corset that bulged about her thighs, under webbed brown stockings. "My garment," she called it. "Like taxes, Sam says. Teeth too, O! Sarah had the same trouble after Bernie, and she took calcium. You ask me I think better injections in the arm, injections."

Dad listened watchfully over the soup in the evening heat. He hunched and studied vegetables in the bowl.

See how I admit the two of them to paper. Put my refusal of their world, which was their deepest gift to me, beside a son's longed-for and imagined love for his parents. "Want to playboy around all your life dreaming smoke in the head?" my father used to ask me, and yet he loved me despite the law that we cannot love someone who refuses our gifts. I did not see the power and light of his world, in which the great issues of birth, love, creation, and death were exercised in action with my mother, vegetables, and the Saturday specials; I had looked for light and power in Pattie and Poe while all the Aristotelian potencies and more lay waiting for me with the combustible garbage swept into the back yard at closing time each evening. He flushed out the reek and drench of the gutter and stood over it with his hose. He held the shiny nozzle and thought forward from the day. The back room, emptied and cleaned, was filled and emptied of carrot tops, beet greens, and the furry blue glow of spoiled oranges. I stalled; my father waited. I looked; my father watched.

A week earlier I had overheard Mother murmuring into the telephone, "So how's your Bernie? My Herbert shouldn't be better, he got a all-A report card and with a B plus in gymnistics, he gained two pounds by the scale but he's full of complexes, still a heartache in the store . . . Yah . . . I read in the paper it's complexes, Sam says he'll grow out . . ."

But only the complexes kept growing out. My father offered me his entire world and I threw it in his face like a rotten orange because he left out one little lump of an Atlantis, my own world.

"Listen to your father he's talking," my mother said. He had not yet spoken, but she knew him well and knew he now would. "You take his fifteen cents for a movie, don't you? Listen to your father."

Still sitting in his washed-out shirt crusted with salt under the armpits, in his old blue serge work pants, once dress-up with the sharpy stripe down the legs, more generous than fathers have a right to be, he tried to help me expiate my sin in a ritual of reprimand. No ceremony could heal him this time, but he waited. This came before the beginning: "At your age I was a man," he said.

He was right.

He swayed over the soup, food breathing back into his body the prayers he had forgotten in leaving his own father. His swaying shoulders heavily sloped and remembered. His father had forbidden him to go to godless America, better to die than to be unfaithful. This too he had forgotten, his father struck down by a Cossack's rifle, but the chant in his voice and the dance of his shoulders remembered.

"Look at you"—he could not. "Are you a man?"

No. Right again.

"A playboy. A nature walker. A eater of ice cream."

All true. I still like ice cream, especially with Hershey's chocolate syrup. He taught me quality in food, my father. I waited for him to force me to make myself what we both agreed I should be; no ceremony could compel it, though only ceremony could confirm it. Still I had to choose. Untheological, without brand names, we improvised ritual.

"A lollipop!" my mother shrilled, thinking she was on her husband's side. Here she was wrong. I was not a lollipop.

"Let me tell it," my father said softly, as if this were an incident of their vacation at Chippewa-on-the-Lake. "It's my turn to tell it."

"I don't care"—me turning in my pointed shoes perforated for ventilation and sweet beauty's sake under the eyes of Pattie. I mourned her now, blaming my birth. I teetered on the edge like the old Peerless on rotten pilings under the High Level Bridge. "I don't care about you." I lowered my gaze to my father's stubby foreign feet in steel-backed boots. "None of the kids have to do it. I don't care about you and your store."

He needed an instant for this. I gave it to him overflowing. "And—your—store."

His hand floated up like a speck fuming on the eyes; his fist crashed down on the enameled table like the plunging claw of a crate hammer. "Oh! Oh!"—Mother. Soup splashed out on his pants and ran weeping with little red carrot eyes.

His gaze was prophetic in mine. *"Some kits help out in the store,"* he said.

"We were practically supposed to go," I said, neither retreating nor regretting, gaining time and learning patience. "Mr. Wilkerson is a teacher."

"Some kits remember their father and mother."

Everyone knows where it hurts when you begin to cry —that place at the back of the throat. Pins jabbed under my eyelids. My palate ached. The tears hurt most in that instant before they break out . . . And then I imagined cologned Pattie's cool laughter at my father's pronunciation of the *d* in *kits* ("—remember their father and mother"), and then drunk with the idea of the murder of someone I loved, my belly awash at the thought, I screamed him to his feet: "I won't, I *won't* work in your store. I don't want it. It's not my life. I hate it. I hate it!"

He stood huge over me, smelling of leafy vegetables and sweat, smelling of his strength and his terror because he would have to beat me. This is the reek of power, what the men at the food terminal understood when Ollie the Agent, Shloimi's man, tried to shake him down first of the West Side men . . . The opponents were uneven. He had wise muscles, protected by years of work and good eating, the skills of use, the satisfactions of his time of life. He had four sons, only one of those baby brothers of mine lying awake to listen. He had had two brothers in America. His swaying body knew it loved me as his father had loved him, the woman carrying her child on a belly or breast, the man taking his son only at the eye or the fist.

As he had loved Ben, as he had failed Ben. How could he know me? How could he know? There must have been a great satisfaction in his fear and love at that moment.

My sole weapon was exactly my dissatisfaction. My father's arms swam with veins among the curled hairs on his bluish, freckled flesh. No bow-straight shoulders like Atlas the World's Most Perfect Develop It! No Culver Academy athlete calling for Pattie Donahue in his uniform at Christmas time! It was a body which had worked well and been used with pleasure, a happy body, soup on the pants, making its own purpose and content with this.

Mine, as I have said: discontented. I looked for a use for it. I said: "And you and your grocery boys and everyone! *I hate you!*"

Mother was crying and stacking the dishes in the sink when his open hand—generous! open!—struck my shoulder. I flew back and then up at him, slipping past his collar rough as a dog's tongue. Mother screamed. I climbed him, flailing; he was planted on the floor and he rocked under my weight for a moment, both of us silently straining toward each other and apart, our sweat pouring together while Mother screamed on and on—the malignant smell of hate and fear becoming the myrrh of two men fighting, the sweet cunning of love and death. I clung to his great neck to strangle it. His beard scratched my arms. He hugged my ribs, forcing them up—cracking!—pushing my hair out, lengthening my bones, driving my voice deep. Savagely he told me his life, wringing my childhood from me. I took this after his long day and had nothing to give in return but my unfleshed arms roped about his neck. We embraced like this.

The broken blood fled for a window into my mouth. I felt myself fainting.

Abruptly I lunged down, perhaps permitted to beg free. His weighty old-country strength: my agile sporting slyness: as he glanced for pity at my mother, I threw myself like a pole against his knees in a playground stunt performed without thinking. The trick uprooted his legs; he crashed; his forehead above the unsurprised Tartar eyes hit my mother's foot when he fell.

He sat up and started to his feet as she held him. I could not breathe, my chest frozen. I turned from his sprawling. I let him hear me choke and then ran to my room. Yes, I had wanted to win, but now, fatalistic, in an instant guessing ahead, I made the highest demand on a father: that he know he had beaten me too, only because he had let it happen.

"What's happening to us all?"—those first tears of old age. "What's happening to us?" Dad was crying in the bathroom with the door shut and the water running in the sink so that no one would hear an old man with an ingrate son. He had locked Mother out, who was dry-eyed now, figuring.

If I am bereaved of my sons, the first Jacob said, *then am I bereaved.* To fight back was all I needed: he had given too much. Economy in Pattie! my father a spendthrift!—such knowledge comes late to me now.

20

There was no moment of reconciliation between my father and me. We quarreled, we lived together, we remained in touch, we warred again on occasion, we made it up, we looked ahead, we walked carefully with each other, we were part of a family. One day I noticed that the war with my father was over. I don't remember when that day came. It came more than once. There would still be quarrels, but we had agreed upon the lines of power. We each had our territory. We could each allow the other to live. We were allies.

Now we come to some other wars. There were many, the Depression, the struggle of family, and the one that rose above our personal mortalities. This is the war which almost made private life seem irrelevant, and then became very personal, forcing itself into the kitchen, as if to demonstrate that we are each of us required as individuals for the grand disasters of the human fate.

September, 1939. A cottage on Lake Erie at Cedar Point. My brothers and I had struggled deep into the beach, playing touch football, sand in eyebrows, shins aching. "See it here! See it here!" the youngest kept yelling. I made myself captain. We found other kids on the beach. Smell of Lake Erie, fish and wind, and a few filmy June bugs who had lost track of time—we called them Canadian soldiers . . . There was another captain down the beach and we chose up sides. Lake-sodden, sand-sodden, we clashed and the score mounted. I sent my youngest brother back to the cottage because his shoulders were sunburned. "Aw, see it here," he said, begging to touch the ball one more time.

We spent a last night in the cottage. The evening breezes came up; we washed; sand in the sink, sand everywhere. My father sat on the porch at dusk, reading *The Cleveland Plain Dealer*. He studied and restudied the large black type, square black letters filled with furry ink—serious news. The newspaper said: WAR. My mother kept asking us to finish the fruit, the nice bananas and pears, she didn't want to have to pack it up for the trip back to Cleveland. My father read until he boiled, and then he threw the newspaper to the floor. He picked it up and read some more. Then, regularly, he threw it down, waited, and picked it up. I took a snapshot of him.

My mother was worrying about whether I had packed my fountain pen, whether the fan belt on the car would last until Cleveland, whether we were men enough to do justice to the bag of fruit she had wrapped together so we wouldn't starve on the two-hour drive back home. She wanted to put butter on my brother's shoulders. He yelled that it didn't hurt. She yelled that a little butter wouldn't hurt. He yelled that it made him feel sticky. She yelled: "What's sticky, you don't want to peel."

I pointed out that there was plenty more skin where that came from.

My father asked everyone please be quiet.

A weekend at the cottage. The newspaper with furry letters. My father was flinging the paper down again and again. I took his picture again.

My mother fought her wars closer to home. I was her battleground; her eldest son was the rough turf over which she struggled toward victory. She determined to root out my flaws before they could appear—particularly the flaw of marrying the wrong woman. There were millions and millions of the wrong women, wherever she looked; they covered the earth, like Sherwin-Williams paint.

Starting from about the age of eleven, I was a worry to her in this traditional way. Would I or would I not marry a nice Jewish girl? My mother debated this question with herself, with my aunts, with my father, and with me. She anticipated the shame, she anticipated the disgrace, she anticipated the moment when my bride would turn on me, holding up one of my socks from the hamper, and crying out that age-old subtitle from the dialogue of an international low-budget nightmare: "Dirty Jew!" Or perhaps it might be metaphysical; suddenly my wife would conclude that I had killed the Saviour. Or that I wasn't good enough for her—a family with a house by the lake. My mother had a nonecumenical view of things.

Like an unsharpened blade, I first must have replied

clumsily, sawing back and forth, looking for my way in life. "Well, Ma, everybody's human, we heard in Auditorium today. All boys and girls created equal. Where's my skate key?"

"Oh! Oh! Aie! Human yes! But marry her, no!"

"What her? *Who?* But it's love that counts, Ma. Hey, the peanut butter's all gone."

"In your own kind you'll marry. Otherwise what will happen to us? She'll turn on me because I don't have an accent, you just say I do—on your father, he speaks worse. I learned it from him. Do you think they let us into their country clubs? Do you think they invite us to dinner? You're an aggravation, not a son."

"Okay, I won't marry anyone this year. First I got to get out of junior high, okay?"

"There's the new jar of crunchy peanut butter, dummy. I suppose you want me to make the sandwich too."

And thus the matter was settled for ten minutes. But then it began again.

"You're only fourteen years old."

"Fifteen, going on sixteen."

"You're too young to marry a shiksa."

"Who said I wanted to marry anyone? Just because I'm in love with Pattie doesn't mean I can marry her." Sadistically, ominously, oedipally I added: "Yet."

"Oh! oh! aie!" sobbed my mother, struck at her core.

"Fifteen years old," I pursued her angrily. "Why can't I be my own age?"

For a moment I seemed to seize the advantage. But

my mother was a Ulysses S. Grant of discussion. Curse the casualties, disregard the losses. She recaptured the terrain, heroic about costs and logic.

"You're a boy!" she cried. "A boy, my own boy. I want you to be a man, a pride to me. Not a baby, a shame—a man!"

"So far," I said dejectedly, "I'm not sure I'm a adolescent."

"Where'd you learn that word? Where? Come on, tell me."

"On the playground. In the toilet. From a kid in tennis shoes."

"Oy, he'll ruin his feet," my mother said. "Flat feet before twenty, and the arch, and the calluses, and that's how the goyim take care. But their feet hurt, they take it out on the Jews. Pogroms. Prejudice. No Jews in insurance companies, no Jews in the banks, not even a teller."

"Mother, I want to go out now. The kids are waiting. I've got the bat."

"You won't go out and play baseball till you promise me. No shiksas. A nice Jewish girl from a good family, plays the piano, not flat-chested, educated."

"Who?" I asked, suddenly interested.

"Promise," she said. "When the time comes, don't worry."

My father participated gloomily, if at all, in these discussions. He could be awakened by my mother's invocations of the sufferings of the Jews. But he looked at me— skinny, knobby, with an oversized Adam's apple and a trombone voice—and was reassured. No one would have me, of whatever race, creed, or color. Also he could not accept these future risks as disasters. Even future disasters were not yet disasters. When the time came, he would think about it.

"Your father doesn't care," my mother said. "I bear the entire burden of worrying."

"Who needs you to worry?" my father asked. "I'll do the work, which we don't need the worry."

"I don't work?" my mother asked. "I raise a son, and he is lost to us?"

"Can I go read my book now? *Lost Horizon* by James Hilton? It's a grown-up book by an Englishman?"

"Lost, lost, lost," my mother said. "What good is it for me to worry and nag and nag and worry if nobody listens?"

My father was behind his paper, *Der Tag*, which came by mail from New York City. I was behind the movie edition of *Lost Horizon*, which had a photograph of Ronald Coleman and Jane Wyatt—or was it Margo?—holding hands on a stone bench in the world of the future, where no one grew old, while old Sam Jaffe, the great High Lama, watched in his robes. ("The years will come and go, and you will pass from fleshly enjoyments into austerer but no less satisfying realms," Sam Jaffe told Conway while I itched with spiritual desire. "Hmm. Chang tells me that Mozart is your favorite Western composer.") I fled the unreality of family life into the reality of the realms of the spirit, where all is peace and tranquillity, and Chang reminisces about Mozart, whom he knew personally.

My mother always sought the parting shot. "But you will," she said.

"Will what?"

"The right girl," she said.

And I responded malevolently, before sinking into eternal truth. "Yes, Ma. First Pattie, and then I'll divorce her. Then Lucille, and then she'll divorce me. And then Pattie again, because I'll always love her, she has such a nice red bicycle."

Lucille, of course, was put into play only to poison the wells of discourse. I didn't want to give away my secrets. Pattie was the only girl I could ever love. She hated me.

My mother took aim once more. "What did we give you for your birthday, lummox?"

"A typewriter," I said. "I already thanked you."

"Yah," she said dubiously.

"Thank you again," I murmured.

"Yah," she said, frowning, having lost her point in a notion about the ingratitude of eldest sons, the perilousness of filial love, the risks of devotion to the cause of that son, the future doctor, the future lawyer, the future pride and joy, the future marrier of a—Ah! ah! She caught the thought on the wing.

"Well," she said cunningly, hoping I would catch all the implications of this news, "I heard about a girl lives up the street, only a year or two older than you, I forgot her name, you know her, I won't tell you her name, you should leave her alone, Anna says . . ."

"What's your point, Ma?"

"For her fifteenth birthday her ma and pa gave her a case of beer. That's the kind of people you're going to marry?"

21

In the next two years my father talked to us a great deal from behind the newspapers. He read the news, and tried Churchill's words aloud, and then put the paper down and fixed me with his slanted eyes and said he was having trouble keeping help. Andy, Ruby, Max were all gone. Only Red Schwartz and Myrna remained of the old crew, and Red was thinking of opening his own place. The young kids worked in factories, bought used cars, went to the Army. From behind the paper, again, where I couldn't see his face, he wondered if I would like to spend part of the summer helping out in the store, good pay, better than anyone, a responsible job—only if I wanted it, of course.

No, I said, I had other plans. I had writen a letter of application. I was waiting for an interview.

"Independence he wants," my mother explained. "He thinks he can be independent at his age. Everything he has he—"

My father stopped her. The newspaper crackled. His face was carefully folded, the eyes thoughtful, a bit malevolent, with a yellowish gleam. "Well, why not? At his age I was independent. He'll find out." And to me he said: "Which I was only asking."

During that vivid, unresolved summer in 1941 before the United States entered the war, I found a job as counselor in a coeducational summer camp near Jackson, Michigan; in fact, near Grass Lake, Michigan; in fact, even closer to Napoleon, Michigan. I had already been there as a camper; now I was a boss, a counselor, an uncle. It was a summer of busy high skies and tireless sun, with times of dust and times of ardent dog-days heat, and the flower of feeling opening. I was moved by green and weather, and even more, by the fact that I knew I was being moved.

I had a friend, I had a girl. I had cash in my pocket. I still wrote poetry and decided that it didn't have to rhyme. Not yet out of high school and too young for the defense plants, I filled in a gap as assistant professor of tennis and journalism. Under the gaudy title of "Uncle," I had power and dominion over a crew of squirmy spoiled boys. Like my father, I was earning money and striding through the universe as a model for others.

Of course, not much cash and awful poetry—and that girl!—and my backhand at tennis!—and those rich kids with their suitcases full of Kleenex! Not much of a rehearsal for being a father. But at least I really did have a friend, a long lazy loony confident fellow named Phil, totally unlike me, who was merely lazy and loony but not particularly long. Together we got the good out of violations of camp laws, rules, regulations, standard procedures, clearly marked signs, mature advice, and codes accepted by all decent folks in the summer-camp business, and so flagrantly much good that on the day when we boarded the bus back to town, the owner of the camp, a physical education supervisor in winter life, put one plump hand on each of our hard heads and murmured, "Forgive them, Lord, they know not what they do."

I knew, of course, what I had *tried* to do. But I left Camp Sherwood in the same poignant condition with which I had entered—an embattled innocent in matters of love. My chronic condition, an absence of excess, a deficiency of sin—in short, the presence of a lack—was complicated by the fact that my friend Phil had become an expert with spectacular gifts of persuasion, who knew how to skinny-dip at night and to stroll intimately in the woods and to row stalwartly across Big Wolf Lake for a frozen Milky Way; and Kate, the girl whose teeth he rotted with candy, was a bouncy and bounceable happy creature who assented to all his suggestions and only entered analysis after she had received her Master's in Sociology (Sosh) midway in the Cold War. *Then,* it turned out, she had done the wrong thing with my friend, but the wrong thing only retrospectively, in a manner of speaking which made him out to be Sibling and Father and Protest Against Sibling and Father, none of which he had intended to be when he strutted in boxer shorts or borrowed my raincoat for a conversation under the pine. In other ways, Herr Doktor, it was the right thing.

But not me. I could do neither wrong nor right thing, it seemed. Limited power and dominion. The girl I tried to outdistance at swimming, who then outdistanced me all summer in every other way, then said to go away even closer, then outdistanced me again, liked to have suntan lotion rubbed onto her arms and legs; I rubbed. "Ooh, ooh, ah, more," she said. But then: "Enough." She liked Clark bars when I bought Milky Ways, Milky Ways when I offered her Clark bars. She liked to talk about art, music, Life; I found difficulty in classifying all these topics.

"Are you sure of yourself?" Sandra asked. "Because I think that's important, don't you?"

I did. Oh I did.

"Do you feel *secure?*" she asked. "Because I think a man should always feel secure."

I wanted to feel secure and to try to feel even more secure. But she always stopped me. "Secure" is not the same as "fresh," she explained with cheerful pedantry. In the English language these are different matters. My grip on the language was almost as unsure as my grip on Sandra, and when I gripped my confidence, I found myself with a handful of air and fingers. And the nails in my palms while Sandra instructed me.

"Because I like a man to be sure of himself, Herb— that's even better than good-looking or a swell dancer. Would you like to put this goo on my back?"

She said "back," but meant more. She said "goo," and meant goo.

There I crouched on my knees on the Outer Raft, breathless after swimming, rubbing suntan lotion, discussing Sibelius and Thomas Wolfe, growing more and more unsure of my certain self. "You don't like the Ruby Yacht any more, Herb? Ooh, that feels nice. A little more up there. *There.* You don't like the Fitzgerald translation from the original Persian any more, Herb?"

"Nope." I was surly and covered with greasy greaseless cream. "All nonsense. Exaggerated. A symptom of nineteenth century British imperialism."

"And another thing I want to have a good long talk with you about is politics, Herb. And also you're not full of self-confidence. You're not really proud of being *you.* Don't get that oil on my latex suit, it stains. You don't radiate energy all the time like a healthy boy, oh, I don't mean that, excuse it, Herb, I mean like a young man should."

But she would not co-operate joyously, energetically, libidinously, as a girl always did, excuse it, a young lady eventually does in the novels I liked in those days. Sometimes I felt as if I had had enough of tennis counseling or mimeograph labors, children making pie beds and children who needed help with letters home to their parents. ("P.S. And mommy lissten, I like my councilor very much please bring him a dozen pair of socks size 12 Davie's father already brought him a sweater.") I wanted to take Sandra away from all this. I wanted to practice radiating energy. At least for an hour or two.

Instead we watched a duck go *squawk,* pulled by the leg straight down into the swampy depths of the lake. "Ooh, listen that squawk," said Sandra.

"Snapping turtle, it's the battle of life," I said, "the

survival of the fittest." I had bought second-hand books about the story of second-hand philosophy, the second-hand romance of art, and the mystery of heredity, explained by a man with chromosomes. A writer with a name like Hendrik Willem Van Loon (witty comments on eternity) had to be a terrific authority, though a name like Amram Scheinfeld (dark ecstasies about gene clusters) ranked pretty high in my psyche, too. "Nature," I announced, "provides a balance of nature in order to—"

"Ooh, I bet those sharp teeth," said Sandra.

"It's all in the jaws. Listen to me, Sandra. It's not teeth, it's the powerful jaw muscles—"

She squirmed away. "I'll listen to you," she remarked, "with your powerful jaw muscles, if you'll first get your greasy hands *off*."

They were greasy, of course, from oiling her packed little body against sunburn. And she had asked me to oil. And now that I had done my work, I had been enticed to play lubriciously. But like some decoy duck, she swam in circles until I grabbed with my snapper's snout; then she derisively let me yank her down to *my* destruction. No, perhaps she did not destroy, but she certainly unraveled.

"I knew this fellow once," said ducky Sandra, "he wasn't a bit secure. A boy should try to be secure." Blissfully, drowsily, she stretched out beneath the sun with her eyes closed, not caring how I looked at her. Her arms were fine, round, ambered by summer; there was a delicate lightening shade into her breasts where they sheltered each other, cradled by latex; her eyelids fluttered to get just a glimpse of me, which was all she required. She said: "This fellow was kind of grabby, but insecure? Oh, honestly. You know, Herb, you sort of remind me of him—" propping herself up on an elbow, examining me through eyes whose intentions were veiled by a thick brush of lash. "Only he was taller." Flopping back down to brown the other side.

I tell the world frankly: Sandra was no joy to me. I wept at night, alone, because the German armies were in Paris.

On Sundays, when the parents drove up from Detroit, Toledo, and Cleveland, we dressed the children in their ceremonial white shorts and white T-shirts with the camp insignia stamped across narrow or pubescent bosoms; we dabbed calamine lotion on bites and then stuffed bananas down throats at breakfast. The kids were supposed to weigh in heavy for their bout with parents. (Today, so much later in history, even the children eat Slimming Foods.) Jokester Phil, my pal, exercised his entire repertory of shoveling, cramming, tamping, and gagging gestures, and said to little Davie Snyder, Lewis' brother, "Swallow, you crud, or I'll tell your mother what you did when you lost the International Afterhours Strip Poker Tournament."

"Oh please, Uncle Phil!"

Phil elaborately relented. "Okay, you're a nice crud. Listen, you have one more banana, hey, and mum's the word."

With gratitude Davie found space to tuck away another few tropical ounces in his endless whorls of childish gut. On weigh-in day bananas plowed sluggishly through tummies all over our camp. Bringing in Davie heavy, Phil hoped to store up a little credit with the head counselor in case Aunt Kate, junior counselor for Girls Group Two, the Brownies, was absent at bed check.

By noon the beastlings had all been shined up and we counselors were ready for parental discussion of heat rash, wax in ears, nervous stomach, and how much progress the heir to a chain of drugstores was making in Crafts. "Not very superlative in Crafts, I'm afraid, but wonderful in Arts-and, Mrs. Snyder. Shows remarkable talent."

Davie's mother was delighted. "Artistic?" she asked. "Is he good with his hands?"

Phil showed me a choked, chortling, warning face: *Don't tell what Davie does with his hands during rest period.* Mr. Snyder, master of many white-coated pharmacists, intercepted our ritual lurch of suppressed laughter. This intuition, passed from Phil to me, probably cost us a box of mints or a carton of chewing gum from the Snyder warehouse. Artistic insights, emotional sensitivity, and having a steady pal like telepathic Phil won't make you rich, but they can keep the old acne from its proper feeding. All right, so Papa Snyder was suspicious. I would eat apples instead of mints, and I hoped the Cuyahoga River flooded all his candies into one gluey mass fit only to be hashed up for Halloween giving.

After dinner Phil directed a program of skits, which is the camp version of classical tragedy, and then we parted the speeding guests from their progeny with many a wave, tear, and smiling, lip-read curse.

Six dozen socks and a sweater. Phil got an electric razor. Hell, wasn't my chin as hairy as his? (Answer: Not quite.) And my hormones even hairier? (Answer: Impossible to ascertain.) Why should he have all the luck with girls and parents?

Here comes that crank with his complicated complaint:

Why the devil should my girl demand programatic assertions that Life Is Really Good, and then barely let me cop a feel, while Phil's girl didn't care if he exhibited a spot of world-historical neurotic indifference—and yet they made out fine together. (This is a statement, not a question.) There was and is no justice in love. Girls who ask, *Are You Happy?* should be forced to *be* happy, like it or not.

The mother who made me promise to hold a wet finger at night near her sonnyboy's head, in order to test for winds invading the channels and by-passes of the inner ear, gave me socks that would have broken my big toe except that my big toe was tough. I was insulted; the rest of me was less tough than my big toe. She should have remembered me with larger feet. Therefore I went to bed nights without wetting my finger to guard against drafts. I should get chapped fingers for a family whose socks didn't fit me? Anyway, I needed all my fingers for poking around the universe and writing poetry. Resolutely I gave up my resentment, which had me imagining an amputated digit, due to horrible chapping, and there I lay in a tent with sneakers and no socks on, thinking about solemn, silly, perfection-hungry Sandra. She had smudged dark eyes, a ponytail, and a way of smiling. Lovely Sandra. Poor me.

Faced by all this trouble, my few prickles of beard peeked out, looked around, decided against venturing into the ungrateful world, and then just burrowed back into my skin for safety. Said my hormones: "HURRY UP PLEASE ITS TIME!" (T. S. Eliot) Said my retracted soul: "Closing up early today." (Bartender, anon.) No razor, no socks, no girl, no truth but words, words, words. *Ow, ouch,* I summed up my life, *I hurt.* (Sandra used the phrase "hurtie feelings.")

I hurt!

I stared into the murky night and wondered if someday I might feel better. My father had told me that things always get better later, if you make provision, maybe. This was definite enough for him, it seemed, but not for me. His pains only hurt him, but mine hurt me.

Expert Phil, my coach, admitted that Sandra would be a tough nut to crack, even for Phil. But of course, between pals and for the sake of perfect honesty, he would never think of her that way in a thousand cruddy years—that Sandra, sure, she reads books and all—but still, that Phyllis Bazelon, the Group One counselor, she looked as if she were getting tired of writing to that crud in the merchant marine. And she was really stacked. So? So? So I still liked Sandra better. Expert advice (an elbow in the ribs) could do nothing for me. Poor sick me, who couldn't be educated.

Self-pity is an effort to make up by loving oneself for

all the love one does not receive from Sandra, Lucille, Donna, or Pattie. Anxiety is a crisis of the fear of loss of love. Back it all comes, back, back to perjured love. My father was too silent, too noisy. My mother was also busy. It came out to my running the dangers of being a sensitive poetry-writing chap. Sophistication, I figured at seventeen, was one of my strong points, just as stupidity was my weak point. However, I could avoid some of the pitfalls, I decided, still heavily thinking, as I led one of my light-kidneyed boys out in his sleep to do his duty in the field. (Enuresis was very popular that summer.)

"But I don't have to, Uncle Herb," he mumbled.

"Listen, you *have* to, Sheldon."

"No, honest, I don't."

I made encouraging waterfall sounds. No luck. A fountain's hiss, a whispering whistle. A drip. A bubble. My entire repertory of magical liquid persuasion. Silence from Sheldon. He stumbled. In slow motion, he crumpled like a melting snowboy against my leg.

"Wake up!" I shook him. "Go now. *Make!*" We were shivering outside in the tall grass. I never led Sheldon all the way across the field to the lavatory, but reserved a nearby patch of weeds for him. Despite his ministrations, it grew untrammeled; it bore its burden of Sheldon with vegetable tact and fortitude, and came to flower in a crown of milky seeds. *A-tchew!* I said, suffering from hay fever, and even in his sleep the brat smiled dimly, blast him. He knew I had my mind, that modified whorl of sinus, on other matters.

"But Uncle Herb, I already did."

Still draped in slumber, he headed back, pushed and shoved and guided and destroyed by my mystic power after a dozen delicate tortures which I had studied while standing up in a little bookstore on East Ninth Street in Cleveland. At his bed I discovered that Sheldon had spoken the truth: "I did already, Uncle Herb." He remembered: he had. Was it not Rousseau who argued that children, in their primal innocence, always know the truth? And mustn't we return at last to that unalloyed wisdom? And put Sheldon's sheets out on the line in the morning?

Sandra drowned me in chagrin while Sheldon merely drowned me.

What I then thought during that cricket-anointed night, however, while the lacewings hollered and the night-sparrows chirped, and somewhere a duck squawked and a train went, *Hooey! Hooey!* was that now I would fool Sandra good. She thought she had my number, and indeed she did; but I would change the number overnight. No longer would I be one of those sensitive poetic chaps. No, I resolved, disgustedly kicking myself into my cot near the door of the tent, pulling the sheet over my head despite the heat, crippling my ears with two well-aimed blows but leaving the mosquito nimble and intact; no! Groaning, swearing, blaming, and desiring. I would not be one of those sensitive poets who tell a girl how brittle, sly, superficial she is, and I can't live without you. No. I would tell Sandra she was sly, but not brittle and superficial, and I would say: "Oh I'll die if you don't—"

Now to poetry. In that tossed midnight hour of rage I composed a poem forever lost to the light. It explained (patiently, logically) to the world of Sheldons and Phils and Kates and Snyders and head counselors and other adults that there were truths of which they did not dare dream, but *I* dreamed, curse them all. I was in tune with nature, blast it. I was calm and all-forgiving. I also had secret weapons which could wipe out everyone.

With shining face I gazed into the darkness and confidently gave that buzzing mosquito one more blow that my ear would not soon forget. Then at last I slept, while the insomniac mosquito chanted its solemn music for dining pleasure. When it alighted to eat, I was lost in crooked sleep, kidding myself, compensatory Herb. Buzz, buzz, whine, and buzz.

The next morning my life cycle, like the mosquito's, went into a new phase. I nibbled at Sandra's ear: I yearned for blood, buzzed, got waved away. I tried and tried. Sandra suggested I not give up. I promised to try again.

"You need practice, Herb. It's called courtship in the old days. You know, I think you're getting a little taller, like this fellow I know back in the city. He's not too much taller than you, and he's a neat dancer, not like you, but you're still growing. And you could learn not to be such a stoop—up on your toes! Up! And you know much more about life, I think. You're a regular philosopher. You're really revealing a great deal to me, Herb."

"You want to talk things over tonight, Sandra?"—the sly philosopher.

"I think I can arrange it. I'm not going to wash my hair, it'll just get dirty again. Yes."

Yes.

When not on duty with our campers, Sandra and I used to Talk Things Over in various hidden spots at night —while swimming in the moonlight and shivering from cold, while lying on the grass at the place where the camp flagpole was impaled (me shivering with futile desire, also impaled), and at the cornfield where I tried to drag her amid the rustling sheaves (she shivered with anger and anticipatory suspicion). Or maybe she shivered with plans, or merely wondered when I was going to figure out how to pry open the lid over a nice, careful, complex suburban girl.

We talked about symphonic swing, about poetry with and without rhyme, about the advantages of photographic memory and perfect pitch; on one particular August evening she did let me coax her into the cornfield. We necked. There was a strange hot wind above us, and below the moving tassels of corn, a still, buggy, expectant coolness. A grammatical progression which is today much clearer to me then occurred: I necked, we necked, she petted. She trembled. *What did it all mean?* they ask about the mystery of life in novels, and I asked in real life: What does it mean? She clutched and swarmed against me in that cornfield; she pressed, flailed, made squeaking noises; a hot swarming fury of girl said yes-yes-yes to a question she was asking herself and bit me hard on the mouth because I didn't have sense enough to do the asking—*Will you, Sandra?*

Abruptly she flung me away and scrambled from her knees to her feet and began walking. She would not speak to me all the way back to camp. She would not say good-night. She turned scowling toward the girls' cabins, her damp hair still hanging over her face (remember Veronica Lake?).

"Goodnight, Sandra. Hey, goodnight?"

No answer. My mouth swelling, my heart in turmoil, I went to bed, confused and ignorant. I learned the obvious truth only later: Girls resemble boys in certain respects. It's not all suing for what you want. Girls want it, too; girls want!

"Hey, Sandra! Goodnight!"

No reply, just those feet in sneakers dragging sadly.

I didn't know. Perhaps even Sandra didn't know enough. We didn't know the truth about desire all two together. I should have learned from my father's way with my mother and Myrna and being secure (insecure). Most things are connected, but how could I see the lines of force between Sandra and my father? Not yet, not yet. Go away now, bedraggled Sandra's body was implying, and come back when you know something which can make me both earnest and hilarious.

Sandra, I wondered in my sleep under lumped-up Army blankets. Sandra, Sandy, Someone, I sighed; and meant the latter especially, draftily calling spirits of Girl out of the vasty deep. I would try again with Pattie Dona-hue. The evening embedded in varieties of corn, jabbed by cob, the moon overhead and bugs beneath, was being worked over by my fantasy of what might happen in some perfect Platonic cornfield. You would think me obliged to recognize the truth, that Sandra and I had made a kind of love together, but on my word of honor—in fact, on my word of dishonor—I had kept my stupidity intact. It was not how I had planned love; ergo, I did not admit it to myself. I was fated to mournfulness; it was not to be; or if it came to be, buffeted by my grieving imagination, it was not to have been was.

The next day Sandra occasionally glanced at my broken lip, grinned wildly, turned away with a look of great intelligence, and said nothing. When I tried to smile, my lip smarted and I didn't really feel like smiling anyway. Sandra was more in tune than she let on. Her suburban gabble and chatter was an attempt to jam the radiating broadcasts of her underground good sense. Dimly realizing this, I nursed my wounded mouth and did nothing to make Sandra live up to herself.

"All right kids, get in line there!"

"Do we have to? Aw, Uncle Herb."

Goofily I let them bunch up for milk and graham crackers. All I really wanted out of life was not money, power, glory, or my kids in a neat line. It was her love, my someone, my meaning of life, my end of the long road. History of birth and death, history of human struggle and aspiration, it seemed to lead me only as far as Sandra. Escape the family, escape the past, escape the home. I wanted adventure in the jungle, but found myself in the cage of join-the-body. I swung on the bars and scratched the fleas on my soul.

"Hey, yah, yah, Uncle Herb, we didn't get in line!"

No. No lines, but bless spirals, whorls, corkscrews, and biding my time.

Then followed the sadness of end of summer, abrupt nostalgia of the uncommitted, withering dry leaves and scattering hopes. The counselors suffered together through a brutal hot spell. We packed up our kids, knowing that the most untenable brat would have to wait longest for his unwilling parents to come after him. A few more evenings I hung double-mindedly over Sandra, malcontent to apply her lotions and unguents, my intentions stagnant with fear. Languidly I stuffed the last banana into the gullet of the last weight-gainer. Joey's parents finally arrived; the hot spell continued beyond the possible; a day of foreboding, heavy sky, laden air, shrill clatter of angry insects and hammer of woodpecker. We badly needed that storm which breaks the thrall of summer just when the seasons have finally been stopped on their rounds.

I closed the car door on Joey, our last camper, and waved goodbye. "A nice boy, he made real progress," I told his parents, "if only he'd learn how to use a handkerchief and stop kicking other children in the head."

"He's so double-jointed," said his fond mommy.

"How was he in interpersonal group relations?" demanded his father, a high school principal.

"You heard Uncle Herb," said Joey's mother, who had not been to college. "He said he gained four pounds and learned how to kick over his head."

I figured they had already decided on the socks for me anyway, so I added, "Interpersonally, he has a lot to learn." In fact, interpersonally, Joey stank. "I suggest you give him some professional help." I was thinking: Drown him, push him off a cliff, draw him and quarter him professionally.

"Art lessons!" cried Joey's mother. "I've always said so. And here is a little token of our esteem for your concern about our little man. On behalf of both my husband and myself—"

Argyles, brutally stamped "Seconds."

That night, in the deserted rec hall, we held the farewell Counselors' Record Hop. We were full of grief for our departing youth, all ninety-eight of them, and hoped to finish off the summer with a celebrational blare of Artie Shaw, Glenn Miller, Harry James, and a brief term of necking after dark, petting after dark, and an analysis of the booty received from grateful parents. We dropped socks as others drop names. I had received eight dozen socks. I put on a new pair. We danced.

"Sandra, will you show me?" I asked her. She knew how to dip and turn in the fox trot.

"Maybe," she said. "I promised to dance a *lot* with Bradley."

"Well, you can dance *a lot* with him," I said with my usual brilliant sardonic emphasis, improved as it always is by jealousy, that is, sapped and bled and shrunken to mere petulance, "but you can also take time out to—oh, never mind."

"Oh, I'll show you," she promised, relenting. She was a woman, protective and tender. "I'll show you Herb," she said, "if you won't say ONE-two, ONE-two all the time in my ear. It isn't like that anyway."

I knew that she would prefer sweet somethings to the sour nothing of my effort to become a swell dancer and a neat date. My cornfield adviser had grown distant. I decided to surprise her with a birthday present in December. Therefore, having already in my mind delighted her with a silver pillbox, I wondered why she had not forgiven me my trespasses as I had forgiven hers. She had a duty to read my mind; our love would be a uniquely binding episode in the history of telepathy.

She danced with Bradley. I danced with Friedel, the dancing teacher, who was also the wife of the head male counselor. He was a muscular old man of twenty-eight, sweaty creases circling his neck above the gym shirt; he practiced the physical education specialist's heartiness with younger men. Friedel held me too close, I thought. "Whoops," I said.

"Only my feet," she remarked sweetly.

The storm broke later that night. But unlike stories, where grave events occur when storms break, real life at our camp did not provide any violent alterations. I remember that Phil's Kate, later to be therapized, had the kind of face—gaggly eyes, crinkly nose—which at least once each evening, a yard or so below, crosses its legs so that you see too much thigh. Goddamn, there it goes again, I thought; and in the meantime, the unconscious face went on smiling. She never learned the graceful art of sitting. She had been taken by another desperate art. Sandra knew how to sit, and wore sensible white tennis shorts, and possessed herself fully with a little pout and smile, but Phil got to take Kate for a walk from which she returned hot and mussed and a few leaves sticking to her back and he broadly grinning.

There he went again, goddamn, goddamn, I thought with green enraged flecks of jealousy and red ones of lust making montage in my eyes. Sandra did not judge Kate, because she had been taught to judge not. She merely looked meaningfully from her to me and said, "Little bitch sure likes to show it off, don't she?"

"Sandra, I think they're in love."

"But I'll go for a *walk* with you, Herb. I shouldn't be too hard on her. After all, she hasn't anything else to offer a fellow."

"Yes, you've read the *Rubáiyát,* Sandra, and really understand it."

For my meekness, she took my arm and hugged it to her as we headed past the swings and the Group Three sandboxes, down past the flagpole to the shore. We stood beneath the scudding clouds, watching the moon rush through. Softly she asked if I would like to kiss her goodbye right now, in this poetic moment, because she might be too busy later to give it her full attention. A few drops began to fall. Haggardly I accepted her offer. We parted.

The dancing moment of Harry James, flies, sand, girl counselors in shorts and halters, boy counselors in shorts and T-shirts, Phil's Kate rashly in a skirt, all of them strolling by lake waters, finally came to an end. We packed away the colored lights in storage barrels. Already we missed the little monsters. We said goodbye with a sense that we had already parted and that this farewell took place after the end. It rained steadily; it drummed and drummed on the flapping tents; I lay awake all night in a rising autumn chill. The summer season of 1941 was over —the last of its sort for me.

That winter, during the immense private hush which

lay encased within the public roar of the attack on Pearl Harbor, Sandra yielded to me again and this time I knew it. I had reached the point of making coherent demands.

At this age my father had already become a starving businessman in New York, "independent," bringing his brother across from the old country. Now he taught me to drive. He knew little of my growing up and I knew little of his, but history entangled us. Neither one of us was independent. He let me use the car although he could not see the point of risking so many lives just to drive out for hamburgers in Rocky River. In America it's like that, I tried to explain. They don't love you unless you can take them out and park in the cinders to have your hamburgers.

By the next summer I was learning how to use the M-1 rifle, making ready to carry it to that far continent which my father had thought to leave forever.

Next comes the history of two linked violences, the first one now seeming comical to me and the second not now or ever. Both of them are family matters about the fate of men. Gradually my father's life echoes in mine; his shadow lies athwart mine.

In 1943, at age eighteen, I entered the Army, continuing at the same time my separation from my father and my education toward him. I could make myself possible by defying him. I could understand him by becoming myself. I could enter his soul, if one enters the soul of another, by suffering his pains. And then I would need defiance of him no longer. To be a father was also my own destiny, strange as he seemed to me with his Tartar eyes, his spells of silence, his intense inward contemplation.

He ran from the Czar's wars, but I quit college in my first year and enlisted. When I told him what I had done, he asked me to go for a walk with him. We walked twice around the block. He wanted to find out what I had in mind. He didn't know how to put the question. I couldn't give him the answer. The second time around the block —once more than usual—he began to whistle and seemed to forget I was there.

The skinny city Jew, wearing glasses, knowing too much from books, spilled head over heels into an infantry company—this is an old story. In the movies it proceeds on ritual lines, with a folk song fresh from the factory and a conclusion in general brotherhood (soft-focus fadeout). In my particular case, I had particular trouble and felt lonely in it. Fort Bragg was a lonesome place, wind-swept, gritty, hot with discipline; and the thousands of men— many thousands, true fodder—made it no less lonesome for the individual eighteen-year-old boys reluctantly handed over by their families. My father remembered the Czar's army and praised history because that time was dead.

Shyly he practiced being proud of me, like an American parent. He did not know about Private Fletcher—my Cossack.

One day, while marching in ranks, a large fat young man named Fletcher kept whispering to me in time as we marched: "*Kike* two three four, *kike* two three four." We were carrying the Garand M-1 rifle. We were preparing to go to Europe to destroy Naziism, and in a few weeks we would be used as replacements as the last convulsions of the horror took the lives of hundreds of thousands, in uniform and out.

"*Kike* two three four—"

I swung on Fletcher. He lurched against the marching line. Metal clattered. A sergeant grabbed me and pulled me out of the company. The sergeant was screaming with rage. What I had done was a court-martial offense and he would throw the book at me.

The lieutenant, who happened to be from Akron, Ohio, a bookkeeper for Firestone Tire & Rubber, heard my explanation. It was no excuse. I had broken ranks. Without discipline, there is no Army. Didn't I know there was a war on?

I knew, but I didn't dare tell him. Talking back would only make things worse. The lieutenant did not require my services as a news commentator, though I would have been glad to show him the big picture with a pointer on a map. I was learning a little bit. "Yes, sir," was a safe comment.

The captain sauntered up and listened to a summary of the situation. He stared eyelessly at Fletcher and me through his wrap-around sunglasses. For some reason, enlisted men were not allowed to wear sunglasses; perhaps our officers wanted to see the whites of our eyes; and so the use of sunglasses implied marvelous powers of decision-making, like those given by a scepter or a miter. The captain decided on an improvement over the normal legal procedure. The G.I. way—boards and hearings—was designed for the Army, not for a war. Didn't the lieutenant know there was a war on?

"Yes, sir," said the lieutenant.

The captain fell to thinking. His sunglasses protected from glare the powerful brain now at work. The eyes were sending filtered signals to the message center; the message center sent a message to the mouth, which broadcast the conclusion of this labor onto the drill field where we stood in ranks, swept by a hot wind, embracing our weapons.

What if the company were to be shipped overseas while I lay in the guardhouse? I would be kept out, preserved by my crime in luxurious punishment while my fellow men risked their hides. Would that be justice? *Would* that?

"No, sir," said the lieutenant.

"Right," said the captain.

"Yes, sir," said the lieutenant.

The captain had a better idea, and being a captain, which is a higher rank than lieutenant and sometimes a quieter, deeper one, he felt obliged to use his initiative as a leader of men. He could act on his idea. I wanted to fight, didn't I? Good. Roger, okay, and over. There would be a fight, but a formal one, with rules, and we would *all*

learn a lesson. (*What* lesson? He didn't say.) Fletcher and
I would do five rounds in the Day Room. He gave us three
days to think about it.

During these three days, training went on as usual.
But not quite as usual. We ran, jumped, crawled, fired,
marched. We listened to lectures and performed gas mask
drill. But in addition to these normal functions of a soldier,
warlike in general, I also thought about murder in particular. While I practiced with the bayonet on a dummy, my
mind was absent. Perhaps our drill influenced my thoughts.
I wanted to kill—to crush, to maim, to destroy my enemy.
Fletcher went through the same exercises. With this special event to entertain it, the entire company was alert
and cheerful. There was a subject for discussion in the
shower, the mess hall, the ten-minute break. The wars
in Europe and Asia were far away and unreal. The war
between Private Gold and Private Fletcher was close and
real. Our captain had won popularity. He was A-okay.

On that fateful evening in Fort Bragg, North Carolina,
a makeshift ring was drawn in chalk on the floor of
D Company Day Room. It was very hot; the sky and earth
were hot, packed in a thick element; flickers of heat lightning disturbed the air billowing over the red sands of North
Carolina. Obeying some deep ceremonial instinct, most of
the men had showered and shaved for this occasion. Even
our officers attended. There was a thin slime of excitement
on fresh cheeks. Bets, predictions, and judgments knitted
the crowd together. When they put fingers in collars, the
lines of tan were revealed.

During the past few days, I should mention, both gladi-

ators had received intense bouts of advice. We each had
our handlers. I must not pass over the fact that I was
not very popular among the men, and this had curious
consequences. Some of the most ardent partisans of
Fletcher—coaching, praising, vociferously justifying—were
Jewish boys from New York. Sons of cab drivers, working
people, they found me as much of an oddball as did the
mountain soldiers from Kentucky and West Virginia. I had
been to college for a few months and talked like it. They
refused to see me symbolically; they disliked me personally,
and that was that. Fletcher was their man.

On the other hand, some Appalachian boys had appointed themselves as my mentors and towel-wielders. For
them, this was mere sport, and used to being quarrelsome underdogs, they took my side against one of their
own. Class distinctions were for the birds. They liked a
fight. They were ignorant and innocent.

Fletcher had maybe forty pounds on me. This is a
good edge, even for a creep. He wasn't much taller, but
he had reserves of blue flesh hanging from his arms and
thighs, and his head was well padded. The Army had
taken his fat and made firm flab of it. Occasionally my
gratitude to the captain for sparing me a court-martial
was tempered by the suspicion that I would be clobbered.
"Hit him first with a right! Cut him with your left! Side-
step, see—like this. Look, go get him right away, but don't
throw all your punches at once. Look, he's got a soft gut.
Look, chop his jaw, he's got a paper jaw . . ."

Both Fletcher and I dreamed in the language of advice.
We took a steady stream of counsel. "Drop him with a

quick one—left, left!" But which would be my left hand when my hour of trial arrived?

The hour arrived. We stood in that makeshift ring with its imaginary, chalked ropes. The captain—in high polish for the evening—acted as referee. The first sergeant had the stop watch. He was memorizing the numbers on the dial, cocking his head a little. We listened to the rules, the gloves were laced on, and we listened to the rules again. The other soldiers hooted, joked, advised, and waited for the show to begin. Fletcher looked blue, plump, sullen, unhappy. I must have looked skinny and unhappy. We were both wearing G.I. khaki shorts, undershirts, and clomping G.I. shoes, all government property. When we moved, the fly of the shorts slipped and the dark sex within, also government property, was shamelessly revealed. Some of us had once been shy about our bodies. We no longer were. We were all "asshole buddies," except for those of us who were asshole enemies.

I felt weighted down by boots and gloves.

Weighted down by the gloves? I began to suspect what the captain had done. Perhaps to spare us serious damage, which would amount to abuse of G.I. property, he had put sixteen-ounce gloves on us. These are not hard to lift—once—they are like pillows. But if you wear them awhile and try to swing, an odd effect occurs.

The whistle. First round.

We wore those gloves awhile and swung. Crazily I leapt at Fletcher. I connected. He connected. I received a lace burn from the glove on my cheek. It stung. I pummeled and heaved at his chest, his belly, his head, anything I thought I could reach. Sometimes I hit him. More often I hit the wall of ballooned-up gloves. End of round one.

Intermission. Laughter and jokes and snatches of song. Fletcher and I panting in our corners, trying to nod to advice. Round two. More of the same. I was trying not merely to knock him out, but to kill him. He was trying to do the same to me, although there was no longer any murder in his eye. His eye was sad and dim. He was depressed. But he did his duty; he answered the murder in me. Also he ran with sweat. Sweat glistened on the hairy arms. Fresh sweat is not supposed to smell, but Fletcher stank, as did I. Sweat mixed with fear and rage is not fresh sweat. It goes back millenniums, and it produces illness.

End of round two and we fell back into our corners. We had not knocked each other out, but we were knocking ourselves out swinging these overgrown gloves. They were both soft and very heavy. We could do a bit of stinging damage with them, but short of a special advantage of skill or luck, it seemed that we couldn't yet decide the issue. Most of the damage was in the form of fatigue in our flailing arms and tensed, harassed, twitching legs.

Third round began. My heart was thumping in its cage. A swift trickle of pain ran up my forearm, jumped the elbow, turned thick and overflowed my biceps and shoulders. I lifted my gloves and pushed them forward. I had no memory, no projects, and hardly knew why I was there. In combat for my life, for the murder of my enemy, I forgot the occasion for the war. Once more, once more, once more.

And then suddenly the other war made its claim. There was a long wail of siren. Air-raid alert. All the lights on the post went off. Blackout, silence, and the clumps of stubborn pine and the red sand of this deserted waste of North Carolina seemed to take over from the temporary buildings, the raucous men, the clank of machinery. The sky above us brightened, but it had the habit of defying sirens and alerts. The silent glint of stars through the windows. Silence. It might be a real air raid this time. In the dark, there was nothing anyone could do.

As usual, we lay down on the floor to await the end of the alert. Fletcher and I flopped out near each other, within our makeshift ring. Soldiers groaned, grunted, complained, and tumbled their bodies about, breathing dust. Fletcher and I, slippery with sweat, listened to our turbulent hearts. Entranced and unthinking, I attended to my body's strange workings. In a few minutes the fatigue always stalking the infantry trainee took over, despite showers and excitement; most of the men were asleep. Darkness and their bodies conspired. In the darkness my body trembled as the chill settled. Glands shut down, organs decelerated, my heart eased. Slimy and filthy, my nose to the floor, I did not doze or dream; I fell into a profound and desperate sleep. Fletcher the same. Silence.

In perhaps forty minutes, the all-clear sounded and the lights flashed on. The captain stood up, instantly awake, and declared that the fight would continue. The soldiers, yawning, privileged to have slower reflexes than their officers, stretched and sighed. "Okay, men! Third round! Where're the boys?"

There we were. Fletcher and I continued to lie where we lay on the floor. We could not move. The sweat and labor and the lying still and the chill had frozen us solid. We were knotted in place. We were so stiff we could barely move.

When our state became clear, there were a few hoots of spite, but everyone recognized that we had worked as hard as we could with our sixteen-ounce gloves. Our handlers helped us up and into hot showers. The fight was over.

The war, of course, was not yet over, but Fletcher and I no longer had dispute together. We marched peacefully in ranks, preparing to kill the common enemy. Lacking a clear victory over him, I did not earn his respect, as the nice boys do in movies. On the other hand, he disliked to start once more this battle without decision. He became discreet; discretion would suffice. The idea of destroying Fletcher warmed me, as the idea of killing Flavin must have tempted my father. But having fought him, I no longer wanted to murder him. Boys will be boy and bigots will be bigots. Together we would do our killing elsewhere.

Since then, I have sometimes wanted to murder my enemies, but I have not been given even sixteen-ounce gloves and the ritual opportunity. Though the writer may believe that his words can destroy his enemies—and he fears this power, too—in fact they do not kill. It is liberating to discover that shedding light is a worthier goal than murdering with words—even worthier than the intention to cause love. Like sixteen-ounce gloves, words are better suited to causing the truth to manifest itself.

Though sometimes, of course, the truth thus manifested is as ambiguous as our frozen sleep, Fletcher's and mine, on the blacked-out floor of D Company Day Room in Fort Bragg, North Carolina.

Now for the second violence in this linked series. The war was over. I was back in the world of a son. Parents gave instructions and I mentioned that I would not follow the instructions. But my father and I had learned caution with each other. No fighting. Sometimes I caught him looking at me, figuring out the connections. On the following occasion I was a bystander, but the event is connected by blood and horror to my own comical strivings.

One of the few survivors among my relatives in Europe was a man named Henry Frankel. This bland, dignified person, with a sudden soft belly in 1946, and pince-nez attached by a ribbon to his vest, and a smooth sallow bald head, had been an eye surgeon before the war, serving on the staffs of hospitals in Warsaw, Berlin, and Paris. His immediate family—none of whom my family in America had ever met—were all dead in the camps, mostly in Auschwitz. He had survived because he had managed to be taken for a Pole; he was captured as a Pole and worked as a bricklayer for the Germans. When he was finally denounced as a Jewish doctor and not a Polish bricklayer, it was late enough in the war, and he was lucky enough in Auschwitz, so that he managed to live until the end. My father and uncles had brought him to the States. At the age of over fifty, he was learning

English and studying American medicine. He had become a ferocious eater. He hoped to be a doctor again.

Imagine him visiting my family, now living in Cleveland Heights—a reserved, silent man, taken for a hero, taken for a mysterious visitor, taken for a victim. He had an angry glare in his blue eyes, but the power of silence in his manner. He was one of those men you can never imagine as a child—you just see him reduced in size, with vest, pince-nez, and bald pate, riding a tricycle. He had put childhood out of his soul. Everyone marveled at his stubbornness in working at English, working at medicine, working as an assistant in a hospital. I studied the hands of this plump, aging man and wondered how they could have survived a lifetime of the nervous work of an eye surgeon, the brutal labor of a bricklayer driven to the pace of forced labor; they seemed markless, smooth. He had gained almost a hundred pounds since his release from Auschwitz. Old, soft flesh, finding place again on his bones. Except when he ate, he looked like a mild bachelor professor, a German professor, in his vest and tweeds. When he ate, his forehead glistened.

And now imagine the scrubbed suburb of Cleveland Heights, far from the war, far from the agony of before the war and after, deluged with evidence but nonetheless cloaked in its film of soap and sleek. Here was this unmarried doctor from Europe. And there were the relatives and neighbors, worried about his lonely life. Naturally, someone had the idea: *find him a bride.*

"He's timid," my mother said, "shy."

"They all are," said my Aunt Sarah. "I've noticed that about Europeans. No get-up and go."

"He's had a hard time. Those camps were no picnic," said my mother.

"They weren't summer camp, they were all year long," my aunt agreed, musing. "That's no excuse he should suffer all by himself the rest of his life. A doctor needs someone to talk to, answer the phone for night calls."

"You forgot," said my mother proudly, "he was a specialist. No night calls."

"Still," said my aunt. "Still, a specialist don't need a wife?"

Although I report this as a fantasy of life in Cleveland Heights in 1946, it was both as I say and different. News had come back of death and desolation, a world snuffed out. For one thing, there was the absence of millions. The millions had not been known personally, but we felt the lack, even across oceans. My father stared at this witness as if trying to see through him to the ancestors dead—well, everyone dies—and then to the murdered, the tortured, the degraded. But no one must die like that. All should be innocent of degradation. My father blinked his dry eyes and watched Henry for some sign or truth or explanation. He had survived; perhaps he knew something. Perhaps no consolation. But some link between the insecurity of a man doing okay in Cleveland, owning land, enlarging the store, and the horror he had escaped—in my father's case—by a mere boyish stubbornness about coming to America. Things as they were in Cleveland—that was one thing—and then there was the abyss out of which miracles had drawn the body of Henry Frankel.

My father was shy with Henry. He disliked to ask questions.

Henry himself, focused and bland, never discussed Auschwitz. It was past, over. In this way he became an accomplice in the events that followed. He gave the family nothing to free their imagination from the bonds of Cleveland Heights. They had prospered in these times, and however rich their sympathies might be, they knew their own prosperity more intimately than the troubles of others. Henry was a little odd; there were years behind him, but blank years, or so they seemed. Old habit enabled the ladies of the family to see him as just a cranky bachelor, needing reform, needing a wife.

"He works too hard," said Aunt Sarah. "Studies all the time. He'll ruin his eyes, get headaches."

"Relax a little," said my mother, "it never hurt a man, even a student. Do you think he's nervous?"

"He don't look nervous. Why should he be nervous?" my aunt asked.

They did not dare introduce him to the unmarried girls of the community. He was too difficult, strange, and foreign, even if not visibly nervous. But it happened that a lady up the street also had a survivor visiting—a woman whose own miracle had saved her. My family and the neighbor's family got together. What luck! Both had cousins from Europe, male and female! They decided that the lady and the doctor might be shy. It would not do to suggest a blind date, a movie. No. That was kid stuff. They were no spring chickens. Better they should meet by accident at a little party, with coffee and cake and friends to fill the gaps in the conversation. It was more mature like that—European. And so it was arranged.

The lady up the street asked one more question: Was he plump? Well, a little insulated, my mother admitted. The lady up the street sighed. Her cousin was *fat*. Good! Good! They had everything in common.

"I didn't say fat," my mother said. "The doctor is just nice, that's all."

But the negotiation had been completed.

As if they were timid children, neither the prospective groom, the fifty-five-year-old eye surgeon from Warsaw, nor his appointed bride-to-be, the plump lady from Lodz, was informed of their fate. On a spring Sunday afternoon, after dinner, my parents suggested a stroll up the street. Henry went with them—a dignified, silent, closed-off man, walking with short steps, with beribboned eyeglasses. A half block farther into Cleveland Heights, where the weekend gardeners were busy and the children playing, the digesting Sunday afternoon walkers out bowing and ambling, my parents suggested that we stop to say hello at the Steins'.

"Oh, yes," my mother cried, shamming, "they told me coffee hour today."

"But not me," said the doctor, "not me—"

She had propelled him in through the open door of the house before he could mobilize himself for protest.

Inside, introductions. There were scatterings of family.

Upstairs, gin rummy. Downstairs, the children were playing ping pong. Hannah Stein, the cousin who had also
survived, was in the kitchen. She too, without knowing
what was happening to her, what was about to happen,
was propelled into the parlor to meet Dr. Frankel. They
met. Their eyes met.

And now it seemed that Cleveland Heights lay not only
in another world from that which Auschwitz filled to
overflowing; it was on another planet, inhabited by creatures which consumed a different atmosphere, an air composed of radium and sulphur. Dr. Frankel drew himself up
like a heavy and dying bird, making its last effort. His pale
blue eyes turned avid and burning. His trembling hands
fluttered in despair. He pursed his lips as if to speak, but
he did not speak. He spat. He spat on Hannah Stein's face
and then walked out.

He did not explain, and after much debate on the subject, no one asked him to explain.

He did once start to tell my mother: "She was in
charge of the—" But he looked at my mother and could
not go on.

The word "*Kapo*" came back to my parents. These were
the prisoners who consented to do some of the work of
controlling, disciplining, or murdering their fellow prisoners.

That the fear of death degrades most human beings is
a fact which has terrible consequences when death is the
immediate condition of every hour. My father, puzzled
and distracted in Cleveland Heights, remarked one even-

ing during the silent week which followed: "Well, not everybody needs a wife." But he knew that the fight to live can cause men to murder and, obscurely, that the purpose of the camps—to degrade as well as to destroy—had been accomplished upon almost everyone. I think he remembered Flavin, the farmer who had forced him to degrade himself.

We cannot understand evil; we can only meet it, recognize it, and live despite it. Some can. In history there are also some who refuse to make the necessary arrangements.

23

If a man finds it within himself to live without others, he can live walled up and quiet for a long time. But then he may make the next discovery, or life makes it upon him —that he cannot—and he grows a rage for connection, communication, personal fact, knowledge of the company he was born to.

It may be too late if he is skilled only for order, not for love. And it may happen just in time if his passion and patience sweep reluctance before him.

My father seemed to be freed by his absolute commitment to insecurity and action, to adventuring in his golden America. At the same time, I believed him to be crippled by the loss of his past: by his choice to extirpate the past as if it were an encumbering organ from some previous incarnation or from some step on the ladder of evolution. Sometimes I envied his freedom and calm; sometimes I pitied his isolation, the steady gaze of loneliness in his humorous eyes. I wondered what he thought about his parents, Ben, Caruso, Flavin, Shloimi Spitz, Henry Frankel, Myrna, my mother, and our struggle against each other when I was a child. Since these matters lay in the past, it seemed that he was saying: No point in worrying. But he had not forgotten.

I was home, waiting to go back to college. I wore my G.I. fatigues, read my old books, drank beer with my friends, studied bop, and wondered if my luck was really so good when they dropped the bombs on Japan that ended the war. My high school friends and I all asked each other: What were you doing when Roosevelt died? Where were you when they dropped the first bomb?

On a parade ground. In a parachute. Thinking: Will I get out alive?

Once during the months I took to become a civilian again, I found an abandoned piece of fruit in the cellar of my parents' house and a line of ants leading to the broken pear, a smell of decay and eating, the ants leading toward it and away, a mindless broadcasting of life, snip and take of jaws and foods. I crouched and stared at the little beasts, trying to see them as individual creatures in their steady track; and wondered if the god who I then hoped watched over us could stop and crouch and stare at me and my father and my grandfather and my ancestors dead and far away as we proceeded with our own steady snip and take of life on the body of the world. Loneliness if I'm an ant; loneliness if I am not an ant and live apart.

To try to answer all this I found the response love, love, love; but love seemed to be a way of plumbing the depths of loneliness, not assuaging it, a snip and take at my mother and father, at friends, at girls, at myself. My father, in his effort at control of the shivering void, silently hunting, had long ago sworn without words to make some abstract unity of the flesh and sense pummeling about him. I swore to try to make, perhaps with words and rhythm, something more than what the ants make in their subtle flow across the floor of the world. Words have no taste and weight, they are abstract, and yet they weigh and taste and curve in the hand like a ripe fruit or the touch of another; they can woo and destroy; a word is a deed. I would seek to make something particular and palpable which might remain on earth beyond the term of my father and the eaten pear, and beyond my own term which, I had only begun to see, was no more permanent than theirs.

If it troubled my father to see me loafing about the house in the springtime of my discharge from the Army, he expressed the trouble only with a daring flight. If I was in a state of loafing and brooding, he could still lift himself toward his old violent will to take chances. He would create renewed intentions about the future. He came home one day from the store—a supermarket now

—in a mood to yell and stomp. "Thiefing! I caught them thiefing!"

"Who? Who?" my mother said, catching her breath.

"Who, what difference does it make? I been in this business too long already. Penny business! Supermarket, feh, it's just a big pushcart without wheels. What I been blind for so long? I made money already, I bought the lots in Cleveland Heights, I made money on the building, why should I stick with the pennies?"

"Who is the thiefer?" my mother begged.

"The help I hired. Listen, the A & P is going to kill me anyway." He grinned. "But they never did yet, they tried. But Shloimi Spitz is bleeding me, he's—"

"You're still making a living, Sam."

"I don't care make-a-living if my blood is bleeding. I'm too old to be looking for spiders in the bananas, stacking cold cereal—"

"You don't stack the cold cereal, Dad," I said. "Other people look into the bananas."

"Shut up, you. Just because you spent some time in the Army you're a hero."

"I never said that, Dad."

He searched my face in astonishment at his own rage. He spoke softly. "It's all right, you did your bit for your country."

My mother muttered suspiciously, with narrowed eyes, "I know you, Sam, when you talk like that. You been busy. What you did already?"

"I been to the library."

"Oh-oh. You're worse than a kid."

"I been reading. I talked with some people. Lawyers. Big dealers."

"Oh-oh, Sam." She was frightened.

"They're no smarter'n me. There's bigger, taller, greener green in Cleveland. I sold the store to the Bruhart Brothers. I'm going into real estate full time. I got a good price. They got a good deal. I shook hands on the deal already."

My mother was weeping as if the earth had shaken under her feet and reality had disappeared into a volcano boiling with options, auctions, title searches, stamped documents, and leering accountants, lawyers, and subtle-eyed promoters. The store? the store gone? the store all gone? Oh, what to think, what does the future hold, what to tell Aunt Anna? Hitler and Tojo had been defeated, but fresh insecurities were rising out of the smoke. My mother made way for the sobs in her throat. She was stricken.

"I just walked out of it," my father said. "I could have asked for the adding machines, the accounts receivable, I don't care. I gave Dave Bruhart everything. Let him get rich on pennies, I don't want it no more."

Once more my mother knew need of mourning garb. Where were the ashes for pouring over her head? Her world lay in ashes. What is real, if not a store? What is dangerous, if not a mortgage? Again my father was being unfaithful to her with his lonely ideas. He must have laid awake in the night thinking; like a bandit, thinking. Just like a son, he must have sneaked off to the library to read. To read about real estate and write notations with a pencil on a tablet. Like a bandit, like a thief, like a son. Maybe the war and the gangsters and the A & P had gotten on his nerves, and then the thieves in the store had made him nervous, and the passing of time was making him old. Could it be? she wondered. She doubted it. But while she was thinking, she wept a little, just so the thinking shouldn't go to waste. It generally led to grief. It led to tears. Thinking plus the gangsters and the war and age and leaky cans and petty accounts receivable and klepto-maniacs and ordinary shoplifters and long hours and trouble with the coolers and the police and, oh, all that. Yes. Plus the thinking. Now my father was embarking again and she was frightened. His way of replying to the midnight voices always frightened her.

For perhaps the first time in this discussion, my mother turned to me. "Tell your father. You're a grown man now," she said, "you can vote and drive a car and shoot off all kinds of guns they gave you. What a dumb thing to do to a kid."

"My mind is made up," my father said, tenderly bring-ing her back to the subject.

My mother pointed a finger at me. "Tell him. Tell him not to be crazy, he knows this business, he's the food busi-ness champ in Cleveland. Produce, staples, meat, the whole schmear. He's well known to be a genius in produce." I shook my head. "Nobody listens to me," she said to the ceiling. The ceiling and Aunt Anna always listened.

"What do you think, son?" my father asked. "You were in the war."

"Why not?" I told him. "All you can do is lose every-thing, so why not, Dad?"

He clapped his hands onto his thighs and gave out his

rich laughter. "I like to hear that, be reminded," he said. "Good, good. Now dry the tears, kotchka."

And so my father went full speed into real estate. Apartments, warehouses, hotels, small buildings. He had a good reputation and he borrowed money. He pyramided. The times were friendly and his eye was shrewd. People liked him, trusted him. The pyramid grew rapidly.

In the meantime, the wars in Europe and Asia had come to a pause. History flowed toward the next mortal crisis. My mother wondered what I was up to in this time of breathing—G.I. Bill and the erratic, jammed campus— and it felt good to let her suspect something which would give her pleasure. I was wasting much of my time, but not all of it. While the ants were busy in the cellar and my father was learning that he had an instinct about bricks and mortar and how to keep up the value of a property by cunning joy in it and Shloimi Spitz was riding out to the West like a cattle rustler in his new Stetson, it would have been absurd of me merely to wear out my G.I. clothes with the ferocious readers of Proust, Joyce, and Bergson who were my friends at college. And so I read Joyce, Bergson, and Proust and was a kleptobibliomaniac too. And joined a movement. (What right had some men to dream of new wars?) And needed an answer in personal fact.

At the end of the first civilian summer my old buddy from camp, Uncle Phil, commanded me to hitchhike to Detroit. There was a girl in Detroit who, like me, was going to school in New York. She read Proust, too. He had propagated my legend, also. Hart Crane was the other poet from Cleveland. I stood out on Route 2 in my whitened khakis with my lyrical thumb extended. I had recently read the scary pages in *Remembrance of Things Past* which tell how Marcel discovers all his friends grown old, and discovers, from the way she looks at him as he gazes into the face of a lady, that he too is withered. Or perhaps bloated. I was twenty-two—perhaps worn out. But Sandusky, Toledo, Detroit: In three rides I flew to meet my old friend and my fate.

The lady who had read Proust gazed at me and in her thickly lashed eyes I seemed young despite my twenty-two years of turmoil. She let me feel this. We drove out to a murky Michigan lake in someone's prewar Plymouth. I was in my uniform of confused veteran and she sat on my lap in *her* uniform, a two-piece swimsuit. She deployed her cuteness and her six years of high-school and college French to console me for my sufferings. She laughed at my jokes and said, "Of course! I should have seen it!" when I analyzed such problems as Stalin's nationality policy, Swann's disappointment in the Duchess of Guermantes, Bergson's debt to Maine de Biran, Leopold Bloom's reluctance to be cuckolded, and the new world which we veterans were determined to create by means of petty thievery and political action. Even more important, she bounced on my lap as the green Plymouth pursued phantoms down country roads.

When we swam, there was amorous water sporting.

When we cooked out, there were amorous exchanges of morsels and bites.

When we drove back, late at night, she let her soft arm fall about me as again she sat on my lap. She showed me the little box in which she kept the two-piece swimsuit. "Look how small," she said. "It folds right up in a little box." And she folded it up into a little box.

I was delighted. "Let me see again."

She took it out and held it up for me. A smell of sun and water. And she folded it up again. "Into the little box," she said sleepily. And I felt her lips against my neck as she dozed and Phil conducted the mighty Plymouth back to Detroit.

I stayed an extra two days in Michigan. We ate melon on the floor of the lady's mother's apartment, and told our stories, and fell away panting. Well, the war was over. This was not another desperate furlough from the Army; it was a case of rejoining the normal world, though of course the normal world also tends to become an imaginary construction. That last remark was also the sort of insight which would lead the lady to look into my eyes through her long lashes, murmuring, "Now I see it. Of course."

On the last day of the visit I drove her to a park in my friend Phil's borrowed Plymouth. We planned to look at the swans and make remarks and neck, but I cut my hand on a loose bit of rusty door when I opened the car for her. This turned out to be a fatal accident, more deadly than the tiny box into which her two-piece swimsuit could be folded and unfolded. She wept over the bloody hand. A large Band-Aid would repair it. But she wept and kissed me for my wound. I was brave. My brilliant masculine insight told me she was weeping not because of the blood and danger, but because we had met and now I was leaving. And so I told her the wound was nothing, nothing, just trivial, I'd had much worse in my time. I had scars I would show her someday.

"In New York?" she asked.

"In New York," I said.

This abruptly consoled her. We would meet again soon. I would show her my scars. Mental, moral, and especially physical. I had something to look forward to.

As my answer to the changed times and the horrors of loneliness, I found the kind of nourishment which the laboring ants discovered in the ripe pear and my father found in his new adventuring with property. We exist on a moving point in time; we emerge from the void and we rush into oblivion. Obscurenesses upon obscurities—obligations to those kisses on my bleeding hand—I felt alive, I felt hope, I wanted to leap into the future—I was in love.

My mother noticed that the summer's moping had ended. It was autumn now, time for the fall moping season. But I was peculiarly cheerful as I packed my barracks bags. She extracted the necessary information from her semireluctant son: Nice girl. Pretty. Clean. Not flatchested. Plays the piano. Good grades in school. "Of course I don't know the family," she told Aunt Sarah, "but what can you do with these soldier boys? They make up their own minds."

"My boys always ask me," Aunt Sarah said. " 'Ma?' they say. And quick as a flash I answer: 'She's not good enough for you.' "

"Well, I feel different with four of them to marry off," my mother explained. "To me she sounds good—plays classical, speaks French."

"Well, if that's the best he can do. But I aim high for my boys."

"Ma!" I said.

"Shush, I was just talking to Aunt Sarah."

"It's too soon to say so much," I told her. And speaking French had nothing to do with it. Eating cantaloupe on the floor of a deserted apartment had much more to do with it. But I didn't tell my mother about that. The luscious sweetness of cantaloupe on a thick rug in front of a fireplace and the word "darling" and the war and my wounded hand. "Mother, you shouldn't tell anybody."

"Who said I'm saying anything? I'm only talking."

And so back to college. I was courting, I was pursuing, I was a veteran wounded by a rusty Plymouth, I thought love could heal all wounds, I was living in a dream, I was carried on a crest of hope and desire, I was marrying a Nice Girl (my mother's definition). She informed my father that he would soon be a grandfather.

"When?" he asked.

"Who knows when?" she answered. "Isn't that up to the children?"

"Then what are you getting excited for, which it is just a lot of talk?"

But he was pleased, they were pleased. It felt good to do things they liked, such as not getting killed in the war, even though I refused to go to medical school and lived in a basement off Amsterdam Avenue in New York and wrote poetry and started to write stories and got arrested for hitting a man who interrupted a speaker for Henry A. Wallace at the corner of 103rd Street and Broadway, near a delicatessen. A Nice Girl would stop me from being foolish. She would make me give my old G.I. boots to the Salvation Army. She would make me dress like a grown man, doing fine in college. She would draw out the good sense which I must have inherited. There was no reason why I shouldn't possess at least a minimum. She would teach me about responsibility. She would be my America, my Delancey Street.

"Then when they make their mind up," my father said, "then it is time to get excited. Before, I got things on the spindle. The building which half of it is modernized, the other half of it is not in such bad shape either. But I got to give it some of my time."

"Dad," I told him on this visit to Cleveland, "would you like to meet her?"

"Please. Tomorrow I can take the day off. The airplane ticket I'm buying."

"I think you'll like her."

He winked at me. "Good taste maybe you've got. If not, you got the same bad taste I got, which it is good enough." Then he took me aside and said, "Look, it's growing. I could use some help. Now you'll want things. You want to come into the business with me?"

"Dad," I said, my heart sinking.

"Wait. Don't talk. I'll talk first. It's not like the food business, dirty. For greenies. Poor. It's clean. You fall asleep one night and you wake up in the morning a decent hour, you're having your breakfast, a second cup a coffee, and there's a telephone call from the Quinn brothers. Oh-oh, what do they want? You talk to them quiet. Pretty soon they tell you, they have big eyes, and you say maybe. But which it means is this: Suddenly while you was drinking your second cup and talking quiet you're a very well-to-do fellow. How about it?"

"Dad, no."

"Let me give you a for-instance, son. I took an option on this big twelve-story brick propitty it had no windows. Standard Storage for forty years, and then they had to go bankrupt. You remember? On Prospect? So what can you do with twelve stories and not a window in the place? Put a lot of Persian lambs in storage. But people got cedar closets maybe, or they spray. Go bankrupt, sure. But I walked around a little on the outside, I walked around a little on the inside, and took an option. You want to know why?"

"Sure I do. Why, Dad?"

He smiled and looked at his fingernails. "It was easy. Nobody thought of it. The plans was lost and nobody thought of it. How it was constructed was this: You could knock out the bricks! You could make windows and it could be anything, a warehouse, a factory, little shops, you know—anything!"

"Are you remodeling it, Dad?"

"Naw, that's the beauty of it. Overnight—the sky's the limit." And he gazed dreamily toward the plaster ceiling on which my mother worked her wall brush against cobwebs the first and third Mondays of every month. He might have been looking at the tattered rooftops of the Lower East Side of New York, where he had worked for pennies, or the black sky of the mid-Atlantic, or the faraway starry heaven of the Ukraine, where he had ridden in a cart with his father to see the wonder-working rabbi. Every sky has its own magic if a man knows how to put it there. He was looking at the strict face of a storage company on which he had seen the possibility of windows. "More I made on just seeing that, telling Phil Larkin about it, selling him my option, listen—how many strawberries you got to sell to make that kind of money? Which it means I slaved in that store for pennies."

"Do you wish you'd quit the store sooner, Dad?"

He shrugged. "That's over and done with." He grinned. "Anyway, I enjoyed. I liked it. Are you listening to what I'm trying to tell you?" He shook his head impatiently. "I'm not *trying* to tell you, I *am* telling you. Which you could live very good. You could help me out, be with me. I'd like to have you in the business, son."

I shook my head.

He waited a moment for me to change my mind. He attended to the mental pictures in the empty air. He cocked an ear to listen.

"I'm sorry, Dad."

"Oh-oh, the boy looks scared. I was only asking. Bricks are very nice. I was inquiring. Putting in a bid, they call it. I didn't think so."

I sighed.

"Never mind, don't I know you already? You want to go to medical school? I'm buying."

"No," I said. "Dad."

"Don't tell me. You just want to get married on the G.I. Bill. That's right?"

"That's right."

He frowned and considered. "That's right. I cocka-meemied around too. That's just what I did, only I did it altogether different." He looked puzzled at what he had just said. How could it bear any resemblance to what he did if it was altogether different? And yet there was a resemblance in our speculations, he believed, and it seems that he was right.

24

When I was a child and afterwards, my father some-times asked me to go for a walk with him. We strolled the streets of Lakewood, Ohio, or the East Side suburb of Cleveland where he later moved, or New York or other places where I lived. His invitation always seemed impor-tant; yet when we walked, the company seemed to be a signal to put his mind elsewhere. It seemed that he had something to say. He knew he had something to say. But he could never say it to me.

"Remember when we went ice-skating?" I would ask him.

"Yah—you still do that?"

"Yes."

"I could still do that. My legs are okay, I just don't have the time. Feels good, don't it?"

"Yes, why don't we try it again next winter?"

And we walked on in silence.

On the day I was married, he looked especially jaunty —a short fat man with a heavy face and a rough thatch of gray, loosely curly hair. He ambled in his peculiarly comfortable gait. He asked me a few practical questions: Where did I expect to live? Did I expect to get a job? What about school? More school? How did I feel about things in general?

I tried to give him both the answer which was true and the answer which he wanted to hear. I wanted to please him, but also to take my new status, married man, head of house, with proper seriousness, which meant no concessions to a boyish eagerness either to please or to defy him. In general, I felt things bore watching.

He was not entirely satisfied with the morning. He was looking for a place for a serious talk. My mother and father had come to New York for the wedding and we walked, looking, while my mother and the bride and her mother took their own counsel together. We strolled past Schrafft's, cafeterias, restaurants. He paused before the automat. No. He wondered if there was still time to buy me a new suit. No, the blue suit would have to do. We kept on walking.

"Taxi!" he said suddenly. We climbed in. He gave directions.

We went together to try to find the tenement where he had rented part of a bed. We wandered the neighborhood. Almost all the landmarks were gone—the kitchens, the bakeries, the night school. The few old Jews in front of the candy store looked at him as at a stranger. They saw a fat, prosperous man with a heavy head, darting up stoops to cock his eye at the street, peering down into basements, curious about the dark faces on every corner. He was from out of town. The old Jews in their caftans and beards saw a tourist. What did he know from bodegas and *carnicerios?* Did he have a brother on welfare? Did he have ungrateful sons? Was his god an avenging one? What could he understand about real life?

Instead, he probably had his own, his American life to live. He had gathered his fortune in the golden streets elsewhere. His sorrows were strange ones. He had abandoned the path of his fathers.

Just off Second Avenue we found a synagogue. Inside there were tailors, workmen, old men, swaying and chanting, calling out to God. We took two skullcaps from the box at the door. I was perplexed. What could he be looking for here? He never sought safety in the synagogue. God did not comfort him. Unsafe with himself was his persistent intention. It was as if God had been broken in his heart, or at least crippled, and he needed to heal himself alone in the jungle of America with the smell of cigars and the glitter of gold. The synagogue was a place of strangers. What could he say to me here? He glanced about as if this were a den into which someone else had led him. But he had brought us both to this place. He stood watching the men at prayers, and glanced up at the little balcony where one woman prayed alone. He sighed. He did not say a word, but waited, he who was so often in fast motion, watching. His lips moved once or twice, remembering the ancient syllables.

Blessed art thou the Lord our God the Lord is One.

What did that mean to him?

His lips moved; he remembered; and then he shrugged.

Then we walked out and our conversation was over. We had not talked very much, but we had come to the end of it.

"Does that place remind you of Kamenets?" I asked him.

"Kamenets is just a story to me. I don't remember it. Yes, it reminded me."

"You never go to shul. This is the first time."

"I think I saw this shul when I was here the first time, a greenie. I think this is the same one."

It was the hour, he noted, to get ready for the ceremony in the rabbi's study elsewhere. I knew that too. In the cab he said, "I think you're right. That's the first time I been in a shul, which I used to peek in that one when I was a greenie." He sighed. As we drove uptown, jostled against each other in the disputatious traffic of Manhattan, he put his hand into his coat and moved an envelope into my pocket. A check. He made a joke of it. "Well, so maybe you'll only get married one time too."

It had been hard for him to say what he wanted to say, and he had not said it. Nonetheless, I understood something of what it meant to him to see me marrying. For a moment at least, it made the past real.

We arrived at the appointed place, a stone temple like a bank. We greeted the guests, mothers, brothers, and bride. The rabbi gazed searchingly into our eyes, trying to make the event new for himself. I was grateful for his effort. We stood before him. He warned us of pleasures and pains to come. He asked us to welcome the future. He saw no reason why we should not be fruitful, and he was glad. He hoped I would go on to get my doctorate at Columbia.

I broke the ritual glass, wrapped in a cloth, using my heel and surprised at the squashed sound of splintering against cloth and carpet. My heel tingled. There were books behind the rabbi. There was family behind the bride and me. We clutched each other's hands. We drank sweet wine. We kissed. Mothers wept. I was a husband.

During the wedding supper at the Tavern-on-the-Green in Central Park, my mother told me a curious story. Just after I was born, my father had been in a motorcycle accident and laid up for months with "a broken back— couldn't do a thing for himself."

"How'd that happen?"

"Personally I think he was reckless. How else do you get in trouble? A truck doesn't have it in for you, a fresh father like that. That's my opinion," she said. "So be careful, remember, you're just a kid."

My father was dancing with the bride. Then I danced with her. We were drinking Rhine wine in long green bottles. We grew light and happy. There was a halo around my wife's hair: I saw it for sure. For some reason the band played "Careless Love" in a peculiar Tavern-on-the-Green arrangement. Violins. I had questions to ask about my father's motorcycle accident, but never got around to it. When I returned to the table, my father was dancing with my mother.

Much later I noticed an odd habit. Each time I am bored or distracted by my life, I find myself looking at motorcycles. I consider it deeply. I take a cycle out on the road and sail free under the sky, my mouth open to the rush of air, the wind billowing under my jacket, and I come back hungry for possession. I am in a great hurry. I must have it right now. I want to take it home tonight. Then, before buying the cycle, I always recall the news of my father's accident and find some other way of satisfying the dream of evasion.

Later he suffered from a brain fever which nearly killed him. He often tells of how he recovered: He heard a click in his head, it was just a click, and then he knew he would be well. It all happened in a moment. *Click!* Just like that.

Still later, in his seventies, active and healthy, he developed glaucoma. This is a disease which can be controlled by medication, though the threat of blindness is continually present. The eyedrops, administered three times a day, keep the channels open, irrigate the eyes, prevent the destructive blocking of fluids. They are also burning and painful to take. My mother and my youngest brothers, who were still living at home, had the job of reminding him to take his drops and giving them to him.

If they reminded him, he groaningly submitted, saying, "Ah! ah! ah!" If for some reason they neglected this, he forgot and missed the drops; there was, later, pain in his eyes and, presumably, some degeneration; yet he would never give himself the medicine or even ask it to be administered. He refused to admit his need; he wanted it to be inflicted upon him; it was an obligation to others, still another duty in his life.

When my wife and I visited Cleveland later, and occasionally I gave him the medicine, I felt both sad and distracted as he lay beneath the dropper, his plump legs spread and his large head turned up, complaining, "Ah! Ah!" and then turning immediately to the papers he was studying or the television. Or, very soon now, to playing with our daughter, his first grandchild.

"We were in a hurry too," my mother said proudly, "couldn't wait to have a kid, just like you. But why don't you finish and get your doctor's before you have any more?"

"Ma, that's our business. Ma, I'm not going to get a doctorate. Ma, I've got other ideas."

"So listen to me: Why don't you just get a doctor's, forge right ahead?"

"Ma, we're going to have another baby."

"Oh! oh! what's the good of talking? I'll have to tell your father."

But he contemplated this news without protest. He could assimilate it. He thought it was okay. He was holding our first child in his arms and watching her wrap her fist around his finger. He asked me: "The kits, when they learn to read, they're just starting out, they still read the story about the gingerbread boy?"

That hour of dusk which, for so many, is the hour of self-examination, self-doubt, nostalgia, longing for love, was for my father the hour to sweep out the store, make sure the sidewalks were not slippery, pay off the day help, make the last jokes, and count up the cash. Perhaps the hour of melancholia came at another time in his life; perhaps driving to work with the fading moon above his truck, through the streets of Lakewood, gave him that time of indulgence and interrogation. But I think not. He was then simply bound to work—enough. Oh-oh: forgot the brooms for Caruso . . . Oh-oh: who took my gloves out of the glove compartment?

He would have roared with laughter at the idea of longing for the unattainable. The unattainable was mere smoke in the head. Security and success: well, he knew what they were, even if they were never certain. Doing well in the real estate business, money magically multiplying against itself, did not change the way he practiced toward his definition of a man's time on earth. Like a solitary skater on the ice, he rehearsed his own gestures, his own patterns.

There were few seams in his perfect control, and like the skater, he practiced to make perfect. When she heard I was to be a father again, my mother gave me a present —evidence of the effort of a husband—a letter he had sent from Indianapolis shortly after they were married.

He was away on some business idea. It is one of the few letters he ever wrote to her:

Kotchka,

I am alone, in the boardinghouse. Dinner was no good, no taste to it. I drank too much coffee, you're right, it keeps me up. They are all talking business. No sense in talking. Tomorrow I'll be doing business, but I don't talk, I am a foolish man, I don't talk or do anything, I wonder if I am alive or anyone is alive and I wish someone would tell me. Why am I here in Indianapolis? I miss you. I am a foolish man. Sometimes I should tell you how foolish if I think of it. Sometimes I wish I still was a baby with a mother and father. That's how foolish.

Stay well, your husband, missing you.

But, she explained proudly, he never found it necessary to tell her personally that he was foolish. Then why did she save the letter if she was so proud? Why did she give me this letter from a man in good control of things, on the occasion of their eldest son's announcement that another child was coming?

25

"The rest of us are bone and muscle," my father was saying to the slow Quinns, "but take that Phil Larkin, he's all nerve—eh Phil?"

It was close on to three in the dim afternoon of Kornman's, a restaurant favored by the small real estate operators of Cleveland. I had come to pay a summer visit with my wife and daughters. Not yet thirty, I was a retired teacher of philosophy, scavenging up a living as a part-time city planner while I planned the future of the universe. We kept our books in orange crates. I had written a novel. I was getting up at dawn to write another. Oddly enough, they hadn't yet put my picture on the three-cent stamp. Our younger daughter was just learning to hold her head up without wobbling. I thought her picture should be on a stamp, too.

My father had invited me to Kornman's to meet some of his new real estate friends—clean fingernails, facial massages. In previous times the Quinn brothers had sold lots on the edge of Cleveland, lots without sewage and electricity, and most of the lots had sunk out of sight for taxes in the Depression. Larkin had sold my father a second mortgage, but paid only the principal, not the interest, and then invited him: "Sue me, Sam."

Quinns and Larkin were loved by their mothers perhaps; as to anyone else, my father couldn't say. There is supposed to be a Jill for every Jack, or at least a Becky, but Larkin had never married. My father was willing to let bygones be bygones, anyway, so long as they contributed to some active current quest. Phil Larkin's conscience was made of gristle, but so what? Should men of mere bone, muscle, and nerve judge him? Didn't he have a heart, too? A soul? A sinking feeling in the pit of his stomach in the black murdered midnights of July, when his dollars and deeds and mortgages lay asleep behind dynamite-proof doors in the safe, and he, lonely conniving Larkin, could find nobody awake to cheat? Poor Larkin, perhaps. Poor Quinns, maybe.

My father was enjoying teasing them with his son as witness. Occasionally he would wink at me. The coleslaw and the butt ends of chicken sandwiches and the wet dust of chopped liver and hard-boiled-egg salads had been cleared away, but the four eaters hated to leave Sol Korn-man's dehumidified air conditioning for the July sun and the risks of business outside. They went on nudging each other, teasing and gossiping with the head-cocked smiles of men who never knew when they might pick up a hot tip.

"Always kidding me," Larkin said to my father, "kidding kidding kidding." He jittered his fork against his dessert plate, puffed from a pipe which had a piece of yellowed adhesive tape holding the broken stem to the bowl, put down the fork and cracked his knuckles. "Anyway, Sam, you can laugh yourself sick, but that's how I made mine—nerve and knowing the truth about people. Laugh, I don't care. I see through. That's a fact."

"See through what? What's a fact?" the identical Quinn brothers asked together, twin sharpies who ate the same lunches, dressed in the same white Palm Beach suits because they hadn't yet caught up with seersucker, and leaned with the same wary pout over the crumbs of their meal. One Quinn clipped the sprouts of gray hair which emerged from his ear; the other let them grow. If you blinked, it was like magic. Identical twins, and they seemed to change ears, so that even if you tagged a Quinn with a sprout, you could never be sure which one it was.

Sam Gold, easy with food, a fat man with a large shiny forehead and a head of curly white hair, was the only one still eating. "Yeah, tell us," he said with his mouth full of cheesecake. "How come you know?"

"Yes, how come, Phil? What? Come on. What's your fact?"

"So how come you know all about people?" my father asked, swallowing and sighing with regret over the last bite. Eating and monkey business were okay together, but monkey business all by its lonesome was just smoke in the head.

"I choose to answer that question," said Larkin. He was having his second bourbon with water. He took it delicately and tucked his novelty hand-painted tie, a scene from the pier at Atlantic City, back into the belt worn high below his pigeon-breast. "All right, no hard feelings, men, but I did better than you boys. Stands to reason.

Look, I never got married, cut down expenses like that, had people figured in advance—stands to reason. No hard feelings?"

"None," said my father, winking to include me in.

"Course, naturally, I pay most of the excess profits to my CPA." He searched each of their faces for an answering smile, found none, forced out the joke: "Seepeeay—Cleaning, Pressing, and Alterations."

"So what do you see through the people?" one of the Quinns asked.

"You mean I can't know it because I got me a wife?" my father inquired, emitting a delicate whiff of pineapple and cream cheese. "Seeing through people, I mean, the truth about the trade. The nerve I already mentioned. Which you mean to tell me I can't, Phil?"

Larkin called for another bourbon, never mind the water this time, hopped his nervous glare over them, made sucking noises in the dead pipe, and said, "Let me give you a frinstance. I had my troubles with that hilly-billy. I make my mistakes like everybody, only less so. What I mean, there's no such a thing as friendship in business. That's what I learned, Sam."

"You learned all that?" my father asked. "You found out all that?"

"I learned it in business, Sam. Backwards and forwards. Listen, they don't mix. You can play gin with a guy got as much propitty as you, that's the limit. The very end. I don't go no farther."

"Where's your for-instance?" my father demanded.

"A hilly-billy?" asked one of the Quinns.

"Okay, okay, what's the matter, you got a deal on?" Larkin thrust his head forward with a don't-hurry-me glare. "Okay, so okay," he said reproachfully to Sam Gold. He put down the broken pipe. He took the drink with a quick jerk of his neck, his Adam's apple suddenly strained and lumpy, then hidden in sinew once more. "Remember that hilly-billy Sawyer I had janitoring for me, Sam? Went from me to you? Clean-cut? Quiet-type fellow?"

"That your for-instance?" My father didn't like Larkin and his nerve because he ate too fast, didn't mind spitting through his talk, lived by the brag in his heart and liked it that way. "Well, I got to leave you boys," he said to hurry him along. He grinned. "Check!"—but he waited.

"Well, I took to him, that Sawyer, yes, I mean it. Wait a sec, Sam. Liked him, no kidding. Really did. Was a former gee-eye, he was, came up from West Virginia down in Virginia there. Didn't have much family either, just like me. You remember—lots of blond and kind of smiley. Well, so . . . He still janitoring for you now, Sam?"

"Nope," my father said. "Good cheesecake that Kornman turns out. Whyjask?"

"That's what I mean about that hilly-billy Sawyer. They're all like that, *un*reliable, *ir*responsible, no good—"

The Quinn brothers were nodding amen.

"Don't care what you do for them. Take an interest in them, then they steal your coal."

Amen—the Quinns were swaying.

"Rob you blind! Steal! No gratitude!"

"They're all like that," a Quinn said.

Larkin turned fiercely on my father, saying, "But not

that Sawyer, that one. He was honest, straight. What do you think, Sam?"

My father shrugged his heavy shoulders and grinned and found a piece of roll to chew.

"I'll tell you what to think," Larkin said. "It don't pay to be good to them. I had him"—and the broken pipe waggled in his mouth. "Does his work good, but he's no damn good. Everybody likes me, everybody says it's a pleasure to work for me, but friendship and affection gets you *no*place with him. Sawyer! All he needs is maybe the right touch of ambition, gets you someplace, and maybe he could stop janitoring and be a manager, but not him. Unsteady. Unreliable. That Sawyer, the whole city should know. Tell you a story about him, Sam."

"Didn't he used to work for you, Phil?"

"That's what I'm telling you"—shaking his head stubbornly at my father's slow grin. "Turns out I already told you he worked for me. Waiter!" Larkin called for another bourbon, the only one of the four to drink in the afternoon, a self-loving thing to do on a heavy afternoon in a season of difficult business. "Worked for me in my Park Villas back in forty-nine," Larkin went on. "Said he didn't like this, didn't like that, didn't care for the suite I fixed up for him. Wasn't a bad suite, Sam. True story. Lots of families would of given their right arms. All right, a man's got a right to live decent, even a janitor. Specially a good janitor, a manager, could be—understood?"

The Quinns understood.

"I went out of my way to please. A nice quiet boy, looked honest. With the result was I liked him. All right, so I fixed him up, remodeled, all new tile shower, big new beautiful Grand gas range, iceless with the deep-freeze attached—"

"So?" my father asked.

"Electrical fixtures, a floor lamp or two, I forget how many, carpeting for his hall—"

"So?"

"They're no damn good, that's what I'm showing. I'm proving it by Sawyer. Kindness don't get you noplace. A lovely suite, sanitas for the walls, fresh linoleum—I ripped up the old stuff and put it in the basement—"

"So why'd he quit?"

Larkin made a wet noise, angry and disgusted, through his empty pipe. "Money," he said.

The Quinns and my father rocked back and forth. This was a ritual laughter, mouths open but silent, unhilarious. "You forgot to pay him?" Al Quinn asked, rubbing at the black mat of hair on his wrist. "He forgot to pay him," he said. It was too hot to laugh aloud. Except for Larkin, they were leaning thick and quiet in the heavy air. Kornman's air conditioning must have gone on the bum. They swayed with their silent laughter.

"A man he can't live by fresh linoleum and floor lamps alone," my father suggested at last. He winked at me again.

"Course I paid! I paid good!" Larkin burst out. The fishbone tendons squirmed in his neck. "That's the whole point of the story. One day I took him to the bank with me, I said, 'Look, see that manager over there? See him? The white collar? He makes no more'n six thousand a year.' So what does that Sawyer say? 'Wish *I* did,' he says. That's what he says. 'Figure it up,' I says. 'Add. Go on, total.' I was as close to him as *this*—I felt like a father to him. 'You do better'n he does,' I says, 'counting in the rent and how he has to buy expensive clothes and put up a front.'"

"You had him there," one of the Quinns volunteered.

"And so?" my father said.

Larkin glared at them in triumph. "So that dummy Sawyer, that no-good, that hilly-billy cluck: '*Can't save nothing*,' he says. Almost like he didn't want to work for me." Larkin took to shaking his head now that the words were out, hardly believing his own tale, fretting anew at the enormity of Sawyer's ignorance. " 'Cain't save nothing, *nawthin*,' that Sawyer says"—and Larkin plucked at the yellowed adhesive tape on the stem of his pipe.

"Who can?" asked my father.

"*Just* what I says to him, Sam. Who can? Who *can?* These days we all got expenses. I'm here to tell you I worry more than any hilly-billy Sawyer. Sure, maybe a higher-type expenses . . ." He pulled triumphantly at the discolored tape. "The taxes, the government, the cost of living."

"Well," Fred Quinn said, "what's the story?"

"He quit. I even offered him his Christmas raise in October, and the whole city knows how it's bad business to show them you need them, you want them. I wanted to do something for that boy. That's how sincere I felt. Yep, after I fixed him up that nice suite, all modern conveniences, he went and quit on me, and I didn't hardly even have time to hire a no-good. I had a run of no-goods ever since. Aggravations all the time. And I tell you I paid good. I was nice to them. My fingers to the bone for them. I would of made that Sawyer my manager, my personal representative in the place, if he'd of only been steady. I extended myself to him. They're all a bunch of drifters—"

"Absolutely right," one of the Quinn boys said.

"Every last one, the good are worse than the bad."

"They get independent," the other Quinn said.

My father, flushing after so much rich food, bent his head devoutly to tip-touch his smile with the napkin. "That what you know about Sawyer, Phil?"

"Worked for you, didn't he, Sam? Janitor in your Friendly place?"

"Phil's right." The Quinns were busy agreeing with each other. "You can treat 'em too good. They take advantage. Eat your heart out. It don't matter how nice you are, they don't see it. They get that way. Just so they got something to eat, got what to drink—"

"Can't trust them," Larkin announced impatiently.

"Why, they don't know how many months there is in the year," Al Quinn said, "those hilly-billies."

"Twelve," my father said, "twelve months to the year, but it feels like thirteen if you count March the fifteen."

Larkin was excited, tapping his pipe against the glass, and the stem separated itself from the bowl. The nervous ting brought the waiter with another bourbon. It was a mistake, but Larkin took it anyway. "He liked me fine, that Sawyer, said so himself, but he just can't stay in one place—a born drifter. No good for nothing, those boys.

Blond hair. Smiley all the time. I liked him! Treated him like a son! You must of had the same sperience, Sam, that why you asked?"

My father's blink said, *Asked what?* Then his smile spread slowly over the plump dark face stained by purple no-shaving. "No, no," he said, "I only treat my sons like a son."

Phil jerked toward him. "Well, I never had a son— no time. No time to get married. Other janitors could of done the job, a clerk maybe—the shortage of janitors— but I liked him, that's why. Shows you can't trust one of them hilly-billies. Just quit on me, Sam!"—and his voice came up shrill.

"They been spoiled," the Quinns mourned. "No appreciation what you do for them. All-tile shower, he said. They don't care. Just so they got a buck in the pocket—"

"Sam!" Larkin cried out. "I actually liked him. I sort of took to that Sawyer, but you see how wrong I was?"

"Dead wrong," a Quinn said sadly. It was the one with the untrimmed tuft sprouting from his ear.

"Everybody in town knows the type. A good janitor, but unreliable. Laziness, not money. Never be sure if he'll show up a Sunday morning after a Saturday night. Isn't that why you fired him too?"

"No," said my father, his forehead gleaming in the yellow light of Kornman's chandeliers, his face bowed toward the napkin now folded into his dessert plate.

Why? That no-good. I even gave him a push-up because he had a nice way. I used to like to see those things, do like that. Now I've learned. Why did you fire him, Sam?"

He murmured softly, "Didn't."

"Didn't fire him? He quit? Run off? Stole money this time, the linens, the tools? You had to learn how to be hard like me, eh Sam? Now it's doggy-dog for you too, eh? Knew he'd come down fast, that one."

"Nope," said my father. He turned the plump smile full across the table. "No," he repeated, "I got him working, he's my Hotel Friendly manager now."

The chair leg squealed as Larkin jumped to his feet, was up, was out. His nose and mouth sniffed and wiggled. His narrow leather heels clacked. He grabbed his hat from the girl, but forgot to pay the check. Was gone because Sawyer liked Sam Gold.

The Quinns, letting their Palm Beach jackets be switched with a brush by Kornman's boy, extending their arms and turning their backs, worried aloud because the heat, and even a heat like this, was no excuse for being so nervous. They remembered what had happened to Joe Rini. Joe had turned out to have blood pressure. "No way you can be sure of the help these days," the Quinns told each other. "Take Phil there, now it's like he says. You got to operate alone."

My father put the broken pipe in his pocket, the lip-soiled ravelings of tape sticky in the faulty air conditioning. He insisted on paying Phil's check. The Quinns argued, but he paid. One of them spoke for both: "Thanks for the interlude, Sam."

On the way out my father said to me: "I want to tell you something about these boys. First thing: You shouldn't ever get to be friends, *friends* friends, with the racketeer who sucks your blood. Second: You should always pay small checks—pay them gladly."

"Okay."

He studied me with a delighted smile on his face. "You don't know what it's all about, do you?"

"It's business," I said.

"Yes, it's business and pleasure. I like letting him know Sawyer works for me, he trusts me, I give him a living wage. But listen—" He signaled to the attendant to get his automobile. We stood blinking together in the midsummer sun of Cleveland. "Listen, I'm glad you went into your own line. We're not so different. You take your pleasure. Which it is you make it your own way."

"Yes," I said.

He stood by the car, tapping the throbbing hood. He gave the attendant a dollar, but didn't get in yet. "Did I tell you the news?"

"What news?"

His Tartar eyes were nearly shut in the metal glare of sunlight. "Myrna, you remember that Myrna used to work for me? You remember? She died from the cancer. Last time I saw her—"

He waited. He seemed to be listening to the motor.

"Yes, Dad."

He thought better of it. He climbed into the car. "Last time I saw her, it was a long time already."

We were heading into the traffic. The nose of his Buick was forcing its way into the lane.

"How's your wife doing?"

I didn't answer.

"You're just like me," he said. "Idiot. Different."

26

There came a time when more and more I wanted to buy a motorcycle. In my dreams I felt the skidding wheels under my feet, the kick of speed, and the cool weight of moonlight on my back. Idly I would sway up the country roads that led to Grass Lake, Big Wolf Lake, and Napoleon, Michigan. I would chew on a blade of grass and stare at the shapes unmoving in the still nighttime fields. I would sail out of Detroit through groves of pine, past regions of sleeping farms, where owls hung from branches, digesting mice all the night long. I had two children, I had a job, I had found my vocation, but I was also distracted by every whimsical fantasy, tick of evasion, tock of salvation, hint of death, suicide, murder. I was sickened by life. Crisis inhabited me, making room for fevers and infections. My wife and I were rending each other. At first there seemed to be some sort of passion in this bloodletting, but then it became habitual, even negligent. A word, a gesture, a glance could set the careless devils loose. Ridicule, vanity, and hopeless rage; echoes against empty walls. The time of divorce.

My parents suspected nothing. When I told them by telephone from Detroit, then the separation began to grow the thickness of reality. It was a part of life. They did not comprehend, yet they comprehended. I was back in the world again; there was power and love in the world.

Occasionally I would have other comforting dreams of flight before disaster—war, plague, earthquake, volcanic convulsion. I would be taking care of my wife and my children, helping them along, all quarrels done. Refugees, we would love one another. There were smoking fires at the horizon, heaps of slag, pits; it was like the industrial valley of Cleveland, the desolation of the Cuyahoga River, but the way of heroic action was clear. The sweetness of survival together.

Then I would wake to disappointment in our upstairs flat in Detroit where all was safe and sound and chaotic and the thermostat switched back and forth in the night while my daughters slept in one room and a helpless enemy slept by my side.

Why describe my trouble? I would ask myself in these suddenly wakeful hours. Why worry and struggle? My father's way seemed much braver to me—no useless fret, anger, or despair, except under the intense shock of an event. Neither fear nor hope. The practice of living was enough.

But he had earned his way by his own history; it was not part of my birthright. He knew what he wanted, he had a definition for success, he knew his own practice. I took refuge in flights, rages, vain hopes and revenges. I could not be as foolish as the man writing to his bride from the boardinghouse in Indianapolis; I could not make sense, either, or put love and ambition together where they belonged, in proper order, with the sweet coherence of which I dreamed.

I moved out. I left my wife and daughters. I was in a furnished room. My father came to Detroit to take care of me. I was ill. He studied me, frowning, with pursed lips. I had a stiff neck: heat treatments. I had an infection where I had been scratched. I had an earache. I was too thin. I saw a doctor who told me to eat more, sleep more, and to relax. He was a Communist. He pulled down a chart of a dog's nervous system and told me that dogs never suffer ulcers, prostate trouble, or nervous breakdowns. Since I didn't have ulcers or prostate trouble, but seemed to have every other disorder, I felt that this observation about bourgeois society was more relevant to his philosophy than my condition. Also I later learned that dogs *do* suffer nervous breakdowns, even in the Soviet Union. I informed him a little stiffly that, although nervous, even a bit jumpy, I had not yet broken down.

"I'll be the judge of that," said the doctor. "Look at the wolfhound. See how sleek its coat. It sleeps and eats its fill, never more, of nourishing food. The nice wolfhound."

The rolled chart flew up in his hands. It snapped to in

its metal case and I pitied the circular dog, demonstrating the virtues of a disciplined society in a state not yet withered away. My doctor sent me a copy of *The Anti-Dühring*, by Friedrich Engels, instead of a bill. Not only a Communist, but disloyal to the AMA.

I sent him a couple of guitar records.

He sent me a ball point pen.

I sent him a sweater.

He sent me two blue chambray work shirts.

Exhausted, I gave up this ideological conflict. Only great nations can play potlatch; I was an emerging state, busy with selfish problems.

My father did better than to lecture me in general. He took charge at a moment when I needed him to take charge. He did not understand power or love, but they were his familiars. Lacking the language for them, he dwelled in these commodities as if they were houses. Cut off from his own family at age thirteen, he lived in the world of do and make. How could he talk to sons? Nothing to say but: "Go out. I give you the stars." And of course no words even for that. "I give you the sky, the earth, the stars, and your freedom. It's all out there." No words.

And how to show that he was generous? With money and energy. He swam in a motel pool with my daughters on his back. He seemed like one of those ageless Galápagos tortoises, living rocks which burgeon out of the sea, encrusted with the centuries, stubbornly enduring and waddling about their beachy turf.

At this time, he also began to suffer loneliness before

the fact of death. Dizzy spells—syncopes—stunningly
empty moments made him grip his chair and a swarming
emptiness filled his head and the world just disappeared.
He repeated this news as if it were a fine wonder. "Funny,"
he said. But as to the person he was talking to, doing
business with—"He never knew a thing. He didn't know.
He thought I was thinking."

He told me this, and then buried himself in my troubles.
He looked over my house, my wife, my children, and the
furnished room in which I lived. He said, "This is a mess."
It was. He had come to clean up the mess.

At first he hoped to rescue the marriage. Divorce was
incomprehensible to him, as it was to me. There were
children, responsibility; there was a history and a contract.
He was not sentimental, but he believed in promises. The
pretty little girl and his son had a long way to go; they had
"problems"; okay, but they could not abandon themselves
in this way.

Then gradually he became aware of the other road. He
invented divorce all by himself. It was his first experience
of it, and it struck him as a fresh possibility. He abandoned
sentimentality, not just for himself, but also for me. "Worse
things than bankruptcy," he said. "Sometimes you got
to admit you're beaten." Having made up his mind, he
was determined not to let me waver. "You're beaten," he
said. I was skinny, boyish, green. "So now what?" he said.

With the stubbornness of the ill or the childish, I
wanted my typewriter and fixed on this with monomaniac
rage. *It's mine!*—the tricks childishness plays on us. I
was willing to leave my books, my records, even my

clothes, but I needed the typewriter I had been given on my fifteenth birthday. It was worth very little, but as much as I wanted it, just that much my antagonist did not want me to have it. There was a scene. Boxes of clothes, debris of abandon, the smell of burnt coffee from the kitchen. Claws. My father stood apart, frowning over this madness. I remember that he looked sleepy.

Even now, I recall with shame his reaching into his pocket to extract a roll of bills. He was puzzled by the yelling going on about him. He did not understand such yelling. It was a practical matter: get them separated. "Wait!" he said. "Stop!" He bought the typewriter back. I looked on bewildered, bereft, as the bills changed hands, and then I took up the black Royal portable—there was silence, silence—and carted it out to my father's automobile.

In Cleveland, his first words to my mother: "Well, I cleaned it up."

"They're back together?"

"They're back apart. It's got to be."

And it was.

Years later, my former wife needed help and went to my father for comfort. "He's a good man," she said to me. They had been estranged; there had been no love between them; there had been anger. One afternoon my father sat with me under the pear tree in his back yard after the frenzy of recriminations and revenges had ended, and the legal business was in process, and life could begin again. He looked at my mother with a glint in his eye. He had few jokes and stories, but the ones he had, he polished.

This was a new one. "Next time," he said, "just make sure it isn't a Nice Jewish Girl."

I remembered this when my former wife remarked about him, "I always wanted to know him better. Even now, why doesn't he let me be his friend? I can be a daughter to him. I'm the mother of his grandchildren. He's a good man."

"I know," I said. Most of the time I sought to be agreeable; just agreeable would be enough.

We pass summarily over wars, time, age, events. But time does not let itself be passed over; time passes us and we remain encased in our histories as it hurtles forward.

It is one of the first days of fall as I write these words. I live in San Francisco, where the four seasons cast light shadows on almost every day; my parents still live in Cleveland. There are new wars; wars never end. The child of a cousin was killed in an automobile accident. A friend was killed in the crash of a Navy plane. I look into a girl's eyes and think I find solidarity, love, the truth of my days and nights, past and to come. The chances for joy and misery remain. We submit to the trials of feeling. We seek to master the sense of our lives, and surely, without even knowing it, we seek to give meaning to the lives of those we love and of mankind.

My father is heading past his eighth decade. In Los Angeles recently his kid brother had a fortieth wedding anniversary. All the relatives gathered—the rent-a-car agency, the liquor stores, the doctors and lawyers ("professionals"), the hypochondriacs and the patients, the one alcoholic (probably a heavy drinker), the successful children and the ones who have not yet become successful. It is a time of expansion—land, outlets, projects, progeny. My father has also kept active. After the party, he wanted to go to Las Vegas to gamble. Money has always been a toy to him, and gambling better than any other activity expresses the playfulness resident in the commodity money. The smell of green, its taste and crinkle, still give him pleasure. After a large family party he wanted to have some fun.

He asked me to join my mother and him for a few days at the Auberge Sandy Dunes (let us call it), one of the piles of pink masonry and violations of symmetry which make up the Las Vegas strip. I stayed two nights, and then we all left for the airport. The visit, I noticed, was an economical one. When the check arrived at the hotel night club, it was marked COMPLIMENTS with a red, smeared, inky stamp. My bill was stamped COMPLIMENTS and so was my parents'. When he strolled from the cages, where he exchanged money for chips, and when he idled among the crap tables, my father was treated with unusual consideration by the girls who brought him lemonade. "Mr. Gold, some lemonade."

"Drink your citrus," my mother said. "It's good for you. I read in a book about scurvy." She gazed about with a distracted puzzlement. Of course, this was not like a shipwreck. Of course, the Auberge Sandy Dunes was not a covered wagon going West, either. Still, a little citrus can't hurt when you're an old man turning on his ankle, saying Hah! and dancing with the flung dice.

On the third day we stood in the lobby with our luggage, waiting to go. My mother and I were amazed that there was no bill. Then the reason appeared. Old Shloimi Spitz came strolling out of his office, alerted by a buzzer. He had shrunk, as the old do, but his bald head with its freckled crown seemed larger, almost dignified. Sober gangster dignity; also a white-on-white silk tie over the white-on-white shirt with ruffles and French cuffs. He was wearing a black Italian silk suit and pointy shoes. The narrow pants gave evidence of the withering his years had brought him. I remembered him as thick-thighed. He had had a bad cold recently; the flanges of his nose were chapped and there was a pale white shadow of lanolin cream about his nostrils.

"Hallo, Sam," he said to my father.

"Hallo, Shloimi," said my father. "I heard you was here."

"You're looking good," said Shloimi.

"You got a good business here," said my father. "How are you?"

"Not too bad. Hallo, missus," he said to my mother. "You enjoy the action?"

"The all-girl violin ensemble I thought was very cultural," my mother said. "Very much."

"Fine, fine. Who's this?"

"Last time I saw you I had the mumps," I said.

"Yah. And now what? You're going to college?"

"I'm forty-two years old, Mr. Spitz."

"Don't remind me. I'm getting on myself. I get a little sinus sometimes—desert allergy. Come here, Sam, I want to talk to you." The two old men strolled across the lobby, arm in arm. "It's not really all my business by myself, Sam, it's a little group of us—"

And they were beyond my hearing. They had the quick waddle of healthy old men. Shloimi was talking, but why? Did he want to recall the memory of his brother, Moishe, dead fifty years now? Had he some need to apologize for the threats and extortions which had bound my father and him together so long?

I watched them as they stood, their reflections swimming in the watery marble of a Las Vegas Doric pillar. My father was listening patiently, impatiently, and touching the marble with his hand. Disapproval. Fake marble.

Shloimi's mouth was moving. His little hands were jerking at the ends of the starched armor of cuffs. His cuff links had stones set in silver: the same stone as that of the Greek pillars of the Auberge Sandy Dunes. My father was nodding politely and looking at everything but Shloimi. Shloimi was working hard on getting his attention. Another man would have gazed at the old gangster on this occasion in order to face the meaning of time and age—to look into the mirror. Here was the representative of the devils with whom he had wrestled, money, power, security, rapid risk, and getting along. Here was his antagonist through fifty years of conflict, his old friend, his enemy, a blotched image of his own history.

Instead my father frowned at his wrist as if he had a watch there and Shloimi followed, a step behind, as he rejoined his wife, his son, and the pile of luggage. My father would still not look at him. Perhaps he was right and Marcel Proust was wrong. Who needs to be so conscious? Who needs the mirror of age when fate must be defied, not ransacked of old sufferings? My father was aware of the flight home. He was thinking of his new projects. Time and luck had rid him of Shloimi; that satisfied him sufficiently.

In the taxi my mother asked, "Did you thank him for the Complimentary?"

"Naw," said my father, and fell to dreaming.

"Well you should—learn to be polite!" said my mother. "It's time already."

"Naw," said my father.

Shloimi stood spraddle-legged in the curved driveway of the Auberge Sandy Dunes (we are calling it) while the hot wind of far Nevada swept over him. He lifted his hand, waving goodbye to my father. I would have liked my father to let the power window of the air-conditioned taxi float down; I wanted him to lean out and wave in return. Instead, he just moved his head in recognition. Shloimi smiled. He gave all he could. He stood in the dry heat and smiled with all his might. An old man smiling hard. He showed his gold tooth.

We had already turned onto the road when my father changed his mind, shifted heavily, and waved goodbye to his gangster. Too late. We were out of sight.

"I don't owe him," said my father, and pressed his lips together as if he understood that his words—the truth of them—hid a different and deeper truth. He owed Shloimi, and knew it. He said one thing, and waved too late, and Shloimi could never see into his heart any more than either of them could see into the hearts of their dead brothers, their parents, their sons. But in their souls the two old men understood that life had joined them in a mutual debt. They had survived together in the world. They had been shaped against each other. Now at the end of time, the most important fact in their past was that they had known one another.

28

I returned to Detroit to visit my daughters during the Christmas holidays. I wanted to teach them to skate. It was a stubborn preoccupation. No matter. We could make health of our tics. The frost of the season was right, but there was a great scramble to find skates, bundle up, and get to the flooded playground. Meaty parental faces and swift kids. There were tumbles, tears in snowbanks, and hot chocolate afterwards in the shed. I explained how we learn to skate later, after trying hard, just as we learn to ride a bicycle later, after skinning the knees. But anyway, we can skate a little right now. "Let's try again."

Triumph when my elder daughter sailed, smiling and blinking, round and round the rink. Suspense while the younger one staggered, complained about watery ankles, finally learned. I pumped along, feeling the easy glide beneath my blades as some sort of validation. It is that pleasure we know in only a few moments of a lifetime—when we discover the soul at age thirteen as we dive into deep water and the water slides over skin. Or when we teach our children to skate, and they learn, and we skate with them.

I wanted them to see, amid the wreck of our life together, how richly nature supplies us with pleasures—love, the course of blood, food, sleep, the use of the body and the spirit within the body. Then someday, when it pressed upon them, they could manage the dark other fact, the inevitable fact, that by these same means, nature takes away life. The years move round, faster each time. I had created a bedraggled family, but weather, food, health, work, relish in the self and the acts of living still gave guarantees of value. My daughters could learn nimbleness on skates and appetite for effort. Perhaps I could offer them something of what I had learned from my own father besides the silence of withdrawal which is the fate of parents and children. Nature guarantees life, and takes it away; and this withdrawal from a father is a dread premonition of death.

"Daddy! I can do it!"

"Daddy, look at me!"

"Daddy, where are you?"

Daddy was traveling. Daddy was out of reach.

"Right here, honey. Look! Backwards!"

And yet there is sadness in this easy pleasure of crackling air and blood in the cheeks. Who speaks of love often has sad eyes. My father, who spoke mainly of trouble and work, pain and disaster, had laughing eyes, delighted from within, not by the spectacle of life, not by the contemplation of it, but by the living of life. I remember why skating with my father gave me such joy. It was the hope of intimacy, waiting to be redeemed. I remember that I always expected more of my father than he gave. I thought knowledge and power came of love. My father found love and power in his mastery of the world. I believed the abyss between my father and me, between others and me, could be crossed. My father did what he could and rested there. He thought he might as well be content in his insecurity.

My father came to the new world with the lessons of history weathered into his body, and thus he was ready to play out his fate. He chose to leave his parents. He chose to leave his past.

I sought to make a peace with my history that can never be concluded. Like a gangster I sought to penetrate my father's secret soul. The limits remained, unredeemed.

I teach my children to skate.

I tell them stories.

I sit with them in hotel dining rooms.

They are left to find their own security and their own definitions of success, as my father did, out of the indecision and cripplings which fate has given them. Fair enough; they are back in history, true to their fathers.

But if there were something truer than history! How sweet it would be. The heart and the will seek to make something more, something that extends further than time, that weighs more than fate.

I look into the eyes of my daughters and see the familiar loneliness and expectant hope. I can give them things; I can take them skating; to them I am still a stranger.

Epilogue and Beginning

Acquired characteristics are not passed on, but children accept them into the hospitality of their souls through the imitations of love and hate. Acquired wounds do not visibly mark the generations which follow after, but the memory of them goads and troubles. Thus history seeks to survive in every birth.

On an Indian summer day of 1938, during the madness of the Munich surrender to Hitler, my father received a last letter from his grandfather in the Ukraine. I was fourteen; we lived in Lakewood, Ohio; the streetcar stopped at the end of the block, near the corner of Clifton Boulevard and Hathaway Avenue. His grandfather had not spoken with his own son after he had permitted the boy to run away to America, but my father's father had been killed during the First World War and now the old, very old man was dying and wrote one final letter to the boy in America.

Not that he knew he was dying. He was one hundred and seven years old, close to God in heaven, addicted to

practical jokes on earth. He had one eye. He liked to fish
a purse on a string out into the dirt road; he watched out
of his one eye until a passer-by noticed and bent to pick
it up, and then he jerked the purse away. And he roared
through his beard with his one-hundred-and-seven-year-
old laughter. Perhaps he meant some comment on the
reliability of purses in the changed universe of Russia.
More likely this was the farce of an ancient creature who
had very little on his mind except memories, and wanted
something to happen today, right now, on the patch of
street which he could still make out. His one eye was
dimming. He complained of this. His handwriting was pre-
cise and small, but he complained that it was difficult to
write beautifully with only one dimming hundred-and-
seven-year-old eye.

My father answered to ask if he would come to
America. He received a brief reply, written by a neighbor,
saying that his grandfather was now too blind to write. He
had a cataract. My father looked up the word: "opacity
of lens of eye, due to toxic states, senility, etc." It would be
very difficult to leave the Soviet Union anyway.

A few months later the old man died, and then the
war broke out, and then all the rest of the Jews of
Kamenets-Podolsk were dead, tumbled into mass graves
by machine guns. My father thinks his grandfather would
have liked to point his beard at the S.S. murderers and see
the end for himself. The circle of life is never completed,
but the spiral turns round, remembering other turnings.

Aside from the fact that he was very old when he

died, and he died, he did not see all that he might have seen of the nineteenth and twentieth centuries because he had but one eye. The other was taken from him a hundred and thirty years ago by a man called The Crippler, who had been employed for this purpose by his parents. These distances are immense, in time, in blood flowing, in the persistence of flesh and soul. Let us try to negotiate the encrustations of years. The path runs steeply down into shadow, up into fear, and we go naked into these realities. His grandfather, whose last letter my father still possesses, was taken to The Crippler in the 1830's. In the woods and villages of the Caucasus, the Crimea, and the Ukraine, where my family lived, 1830 might as well have been the twelfth century. The people still recalled the dominion of the crazy-hatted Turks. They knew the marauding Cossacks as occasional destroyers, not as neighbors. The sunlit woods were a place of menace. The narrow mud streets ran as readily with gore as with commerce. The people spoke Yiddish. The rest were strangers. The Czar and the Russians were utter strangers. And the work of The Crippler was as essential as that of the undertaker. Like the undertaker, he served the living.

The Great Imam, Shamyl, was just then preparing to lead his Moslem mountaineers in their war against the Russians; the holy slaughter would provide a great victory for the Little Father in 1859. There had been other holy wars for faith and land, and other great victories; dominion on earth must continually be reaffirmed. In this land where Prometheus once lay in chains, where Jason once sought the Golden Fleece, strange waters bubbled in underground springs; pastures, oil, and precious metals lay waiting for human use; the earth was enriched by bodies and pieces of bodies—the Tartars, the Ruthenians, Mazepa's bands, the Poles, the Turks, the Russians, the Jews. The Chazar khans now lay mingled with the dust. The Scandinavian house of Rurik had first conquered, then disappeared. Yesterday the Golden Horde of the Mongols rode their fierce little ponies down the Mamison and the Daryal passes, hoofbeats echoing on rock. Now Circassian princes, married to blond northern ladies, conceived children who ruled, or seemed to rule, or tried to rule. Anarchy gave way to chaos, gave way to bitter autocrats. In reality there were two rulers—swift fear and slow fear. Revenge was utter. Then for a time everyone bathed in the golden sunlight and harvested the swaying grains that replaced some of the pastures.

But always there remained this nostalgia for death and destruction. Precarious life could be reaffirmed by murder. *I* live, *you* die. *You* die, and I can risk turning my back on you. *You* are crushed, and I can walk less warily.

Everyone waits for death, whether he knows it or not, but the Jews waited especially for murder. They bargained, sometimes with mutilations—in this place with mutilations—against the universal fate. In his own way The Crippler intended to save some of the sons.

The Crippler was an old man who lived alone in a hut in the woods, separated from all the world by the horror of his vocation. His job was to cut off the hands and the feet of Jewish boys; he deafened with a little stick, he blinded with another; he cut tendons and he created limps, twisted arms, broken bodies. Did he choose his vocation or was he chosen? How does a man become a crippler? I imagine that he had no wife or children of his own. There must have been some awful consecration in his heart, deeper and more terrible than that of a rabbi. He was the surgeon who treated a fatal malady inflicted upon the Jews by those strangers who carried the plague.

In those days, and for long afterwards, the Czar attempted to settle the irritating matter of his Jews by drafting all the able-bodied men among them for a period of twenty years. An officer rode up and said, "You! you! you!"

"Oh sir, he can't because—"

"Who are you?"

"The child's father, please, Your Excellency, he—"

"The recruit will stand on this spot tomorrow morning." The officer's long Cossack body leaned down along the heaving flanks of his horse. He made a mark in the dust with his sword. "Here! here! Understand?"

"No, sir, he's only a child."

The officer sat immense on his horse, noting it all down. "On this spot tomorrow morning!" And in a swirl of dust he was gone. But the Jews stood silent among the turning motes in the air. He would return as he promised. There was no more hope.

When a boy was taken, his parents brought him to the rabbi. The rabbi pronounced the service for the dead over his head. They would never see him again. Most likely they would never hear from him again. Almost at once, in the Czar's army, he would be forced to eat non-kosher food; other soldiers would sit on him and they would hold his nose until he swallowed and choked on cabbage soup floating with lard, on kasha mixed with bits of pork. The desecration ended his brief life as a man. He would no longer know who he was. He was cast out, he was submitted to use, he was a thing. What defined him as a person had been profaned; he profaned God; he had eaten unclean and forbidden things.

Much of a child's discipline in virtue, obedience, awe, and worship was joined to the duties of food: of cleanliness, of care, of prayer over food, of the appointed time for certain dishes and the absolute rejection of others. Milk and meat were never eaten at the same meal or with the same utensils; the blessed white bread, queen of the Sabbath, was taken with joy and wine on Fridays at sundown; pork and shellfish were abominations, cursed, forbidden; certain blessings had to be performed and rules obeyed in the preparation and the cooking. To violate these commandments was an insult flung in the face of God; it was unthinkable, filth, a horror, obscene. A Jew who could eat pork might do anything, or anything might be done to him. He was lost to humankind. His body would wander the earth like a wild pig's body. He would see the knives stuck in the earth near the Jewish huts—this was one way of cleansing them—and he would blush if there was still blood in his veins. But in his veins ran only madness and despair. He wore the Czar's uniform. He ate pork. He was worse than dead: destroyed, a walking shame to God, a man without even the privilege of martyrdom.

And then, at some indeterminate future date, he would

finally die in one of the Czar's wars if he happened to survive the cholera, dysentery, and smallpox which periodically swept the Czar's army. Or if he was not first killed by an officer, a noncom, or a non-Jew. Or perhaps, in the despair of that living death, even by a faithless Jew. But all this, of course, came after the end of his life, since on his very first day under the Czar's dominion he was forced to eat non-kosher food as the symbol of his bondage. His body lay in bondage, waiting to be devoured; his soul was fled. Grief alone remained in his heart. The service for the dead provided for all temporal contingencies; it dealt in the ultimate matter.

The Crippler explored a means to postpone the service for the dead for many of these children. The Czar hungered for healthy Jews, he loved to crunch up their bodies and spit them out, but he had no taste for defective ones. The Crippler manufactured defects to thwart the Czar's appetite. When the time of the boy-collectors arrived, the parents took their children to the hut in the woods where the ferocious old man waited with his instruments. They stood in line, weeping, the boys clinging to their mothers in terror, the fathers morose and determined, the mothers wailing in the birch and pine forests of the fertile Ukraine. Few dared to pray as they waited—would this not be sacrilege? They knew what they were doing, but they did not ask either divine sanction or divine forgiveness. It was a decision on earth. It was polluted, as decisions must be on earth. Oddly enough, when the moment came, the boys marched into the bloody room without tears, and the mothers stopped weeping, and sometimes only at that time did the fathers begin to wail like women. They saw their sons look brave and manly. The sight undid them.

Within this collaboration in a custom, it was necessary, of course, to be reasonable. The State could not brook ridicule—a rabble of Jews all missing the index finger. That would be absurd. An entire village of invisible fingers pointing toward the sky with invisible reproach—absurd! The Czar's collectors knew what was being done, but they hardly minded, so long as the forms were obeyed. These gentlemen preserved their dignity. If the Jews chose another way, the battle was won. And if the Jews chose to destroy themselves, why, so much the better. The Little Father in Moscow, in his great wisdom, would smile at how the cursed ones insisted on reading their strange books, babbled their strange prayers, wore their magical long black coats and sideburns, but then could be led to devour their own young like beasts. Let them fabricate a race of cripples. Then they would not have to be fed by the army. They made poor soldiers anyway; few were converted, few became Russian; and they died miserably later, sullen, closed in, deaf to the Little Father's holy will for them.

And so they would rather punish themselves by their own hands? They would rather invent and choose their own grief, like Jews, like Jews always, like Jews since the time of the Refusal?

Fair enough. Good. Delicious.

The provincial officials winked at the game. Some officers found it a marvelous joke over vodka after wearying themselves in obscure struggles over the cold bodies of

the sluts of the village. Some pious ones discovered an
obscure justice in the way of the world. The way of the
world must mean something. The world could not run this
way without some intention. *Slava Bogu:* Glory to God.

Still, the papers had to be filled out, the bureaucracy
had its regulations. In this complicity between victim and
oppressor, it was the duty of the victim to make his wounds
interesting and varied. The Crippler performed the ceremony, and also made the rules within a general code.
Judgment was delegated to him. It must seem like a set of
accidents. As the boys lined up, he looked them over and
told the parents, without any expectation of contradiction:
"This one I'll take two fingers. This one I'll take the foot.
This one I'll deafen." He looked sternly at my great-grandfather's parents. If the aggregate of horror did not satisfy
the Russian inspectors, they might come down drunkenly
in the night upon the entire village. "Your son," he said,
"I will blind in one eye." And for the first time he faltered.
He added a few words which might serve as apology.
"Only in the left eye."

My great-grandfather's mother was weeping. His father
accepted fate, but with a murderous withdrawal. He could
do nothing for his son; he was unmanned, as Abraham
must have been with Isaac. But then it was God who demanded the sacrifice. And God asked only assent to the
sacrifice; then He relented.

The boy clung to his mother. The Crippler paused
because he had to justify himself to no one, and yet he was
human too, although a crippler. He had been crippled

himself—he walked with a limp. He fixed the child with his fierce gaze and said, as if to give him courage:

"Out of the right eye he will see like a tiger. How many sights can you see with two eyes? No more than with a good right eye. I'll only take the extra one, come here"—and he bent with his beard jutting toward the terrified child while my grandfather's father suddenly wept and prayed.

"Come here, son. Come here. Here."

Blessed art thou the Lord our God the Lord is one.

The boy screamed.

The Crippler did his deed.

When my father wanted to come to America, his grandfather hissed with rage at the boy's father. Godless America! He showed his scarred socket and said, "I see! So he can escape the army? I see anyway. Is he to be more free than I am? Does he have a right?"

His rage, his fear, and his hurt clinging to the reality of the past was given to his own son as a cautious passivity, and then transformed by my father into its reverse, a controlled will to make his own life; and then somehow, in some other way, it was transmitted to me. The Crippler is an instrument of the way things are, and so are the crippled. We are chosen. Also we sometimes manage to choose our sacrifices—eye, toe, ear, hand; we risk our members—heart, soul, memory, will; we risk our brothers and ourselves; we each of us bear the many marks of sacrifice, compromise, and accommodation.

On his last visit to me in San Francisco, when he stood on my little terrace looking after the Japanese freighter heading east through the Golden Gate, my eighty-year-old father was still plotting his victories for the next twenty years. He had taken great pains to stay alive in these times. He had dared the world and his own weaknesses to defeat him, and sometimes he accepted a defeat, because his failures were as necessary to him as his riding free.

For his pains my father did not resolve the quarrel with death. Nor will any of us. But he sought his own way to the common end, carving his will out of the dreadful void, and may I and other fathers do as much.

about the author

Of *Fathers*, HERBERT GOLD writes: "This is a novel in which I have used real names and the sense of some real people in order to make a particular bridge between history and the shaping imagination. The several fathers and others in the book, including the teller of the tale, are imaginary immigrants, travelers, cripplers, strivers, children. Like all novels, this one has a basis in fact, and perhaps more of a basis in fact than some. It did not happen like this, but it might have. Perhaps it once happened *almost* like this. I have chosen to tell it as a novel in the form of a memoir. Like the name 'Gold,' which is an imaginary name, this is an imaginary history. And real. And twice imaginary."

Herbert Gold has written eleven novels, and his short fiction and essays have appeared in America's leading magazines. For his work he has received many important literary prizes—among them Guggenheim and Hudson Review fellowships, an award from the American Academy of Arts and Letters, an O. Henry prize, and a Ford Foundation Theatre fellowship. He has several times been an American delegate to the Formentor conference.

Mr. Gold was born and raised in Lakewood, Ohio. After taking B.A. and M.A. degrees in philosophy at Columbia, he studied at the Sorbonne in Paris. He has been a soldier, hotel manager, city planner, and college teacher—the latter at Harvard, Cornell, the University of California, and the University of Iowa, always briefly.

He now lives in San Francisco.